The Legends of Caraigdun

The Legends of Caraigdun

Quest to Slay the Dragon

Jane Cleere Johnson

Mushroom Manor Books

I dedicate this book to my own six children:
my inspiration, my muse.
Always remember bedtime stories in the hallway.

{ 1 }

The Wizard's Shoes

The sounds of the forest exploded. All creatures bellowed the warning call as Erik drove his steed on. Holding his head high, he kept his sword sheathed. Suddenly, the trees came to life, throwing dead branches at him as if they were arrows. Erik dodged the arrows and rode like the wind. The arrow branches caught fire, one sailing quite close enough to singe his curly hair. Never breaking stride, Erik slammed his body flat against the horse's back. Large rocks closed the path in front of him. Erik's virile horse jumped over each one with ease. A small crimson dragon appeared out of the sky and swooped down. Erik could feel talons scrape along his back as he swung his body to the side of the horse. The dragon hovered overhead, wings flapping like an eagle preparing to snatch up his prey. The horse reared up on his hind legs and whinnied anxiously. Erik pulled up on the reins, set his piercing gaze upon a cloaked figure perched high in a gnarled oak, and yelled, "I've no time for this!"

The sounds of the forest ceased.

Suddenly, the cloaked figure was standing right in front of Erik. She held her hand up and walked slowly around him. Erik found it difficult to look away from her piercing gaze. Through his eyes, this strange woman seemed to enter the window of his soul. Sure, that she would conjure a spell, causing him to meet the same fate as many of the townspeople who came back with tales of horror, or never returned at all, Erik's first thought was to reach for his weapon. He resisted the urge and kept his gaze steady. Solon, the hermit woodcutter, had trained Erik in using weaponry, but had also advised him not to draw his sword if he met the dark-haired woman. When she lowered her hand, Erik realized he had been holding his breath. He exhaled.

"Bare feet," she observed. "If it wasn't for your tattered clothing, and bare feet, you would seem of noble birth, the way you carry yourself through the thickest part of the forest, with no thought of your safety."

The forest came alive. Screeches, hoots, scratches, and rustles filled the air. The stranger raised her hand, and all were immediately silenced.

"Arrogant, brave, or stupid. Time will tell," she muttered. "Stop and sup with me, young man. I am intrigued by your manner, and would like to know how you spotted me," she added, glancing past the many leaves to her hiding place atop the gnarled oak.

Erik was sure he saw the giant tree smirk as its branches reached uncomfortably close, and a protecting cloak of leaves fell around the woman. When Erik left Cathair that morning, Solon had convinced him to take the path through the Forbidden Forest. Normally Erik would have ridden north across the flatlands, taking the long safe way around, but he was determined to bring the herbal remedy, made by Solon, to his mother in time to save her life. Cutting through the Forbidden Forest would shave a day off his journey. Stopping and speaking to this stranger was against Erik's plan, but Solon had instructed him to watch for her. Somehow, Solon knew she could help him.

Be truthful, yet polite. Solon had instructed. "Thank-you, but I don't have time to rest and I can't think of eating when I have just received word that my father is dead and my mother is swift on his heels." Hearing himself say the words made Erik's heart skip a beat. With a tug in the pit of his stomach, his mind raced home to his family. Earlier that day, he had received a note from his mother relaying the horrible news about his father, as well as a message from his sister Aimee with news of his mother's illness.

"I entreat you to find it in your heart to let me continue on this path." Erik bowed a low deep bow, sweeping his hand across his torso and lowering his eyes to the ground. "I can pay you in gold, my good woman."

"If what you say is true, your cause is noble. Yet, I have no use for the soft metal that so many deem precious. I am Athena, Keeper of the Deep, Dark Forbidden Forest." Pulling down her hood to reveal a mane of long unkempt black hair, with a gray streak winding down one side of tangled bangs, she continued. "I will get you home quickly."

Erik almost fell as he slipped off the sleek black stallion. "I am fine." He insisted, ignoring his own weariness. "Wildfire could use a drink and a quick rest."

Erik felt the urgency to jump back on Wildfire and continue his journey, but he trusted Solon, and for reasons he could not explain, he felt compelled to speak with this woman. "I am Erik, son of Denis of the Valley of Caraigdun, that lies on the other side of these woods."

Erik glimpsed a look of recognition on Athena's face before she turned away and ran her hand up and down the leg of the sweating horse. He was sure he heard a crack in her voice as she spoke. "Come see," she beckoned. Taking Erik's hand, she ran it across the right foreleg of the stallion. He could feel a slight swelling.

"I suggest you leave him in my care. There is a poultice I have used with success. He will mend with a few days' rest."

"Wildfire will have to rest when we get home. It is but half a day's journey through these woods."

"As I watched you dodge flaming branches and clear the boulders that rose in your path, I thought for sure you were arrogant or foolish. Surely you have heard the stories of dangerous and ominous creatures."

Erik's gaze met the dark eyes of the keeper of the forest. "I do wonder what became of the crimson dragon." He kept his gaze steady, looking for anything he could learn from the reaction of this intriguing woman. "Of course, I have heard the stories. We hear them all the time in Caraigdun, and now it seems I have experienced some for myself.

'Tis strange. My brother and I played on the edge of these woods for years and no harm befell us. Alas, no matter what dangers befall me, this path through the woods is the quickest way home. I have no time to waste."

"Trust me Erik, son of Denis of Caraigdun, if you have faith in me and faith in yourself, I will have you home within the hour."

"You must have a very swift horse. He would have to run three times faster than Wildfire."

"I have my methods," she said. "Come in and rest by the fire, young Erik. I have some stew on, for though it is barely fall, the icy fingers of winter have already grasped firmly to the reins of seasonal change this year." Athena opened the door to her small cottage. Leaving it open as an invitation for Erik to enter, she hurried to stir the stew.

Erik stood at the threshold; the warmth emanating from the cozy room beckoned his weary bones. The savory smell rising from the cauldron tempted his hunger-gnawed belly. "Yes, that is true. That may be why my mother has fallen ill. Her health always fails in the winter. She would rather be out in her garden harvesting a full crop." Erik grimaced as he thought of the garden spot.

"I hope this early frost doesn't spoil the harvest. With father gone, it's in Brian's hands."

Athena stirred the stew in an enormous pot. So much stew you would have thought she had been expecting company. Putting down the ladle, she looked up at the handsome young stranger. "Tell me about your family," she said.

"Brian is your brother, I presume."

Erik was almost unaware as he made his way into the room and was now sitting at a small wooden table. He looked down as Athena filled the bowl in front of him with scrumptious smelling stew. The thought that she had poisoned it crossed his mind. Maybe he'd fall into a deep sleep and never wake up if he ate. Somehow, he trusted this hermit woman. It was almost as if he had known her his entire life. "Yes, Brian is my younger brother. My father is, I mean, — was a sailor. He was gone for weeks on end, leaving Mother to care for the six children. She was always very frazzled by the time he returned. I remember once when I played a great practical joke on her. She had just pulled all the dry clothing from the line. She went into the house to tend my little brother Adam, who had woken up and was crying. I took all the clothes, dipped them in the water barrel and put them back into the basket. You should have seen the look on her face when she finally got the little guy settled down and came back out to bring in the wash. She was hanging it all back on the line, mumbling to herself about how she was sure she had just taken it down. I would have gotten away with that one, but when she went to get water from the water barrel later that day, she found a stocking in the water. She threatened to send me away to learn a trade. I always could get on her nerves. I was just trying to have a little fun. Father came home that time and brought her a beautiful silk dress from the Orient. She threw it in his face and said, 'Your gifts do not appease me. You go away on these long journeys and adventures and leave me here with your son...!' And she stomped off. The girls told Father what I did, and I had to do everyone's chores for ten days. My sisters didn't get a break, though. They had to do all of Mama's work. She went off and hid herself in a cave for three full days before Father could get her to come home. I'm sorry; that's a boring tale to you, for sure."

He looked closely at Athena. She scurried around the room, rummaging through an old trunk, looking under a bench, reaching high on shelves. What was it about this woman that made him feel so comfortable? Glancing around the room, he realized how much everything reminded him of his friend Solon. The quilt thrown over the bench had the same pattern and colors as a quilt Solon used for his modest bedding. The leather working on Athena's money bag, the pottery on her shelves, all reminded Erik of Solon. Yet they could have merely shopped at the same merchants. It could have been a coincidence. Then Erik's eyes fell upon a shield standing in a corner. A family crest adorned the shield; engraved with the forms of the four great birds of the sky, the eagle, the falcon, the raven, and the hawk. The same family crest Erik had seen once when Solon had asked him to retrieve a knife from an old trunk in his hut.

Athena stopped searching. "No, it is very interesting to me, Erik. I haven't heard a truly good story in...." The look on Erik's face stopped Athena mid-sentence. She followed his gaze to the shield.

Erik stared at her in astonishment. "How are you related to Solon?" he asked.

Athena walked over to the shield. Picking it up, she traced the outline of each of the magnificent birds. "You have been open and truthful with me, son of Denis. I will tell you. Solon is my brother."

Erik was happy to hear this news. He had known Solon only a year but had felt he had known him his entire life. Solon had given Erik good advice about dealing with the hardships of the life of a blacksmith apprentice. Erik's master was a skilled man; the training he received at his side was invaluable, but he drove Erik relentlessly. For a few minutes at the end of each sixteen-hour day, Erik found solace and respite in the small home of Solon. "I knew there was something familiar about you, my lady." Erik proclaimed.

"Yes, Erik. When you mentioned the hermit woodcutter, I knew you had met my brother, but we have our reasons for staying apart."

"Staying in hiding, it seems," said Erik. "This explains why he insisted I take this path, when the townspeople all warned me against it. They all have tales of danger in attempting to cross this wood."

"You said you have played in this forest all these years and nothing strange happened to you."

"Yes, but I figured we never came in deep enough. I was not afraid to enter today because Solon told me that if I rode with my head high and my sword sheathed, no harm would befall me. I knew I had to get to my mother as quickly as possible, but I have heard many strange tales and my parents have forbidden us from entering these woods. Now, as I think back, each time I told Solon the stories reported by the townspeople, he would snicker or smile. He knows you live here, doesn't he?" Erik took a large bite of stew. Although he should have felt tired from the warmth of the fire and the warm glow in his stomach, he felt invigorated and ready to start home.

"Yes, he knows I live here, but what could I have to do with these strange tales? I am but a simple peasant woman, living a quiet secluded life."

Erik thought about Solon. How strange things happened around him. He said he wanted to be left alone, yet he allowed anyone with a need to visit him. Although he called himself a wood cutter, Erik had never seen him chop wood. He was skilled in the healing arts and had given many remedies to people who came from far and wide to seek his kind heart and skilled hands. Yet, occasionally, there were those who had entered back into the town with tales of not being able to find Solon's dwelling place. Others claimed he had put a spell on them. Many exaggerated the tales, compiling them together and claiming him to be a sorcerer who could make himself and his dwelling invisible, and that he could heal with magic.

"I am not sure about everything that happens in the forest, Athena, but I am pretty sure the things that happened to me today were illusions, most likely conjured by you."

"You are clever, Erik. I have always loved a practical joke, as I can tell you do as well. I also love the harried expressions on some faces as they run from a specter I have conjured up."

"You are a witch, then?" Erik stood and walked around the room reading the carvings on the jars lining the shelves: elixir of scorpion tale, fermented powder of cocoa, dried wort of John the Saint.

"I dabble in sorcery, my lad, but mostly I have found that magic is something that lies within the souls of many. Certain situations bring out unique gifts that the bearer may or may not learn to use. But enough of that, I promised I would get you home quickly."

Turning to look at the mess she had made, Athena scratched her forehead. Opening an old trunk that she had already pulled stuff out of; she called Erik over. "You have long arms. Reach to the bottom and see what you find."

Erik reached his hand down into the trunk. When he thought he should hit bottom, his body lurched forward. Something was pulling him down. "he—ll-p...!"

Athena grabbed him by the legs. "Let go of him, or I won't share my stew with the likes of you!" She yelled.

In an instant, Erik felt the release of his arm.

"So glad he didn't rip it right out of the socket," she said, giving the arm a once over. "Now hand up the boots!" She yelled into the trunk.

Suddenly, a pair of worn brown leather boots came flying out of the trunk and landed on the other side of the room.

"What is that creature? What..., how?." Erik stammered.

"Don't worry about him. He's brutally strong but totally harmless, as long as I keep him fed. Take the pot of stew around back and you'll see a chute to pour it down. I'll examine the boots; make sure he hasn't damaged them."

Erik found the chute and heard the snarling of the hungry beast. He used his finger to take one last taste of the scrumptious stew. Such a waste to throw it away like this. The beast snarled more loudly, as if in response to Erik's thoughts. Erik poured the stew down the chute and returned to the warmth of Athena's cottage. Athena was sitting on the bed polishing the boots. "An old friend left these in my care many years ago."

Erik looked at the tattered boots. "I am sure Wildfire will make the journey, ma'am. On my best day, I could never outrun him. I thank you for your offer but. ..."

"Even the swiftest steed would not get you home by sundown, my young friend. Wildfire will need to remain here and rest until you return in a few days. I know these boots look worn, young Erik, but a great wizard used them only once a long time ago. He knew he would wear them only once, so he conjured them well-worn like this to avoid hurting his feet on the long journey. When the journey ended, he gave the boots to me. He thought he would never need them again and said I could destroy them. I am glad I have saved them all these years. You will be amazed at how swiftly your feet will carry you in these shoes."

"I have nothing to pay you with."

"No need to pay me," said Athena. "I think they will find a good home with you."

Erik was eager to get home and glad that Wildfire would not have to risk the chance of breaking his leg altogether. "I am very grateful to you Athena," he said, his brown eyes smiling.

"I am glad to see that I could cheer up a young traveler. Most people who enter this forest are so selfish. You are one of the first I've seen who has no thought for himself. Wait, there is one other item in this old trunk that I think will be useful." She pulled out a magnificent cloak.

Erik pressed the shimmering material between his fingers, sure that he had seen this fabric somewhere before. It was a flash of a memory and then it was gone. Probably just similar to something Father brought back to Mother on one of his long journeys.

Athena draped the cloak around Erik's shoulders. A comforting warmth spread over him. "This will keep you warm until you end your journey."

"I shall return soon," Erik called as he ran forward onto the path. Somehow, his feet felt light and his head clear. Holding on to the hope that Athena was as honest and wise as her brother Solon, he pressed forward. Could it be that these two held the secrets to magic, an ancient art only heard of in legends and stories? He placed his hand on the pouch that held Solon's remedy. After this brief meeting with Athena, the suspicion that Solon was more than a mere wood cutter who dabbled in the practice of healing expanded in his mind. He had received two notes that morning, one from his mother telling of his father's death and one from his sister Aimee, saying that his mother had been ill for a while and although she had forbidden her from telling Erik, Aimee would never forgive herself if their mother passed away before Erik had bid her farewell. It seemed odd that Aimee had not mentioned their father's death. It also seemed strange that the two messages arrived on separate posts. A centaur had delivered Mother's note; a creature he had heard of but had never seen before. Erik's thoughts continued between the two places he called home and the events of the past few days. Uppermost in his mind was his main purpose—to get the remedy to his mother by sundown. He gazed overhead. The sun was high and a bit to the west. I hope these boots are magic indeed, he thought, because there is no way my own two feet will get me there in time.

{ 2 }

The Magic Within

The cottage of Denis and Jaynea of Caraigdun was a peaceful sight, situated upon a grassy knoll and surrounded by rows of apple trees to the south, oaks along the north, and pines along the back. Berry bushes, usually overflowing with blue, black, and huckleberries, provided a natural fence around the yard. A large garden provided vegetables for the family and was usually thick and ready for the fall harvest by this time of year. Erik slowed down as he crossed the property. His heart fell as he saw how the long drought had affected everything. The place looked like winter's barren state rather than autumn's joyous feast. As Erik approached the cottage, he imagined his sisters Aimee and Becka taking care of their mother. He opened the door and saw Becka with a duster in her hand. He spoke her name, and she turned but kept dusting. "Erik, you are here," she said, as she put the duster down, gathered some dishes and started walking toward the kitchen. "I need to clean up before Mama wakes up."

Erik took the dishes from her. "Becka, it's okay," he said. "These can wait." He could see from the bags under her eyes that she had gotten little sleep. He knew that his sister, who was just a year older than him, would need to keep busy.

"My friend Solon gave me these herbs for Mama. He says to seep them to make a strong tea."

Becka seemed to wake up. She snatched the pouch out of Erik's hand.

"The doctors say there's nothing they can do. Once the rash starts the infection will only worsen. Mama.... We may lose her..."

Erik placed his hand, gently on her shoulder. "Make the tea, Becka. Solon is a healer. I trust him."

Erik stood in the doorway of his mother's room. Aimee sat slumped in a chair asleep. Only one thing could have allowed her to claim such respite. She must have come down with the dreaded sickness.

Erik walked past bowls of untouched broth. His cloak knocked a spoon to the floor, and Aimee stirred.

"Becka, what are you doing? Go get some rest.... I'll...Erik! I'd throw my arms around you but I don't want you to get sick."

"Yeah, I don't want to get what you have." said Erik. "Whatever it is has made you shorter."

"Ha, you would have me take that as an insult, and yet the best things do come in small packages," said Aimee.

Aimee dipped a cloth into a basin of water, wrung it out, and placed it on her mother's forehead.

Erik could feel his insides clench as he looked at his pale mother. He gasped as he noticed the small form snuggled next to her. "Not Adam too," he whispered. "Not my little warrior."

"Mama has suffered through many restless nights coming in and out of fitful dreams," said Aimee. "Adam's small body has been curled up next to her for three days. He holds on to her hair as he sleeps like he did as a small baby. We couldn't keep him from visiting her. He and Kami have gathered flowers and brought them in each day. Not knowing what else to do for the mother they love so much."

After the invigorating run he had just experienced with the magic boots, Erik felt that the world had come to a complete stop. His mind slowed to one thought. That he was too late.

"All night as I stayed with them, I listened for their breathing to make sure they --" Aimee's voice cracked as she struggled to tell the tender tale. "Each time our dear mother breathes in deeply, her little son breathes in deeply; simultaneously, as if he were still in the womb."

"Mother, it's your Erik. Home to save you and our little warrior, Adam."

"She can't hear you," said Aimee. "We haven't been able to communicate with her for over a week. Nothing can help them."

"Becka is making a tea from herbs my friend Solon sent," said Erik, wiping the worried look off his face. "They will get better," he said, as he threw his cloak over a chair, sat down, and took off his boots. His feet were not sore at all. Having made it home in only an hour was amazing. He decided Athena's cottage must have been closer to home than he thought.

"Aimee, you can rest now."

"You are the one who has had a long journey, Erik. You should rest."

As Aimee spoke, Erik noticed her words slurring, and her eyes drooping.

"I have had help on my journey, and you look half dead."

"Thanks a lot," she said. "For once, I know you are not teasing, Erik. I'm sure I look as bad as Mama and little Adam. I guess I will get some rest, but you must promise to wake me if they come around."

"I will, but you need your beauty sleep. Wouldn't want the poor dolt of the month to come courting with you looking like that now, would we?"

"I'm glad you're back, Erik. We need a little humor around here." She started to leave the room. "I'm going to want to hear the story of how you got here so quickly," she said, yawning. "When I wake up."

As soon as Becka brought the tea, Erik took some into Aimee. Waking her slightly, he lifted her head and poured some of the tea down her throat. "Just in case," he said.

"Thanks, little brother." And she closed her eyes again with a smile on her face.

Erik smirked. "'Little brother', huh?"

Erik looked in the sickroom and saw that Becka was sitting quietly by the patients. "I've only given them a few sips each," she said. "Maybe you could help me hold their heads."

Erik walked over and gently held his mother's head. She felt so fragile. "Maybe you should hold her head. I feel like I might break it like I did your China doll."

"Don't be silly," said Becka. "You weren't holding my China doll gently when it broke. You threw it across the room because I told Father you emptied all the milk pails and convinced Brian that he hadn't yet milked the cows."

"That's right. That was so funny. He had gone back to sleep, after completing his chores, early on a winter morning. He is always so quick with his chores. I woke him up and told him he had to get up to milk the cows. He said he had already milked the cows. I said, 'you must have dreamed that you milked the cows because the pails are empty'. He went to milk, and the cows were furious with him. They bolted and kicked and must have thought he was out of his mind."

"It may have been funny to you, but Brian still hates you for it."

"I know." Erik was quiet for a moment, remembering all the horrible stunts he had pulled on his younger brother. At first Brian came back for more, like some people Athena told him about who entered the Forbidden Forest. They want an adventure. They want a story to tell. Then they get enough of it and they don't want to go near it again. Mother had told Erik for years that his jokes would drive Brian away.

"He doesn't really hate me, does he?" Erik asked as he lifted Adam's delicate head off the pillow. Adam stirred and grabbed his mother's hair. "It's okay," Erik whispered. "Your big brother is here."

"He doesn't know you." A tall young man with blonde hair and blue eyes had appeared in the doorway.

"Brian!" said Erik, rising to greet his brother. "You're right. I guess you're his big brother now that I've been gone for almost a year."

Brian said nothing. He just glared at Erik.

"Kami and I have brought carrots and potatoes for dinner," he said to Becka. "I'll go out again because I know it's not enough. But it is cold out today. I thought I'd better bring Kami home."

Erik looked at his brother, who had grown almost as tall as his own 6-foot frame. "I'll come with you."

"I don't need your help."

"Look Brian, I know you were angry with me when I left but I have been sending home everything I earn. Times are hard now, and we have to pull together. With Father dead and --"

"What do you mean 'Father dead'?" Kami had just come around the corner. The look on Becka's face told Erik they didn't know.

"I thought you knew." He ran to hug Kami, who stood stunned in the doorway, tears swelling in her big blue eyes. He swept her up in his arms.

"How did you hear this?" Becka asked.

"I got a letter from Mama."

"Mama has been in this bed for a month and couldn't possibly have written to you."

"Then who could it have been? The letter is in Mother's writing, see?" Erik pulled the letter out of his pocket.

Becka took the letter and turned it over in her hands. "This looks like Mother's writing, and I feel like I've seen parchment like this somewhere before. I can swear to you and the rest of these children are my witnesses. Our mother has been lying in this bed, delirious. She has spent several nights in fitful dreams. She could not have written this letter."

"Mama has been talking in her sleep a lot." Kami's voice was small, and she was still sobbing. "She keeps calling out for Father."

"You've been in here?"

"You and Aimee tried to keep me out, but I snuck in and curled up on the floor on the other side of the bed. I had to be near my mama," she said, through tears.

"I understand," said Becka, and she bent down to hug her tender-hearted sister. "Kami is right. Mama has been restless. She keeps calling out, 'Denis, my Denis, the dragons has my Denis.'"

"Yes, that's right," said Kami. "And then she stopped dreaming about Father and started calling out for Erik."

"Yes, she wanted you home," Becka looked at Erik. "She awoke for a few seconds and asked for you. Somehow, she got this letter to you."

Erik gazed at the letter. He remembered the strange woman in the forest. "Maybe by magic," he said, not believing his own words.

"What do you mean?" said Becka, incredulously. "Our mother is a simple peasant woman who loves to garden and have picnics with her children."

"I met a woman in the Forbidden Forest and --"

"Oh, now you have an incredible story to tell about that fake forest," said Brian. "This whole thing is totally ridiculous if you ask me. If our mother had used magic to call someone to help, I'm sure it would have been Father and not you."

"I was deep in the Forbidden Forest just over an hour ago. Wildfire had a badly swollen leg, so a strange woman gave me these shoes."

"I suppose you are going to tell us you ran here in one hour's time, when the center of the forest must be several hours on a swift horse."

"Yes. I can't believe it myself. But it's true."

"I don't believe it. You probably forged this letter to get your lazy hide out of smoldering hot apprentice work."

"Brian. Let him finish. Something tells me Erik is not lying." Becka's voice was stern but calming. "Tell us about this woman, Erik."

"Her name is Athena. She gave me the boots and this cloak and said I would get home quickly, and I did, but she said something else. Athena believes that many people in this world carry gifts. Gifts that can become magical if they realize what they are and fine tune them. She asked me who my mother and father were, and I told her. She wouldn't look at me when she heard their names. I think she was trying to hide something from me. I thought she sent me on my way quickly because she knew I was in a hurry to get home to my sick mother. Maybe she was in a hurry to get me home to her sick friend."

"But wouldn't she have come here and tried to help you if she really had been friends with our parents?" Becka asked.

"She helped me, but — I don't know. I think she could have healed Wildfire, but she kept him and gave me these things. I think she wanted me to return, but she couldn't or wouldn't leave."

Erik unclasped the cloak and held it in his hands. He could feel the warmth coming from it. The material was soft and silky, and the color reminded him of a clear mountain stream. Although the cloth seemed transparent, he could not see his own hand through it.

"If this sorceress of yours really is magic, then this must be an invisibility cloak, right?" Brian took the cloak and threw it over Kami's head, almost expecting her to disappear. But Kami did not disappear. Her sobs grew louder. Erik pulled the cloak off and picked his little sister up again.

"Athena said that magic is something that lies within each person's soul. She said that everyone has gifts and --"

"So, you think our mother magically sent you this letter from her dreams?" Brian demanded.

"I don't know. I can't explain it any more than I can explain these shoes, but we don't know what Mother does when she goes off to that secret place of hers. Maybe she's kept up with something she and Father started years ago but had stopped."

"I know what Mama does in her hiding place." The group thought they had been keeping their voices down so as not to wake the others, but Aimee, as tired as she was, hadn't been able to sleep through it.

"Wow, the color has really returned to your cheeks," said Becka. "You haven't come down with the fever, have you?" she asked, placing her hand on Aimee's forehead.

Aimee swept Becka's hand away with a flourish. "That was some concoction that old hermit friend of yours put together, Erik. I feel like the Goddess of Rejuvenation has smiled down on me and given me a new life. I could run to town and back with supplies, do everyone's chores and --"

"Oh, quit being so dramatic," Becka felt weary, even though Aimee had let her sleep the whole night before. "What did you mean, you know what Mama does in her hiding place?"

"Oh, Becka, you were tiny, and Erik was too, but I think I was four years old the last time she took us there."

"What, I've been to the cave that Father has protected for all these years? What are you talking about? Brian and I searched for years. If I had been there, I would have remembered." Erik stood by the open window, looking out at their property.

"You were a newborn baby, little brother. She took all three of us there and she worked her magic. That was the last time."

"So, our mother is magic?" Kami asked. Her sobs finally stopped as she listened in awe to her oldest sister.

"She is magic with her hands. She sculpted statues of each of us. And I remember my favorite one was the last one, a grand statue of a magnificent dragon with Erik and Becka and me riding on his back."

"That is magical, but why did she stop taking you? That means I've never been to the cave," said Kami, frowning again.

"She may have taken you there when you were a wee babe, my little Kami. I just know that I was getting too old, and she waited too long if she didn't want me to remember anything because I do."

"I do too." Becka was smiling. "This parchment came from Mama's cave. Now, I remember being there with her. She was trying to get me to sit still, and she handed me some parchment to draw on. I was three or four then, I guess, and I'm sure Aimee wasn't there. I just remember that Mama was so proud of my scribblings. She had Father bring me a drawing book from France so I could practice my art. I remember the dragon with the three of us on its back, and I remember she had a baby there. But it wasn't Erik. It was Brian."

Brian said nothing, but Erik could see a faint smile cross his face.

"Yes, yes, it all makes sense. She has taken each of us there and used us as models for her sculptures. She just stops taking us when we get too old." Becka was looking at her mother, still wondering and hoping that she would recover soon and tell them all about this cave and explain the magical happenings.

"She doesn't want us to know about her special place," Kami said. "I don't remember this at all. Maybe she never took me."

"Kami, do you remember that dream you told me about, the one where the flowers blossom and speak to you?"

"Yes, it was a very fun dream, until the trolls came and began eating the flowers. I ran and tried to gather them all up to take home to Mama. She loves flowers so. But the trolls chased me and then a great dragon came, and I woke up."

"I think your dream came from a story that Mama told you while you were at the cave with her."

"I think I remember too. She would make up stories to get me to sit still while she sculpted." Brian smiled.

"See, we've all been there," said Aimee. "Adam was probably there recently." She looked at her baby brother and saw that he was stretching and squirming, coming out of a deep sleep. He had finally let go of his mother's hair. Erik noticed and spoke to him.

"The Little Warrior awakes."

Adam sat up with a big smile on his face. "I was riding a pony, and we flew up high into the clouds... and... Erik, you are home! Mama asked you to come home, and you did!"

Erik picked up his little brother; amazed at his light frame. But the heat of the fever had gone from him. "I came home, and it looks like my little warrior has grown into a big warrior."

"I am big. I can fight the dragons, but you and Brian can help. We must save Father."

Becka came and lovingly took Adam out of Erik's arms. "Adam, you and Mama have been very sick. I think you both have had some terrible dreams."

"Yes, I'm sure our father is safe and on his way home to us," said Aimee. "The letter she sent to Erik told her worst fear, that her Denis had died."

"Father is not dead. He has been captured. Mama is afraid in her dreams that he is dead because he is in the dragon's cave. Adam slid out of Becka's arms, walked over to his mother, and kissed her. Mama, open your eyes. We are finished sleeping."

The herbal tea had taken effect quickly on Adam's young body. "Give her more medicine," he insisted.

"How he knows we gave them medicine, I don't know, but I think we'd better listen to him." Aimee left the room and went to heat the water again. "Becka," said Erik, "you'd better have some tea too. You look more than half dead."

Becka shoved Erik as she walked past him. "I'll have some," she said. "And I'm sure we all could use a good meal."

"I'll go out and hunt us up something to eat," said Brian, "I think I heard a wild turkey when Kami and I were out earlier. I'm sure Mama will need to eat once she comes around. She has had little, if anything, in two weeks." Brian glanced at the cloak.

"I'll go with you," said Erik. Standing next to his brother, he stood eye to eye with him and knew then that they were almost the same height.

"Thanks Erik," said Brian. "But I think you'd better stay here with Adam and Kami. They need a man around right now."

"I didn't expect you to call me a man, little brother," Erik said, standing up as tall as he could and patting Brian on the head like he used to just last year, when he must have been a foot shorter. "Although I hate to admit it, you're right. Adam and I will have a game of chess."

"Yes, anything to keep him calm," said Becka. "We don't want him to get sick again and we have to keep the little monkey from jumping all over Mama. She's still feverish."

As Becka shooed the boys out of the room, Erik tossed the cloak to Brian. "For warmth." he said.

Becka pulled Kami close to her. They both sat down by their mother. "She will be happy to see your pretty face when she wakes up," Becka said.

"Your pretty face too," said Kami, hugging her sister.

{ 3 }

The Origin of Magic

Erik allowed Adam to beat him at chess several times, before the little boy got tired of playing and went back to lie down by his mother. Once Adam settled in, Erik set out to find Brian and try to help him hunt that wild turkey. He made his way through the fields and up the slope quietly. He didn't want to scare Old Caesar away. Brian had named the bird Caesar, not the usual Tom, because he didn't like to kill anything, so if an animal had the name of a villain, it made it easier.

From the top of the slope, Erik could see all the lands of his father. Over two-hundred acres. He and Brian had covered every inch as children. Erik never understood why his father wanted to own so much land when he would never farm it or keep livestock there. The garden and the livestock they had was close to the house, and just enough for their family. From the top of the hill, he could see that the house was in the exact middle and was also on high ground. The wooden fence, trees, and eagle's nest on the top of the house made it look like a fortress. Looking east Erik spotted Brian, he was a good distance away—in the precise location that Erik would have thought Caesar might be at this time of year. Erik studied the terrain to determine the best approach. He decided to come up from the south. He knew the boots would keep him light on his feet, and hopefully keep Caesar and Brian from hearing him. When Erik was within one hundred yards of where he had spotted Brian, he saw the turkey hiding in the thick brush. He didn't see Brian but knowing where he had been, he threw a rock into the brush. The turkey gobbled wildly and scurried further into the thicket. Exact opposite of what Erik hoped he'd do. He made his way around to the north side of the bird. Still no sign of Brian. Erik gave his best turkey call, and the large bird came running across the open field. Suddenly a swift arrow met its mark, and the bird fell. Erik wanted to shout "Bravo!" but he refrained. He wanted Brian to think he had bagged the elusive bird on his own, but he still didn't see his brother. Suddenly he saw the turkey move across the field. Erik stifled a gasp. He was sure that one arrow had killed the turkey instantly. A gunny sack rose, and the bird fell inside. "What sorcery is this?" Erik whispered and then did the best he could to stifle his own laughter. "It must be an invisibility cloak after all." Maybe Brian would believe in magic now and more importantly, maybe Brian would believe in himself. Erik knew his little brother had always felt like he was in his shadow and didn't have talents like those of his sisters. Aimee with her singing and storytelling, Becka with her drawing and baking, Erik could beat everyone at everything, jousting, swords, and chess; Adam only beats him because Adam doesn't have to follow the rules. Kami, well Kami is just so nice, always bringing flowers to everyone. She can talk to anyone about anything; every stranger is her immediate friend, but Brian acted as if he had no talent at all. So, this contribution. Bagging this bird. This would mean everything to him.

***

Erik used the boots to get back to the cottage quickly. He sat by Kami and watched their mother continue to sleep. He smiled when he heard Brian come in and tell Becka that he'd be preparing the bird for her to cook. When Jaynea began to stretch and yawn, he sent a silent prayer of thanks to the Heavens. Jaynea opened her eyes slowly.

"Mama, are you okay?" Kami leaned forward to hug her mother.

"Yes, my little Kami. I am going to be okay. My head feels like a herd of elephants is stampeding through it right now but... what about Adam! Is he still suffering?"

Erik took his mother's hand. "He has already beaten his big brother at a game of chess."

"Oh, Erik you came! You got my letter."

"Mother, I'm so glad you've finally woken, but when did you send Erik the letter?" Aimee was standing in the door with more tea. She walked over and gave a sip to her mother before she let her answer.

"I'm not sure when, but I was in the cave, and I wrote it and sent it along with my friend Didean."

"Mama, we think you are delirious," said Aimee. "You have been talking in your sleep and well... you have spoken of dragons, and you called out for Father."

"A centaur delivered your letter to me this morning," said Erik.

"So, I must have written it a few days ago. Yes, that's when I called for Didean."

"But Mama you were in this bed sleeping all week and the week before," said Aimee. "Becka or I was with you continuously. No one by the name of Didean came here and we can't understand how you could have written this letter."

"You know silly girl," she said. "I wrote it in my dreams and Didean came and took it from the cave. You've been to the cave Aimee."

Everyone in the room became silent. Erik saw a look of realization in his mother's face. He knew things would change while he was away, but this was unexpected. First Athena and the magic boots and a cloak that made his brother invisible, and now his mother talking about dreams, caves, and magic. "Mama," he said, placing his hand on hers. "Your letter said that Father is dead. You didn't say how, just that I needed to come quickly."

"I.... oh, I must have dreamed...I must have been...I must be delirious," said Jaynea looking away.

"Well, that's how it seems." Aimee sat down by her mother.

Erik wished he could talk to his mom alone. He didn't know how much he should share about Athena, and the magic boots.

Jaynea sat up slowly, rubbing her head. "I need to think."

"Mama!" Adam came running through the door and threw himself onto the bed. "Your eyes are open!"

"Yes, my sweet little snooggin in a booggins," she said, and she shook her head at Becka who was about to pull Adam away. "We are both finally better."

"I beat Erik at chess."

"Yep, he's learned some fantastic strategies in my absence." Erik stood tall next to his mother's bed, bending down, he hugged her gently.

"He still cheats," said Kami.

"You know he doesn't have to follow the rules, Kami." Jaynea smiled at her daughter. "You didn't have to follow the rules until you understood them either."

"But I don't remember that. It seems like I've always known the rules."

"Now Erik and Brian and I will save Father from the dragons," said Adam standing next to Erik with his hands on his hips.

"You are my little warrior, aren't you Adam!"

"No. I'm not little anymore."

"Adam must have heard me talking in my sleep," said Jaynea.

"No, I saw Father get captured by the dragons, Mama. If we don't save him soon, the dragons will eat him for breakfast."

"It seems like you and I need to compare dreams, Adam. In my dreams the dragons took your father. It seems I thought they had killed him. I suppose I thought it really happened. I'm not sure. I don't really remember very much of those dreams now. Someone must have heard that I was ill and sent for Erik."

"So, Father isn't dead or captured?" Kami sat on the edge of her chair and clapped her hands before throwing her arms around her mother's neck.

"I hope not," said Jaynea, and her eyes looked upon Adam. "I mean, of course not. I'm sure he is on his way home right now with gifts for all of his daughters and stories for all of his sons."

Becka stepped out of the room and motioned to Aimee and Erik to follow her. As they stepped into the kitchen she said, "It seems Mama is keeping something from us."

"I know," said Aimee. "I am so glad she is awake, but it is hard to know what to believe."

"I'm not sure she knows what's reality and what was just a dream," said Becka, pulling plates out of the cupboard and placing them on the table. "We need to finish our conversation with her after the little ones go to bed tonight."

"I will have to tell her more about my journey here, and my friends Solon and Athena," said Erik. "All these years, we've heard of magic, and even met some magic creatures, always outside of our property though."

"Mostly large odious creatures like ogres and giants. Never anything wonderful like a unicorn," said Aimee.

"That's true," said Becka. "Now I have a feeling Mother and Father have been keeping something from us."

"Yes," said Erik, thinking about the cloak and shoes Athena had given him that very day. "Let's eat a good dinner and let Mama recover a bit."

"And then we'll ask her about the magic," said both girls together.

"Yes, the magic," said Erik.

{ 4 }

Secrets

"How in the world did you snag this one?" asked Erik as they sat down to the best meal any of them had eaten in weeks.

"Wouldn't you like to know?" asked Brian half smiling, half scowling at his brother.

"Exactly what I needed after a month on a starvation diet," said Jaynea.

Becka noticed that her mother's appetite was anything but returned to normal "You're eating like a bird," she said.

"No, she's eating a bird," said Brian, and they all smiled at the joke.

Everything seemed so perfect now. Mama and Adam were getting better; Kami had gathered blooming wildflowers of Autumn and made an aromatic bouquet as a centerpiece. Erik was home with plenty of stories to tell. He made jokes about the people of Cathair and had the whole family rolling with laughter when he told them how he had convinced a giant not to eat him. "I told him I wasn't really a human being."

"Well, that part's true," said Brian.

Erik ignored his brother and kept talking. "I told him I was really a giant watermelon that was enchanted by a witch with a poor sense of humor. Of course, he said, 'Watermelon will do just fine'. I convinced him that if he ate such a humongous watermelon, the hundreds of seeds would grow in his belly and entangle in his entrails, and he'd never be able to eat anything ever again. You should have seen the look on his face as he rubbed his hands all around his humongous gut and said, 'I don't feel so... good'."

Adam started giggling wildly at the way Erik twisted up his face as he rubbed his stomach and groaned.

Between his own chuckles and snorts Erik could barely finish the story. "He turned a very — delightful shade of green — and sat right down on the grass. Wildfire took me out of there fast, before that overgrown brute had a chance to change his mind."

"Not like you have to be brilliant to fool a gullible giant," mumbled Brian. Who despite himself couldn't keep from snickering at Adam, who seemed like he would bust a gut rolling with laughter on the floor.

Once he calmed down a bit, it was Adam, in his innocence, who threw in the snag that stopped the laughter.

"I wish Father was here," he said.

"But he is on his way," said Jaynea, taking Adam on her lap. "He will be here soon."

"No, I told you! He is with the dragons," the little boy insisted.

"Adam, you had a bad dream," said Becka, "You must have heard Mother and somehow her mumblings found their way into your thoughts."

"That's right," said Jaynea. "We both just had some very disturbing dreams."

"I had a bad dream, and the dream is for real. Father will be eaten if we don't go and save him."

"Adam, that isn't funny," said Kami. She kicked him under the table and the happy reunion was over.

"I know it's not funny. It's true. I can show you where the dragons live." With that, he left the table and went into the room where he had slept next to his mother all those nights.

The others followed him and watched as Adam reached his small, yet confident, hand under his pillow and pulled out a map. It was on a large, thin piece of leather.

"I didn't dream that up," said Jaynea.

"Oh, he's always drawing treasure maps, ever since Erik and Becka sent him on that treasure hunt last year." Aimee grabbed the map out of Adam's hands. She stood and stared in awe at the creation before her. "This is definitely not anything Adam drew," she said, handing the map to her mother.

"No, he didn't draw it with his hand anyway," said Jaynea, bending down to look into her little boy's eyes.

"Where did the map come from, Adam?" she asked, trustingly.

"I found it in my dreams, in the cave."

"You've been to the cave?"

"Yes Mama, I saw Didean there. He told me he had delivered the letter to Erik and that he would get home in a few days. After I saw Didean, my dreams weren't scary anymore, Mama. He told me you would be okay, and that Father would be fine. He said we would have to use our magic to help him, but he would be fine. I like Didean a lot. He is the pony that gave me the ride home."

"The pony with wings?" asked Becka. "You told us about him when you woke up."

"Yes, he is the pony with wings and a boy's head and arms."

"Didean always wants to look young," said Jaynea.

"Mother, I don't understand," said Aimee, sitting down on the bed next to Becka, who had already collapsed.

"You have to explain what's going on here," said Erik.

Kami held on to her mother's skirt and Brian held tight to the cloak under the table.

Jaynea looked around the room at her six children. "We wanted to protect you all," she whispered.

"Mama," Aimee whispered.

"Give me a few minutes," she said, her eyes pleading with Aimee.

"Erik, help Mama back to her bed. We will clean up and I will speak with you later, Mama. We don't want you to have a relapse."

"Everyone let Mama rest," said Becka. "You little ones wait by the fire and perhaps Erik and Brian can tell you some stories of their adventures."

"I haven't had any adventures," said Brian.

"Hunting this turkey today was certainly an adventure," said Jaynea, as Erik helped her up.

Brian glanced at his mother. She ran her hand across the silky fabric of the cloak that lay across the back of his chair. A look of recognition spread across her face, but her shoulders slumped as she walked to her room.

After they had cleaned the kitchen and Brian was busy making Kami and Adam laugh whilst he concocted an alternate version of how he caught the turkey, the three older children went in quietly to see their mother. Jaynea was sitting up in bed and though awake, she looked worse than ever.

"Mama."

All three children ran to her side and asked her to lie down.

"You look wretched," Erik's insides churned. What if the wood-cutter's remedy didn't work after all?

"We need to let you sleep some more," said Becka.

Aimee got an extra blanket. "Erik, we need to keep the fire in here going tonight."

"I'll chop more wood right now," he said.

"No." Jaynea's voice was quiet yet firm. "I have just tried to contact your father with a mind reach. He is not alive in this realm of exis-tence, or I am sure I would have been able to reach him. I am just worn out again because it has been years since I used such intense magic."

The children stared at their mother. Did she really just admit she could use magic? That the legends and tales of magical creatures told by villagers and passing travelers were true?

"Mama, you are so weak," said Aimee. "I think you may be delirious."

"You have used magic today haven't you Erik?" Jaynea put her hand on her son's shoulder.

"The sorcerous Athena loaned me these," he said, holding up the worn leather boots.

"Your father's shoes."

"Father's?" Erik asked. "Father is the old friend Athena spoke of?"

Aimee sat down next to her mother. Becka walked over to the fire and stoked it a bit. It was too much to sink in so quickly. Both girls had a feeling they wouldn't have much time for any of it to settle.

"I need to talk to all of you."

Becka started to go and get the other children.

"Don't tell them what I just said about your father," said Jaynea.

"I won't Mama."

Once all her children were together, Jaynea took a deep breath. "You have all grown up so much," she said, placing her hand on Adam's head. "I never thought this would happen, but I believe it is time for you to know about the past. The best way for me to explain is to take you all to the cave. I really don't want to show you my secret place, but I have a feeling our lives are going to get a bit crazy. Once the magic starts, it's hard to stop. You may all have to tap into a few of your gifts before things get back to normal."

"Do we get to go there right now?" Adam jumped up off the bed. "Will Didean be there, Mama?"

Becka started, "Oh, Adam, it's already so late. The sun sets soon, and Mama must rest. We will go in the morning."

"No, Becka," said Adam. "I know you are still exhausted, but the dragons will eat Papa for breakfast soon if we do not save him."

"How does he know all this?" asked Brian, smiling at his little brother. "Maybe he knows where Mama's cave is too."

"No. Mama's powerful magic guards it," said Adam looking up at his mother for her approval.

"Mama!" said Becka. "You said you hadn't dabbled in anything intense in years."

"Oh, that's an old spell," said Jaynea. "It's held out for such a long time because you children have never been curious enough to find it."

"Erik and I have spent hours searching for that cave, Mama," said Brian.

"Yeah," said Erik. "I've pulled some of my best pranks on him while looking in the forest."

At this Jaynea laughed quietly. "Why would you think the cave is in the Forbidden Forest?"

"Well, we've searched in the foothills of Mount Sheldon too," said Brian.

"Not there either," she said.

"Then where?" asked Erik.

"You have traveled so far," she said, smiling a smile that was almost a smirk, "when the cave is right here in your own backyard. Brian, could you give me a hand?"

Brian took his mother's hand but as she tried to stand, she fell back into the bed.

"Mama," said Aimee, putting a hand on Jaynea's head and then her chest. "It doesn't feel like the fever has returned. She must be completely exhausted."

"We'll find the cave," said Erik.

"She said it's right in the backyard," said Adam heading out the door.

Brian and Erik followed.

The backyard of the Caraigdun house was a sloping hill of grass. Open fields of wildflowers covered the acreage leading into the forest behind.

Erik scanned the yard. A water well. Clothesline. Old stone wall surrounding... "The old oak tree." He said. "That has to be it."

The three boys ran to the tree. Adam started climbing; Brian checked the base.

"We've climbed this tree a million times," said Brian, amazed at his mother's cleverness.

"But where is the entrance?" Erik thought about the many times he had climbed the sturdy branches of this ancient oak. "How does our clever mother enter the caves from here?"

"Ha! She is clever." Becka and Kami had come from the house.

"I don't see any cave," said Kami.

"The first thing we must think about is that our mother is magic. She has always been magic, and she hid it from us," said Erik. "But there must be some clues, we have to think."

"Think back over our lives...." said Brian.

"I only have five years and I can only remember some of that," said Adam.

"Yes," said Becka. "But you were the last one to enter the cave with Mama. It would have been recently."

"Yes," said Erik, "maybe within the last year."

"You have to remember."

Adam closed his eyes. "My memories get mixed up with my dreams," he said.

"You could have dreamed something that will help us," said Brian, still rummaging around at the base of the tree. "I mean maybe one of these branches is a lever that opens up the entrance."

"Oh mother, you have us all so confused and we are all so tired." Becka had only drunk a little tea and she was feeling very lightheaded and sick.

"Yes, we have to figure this out," said Erik, "If Adam's dreams are correct, our father could be dragon toast in only a few days. Adam, close your eyes again. Try to remember the dreams you had when you were sick. You said you visited the cave in your dreams and that you met Didean there. How did you enter the cave?"

Adam closed his eyes. He scrunched up his face. Thinking hard. "Didean said I had to clear my mind of all evil," he said.

Aimee came out of the house. "Mama is mumbling in her sleep again. This time she is ranting about being captured. She keeps saying that the dragons are coming."

"Has her fever returned?"

"Yes, Becka, I'm afraid it has."

"I searched her room for some clue to the magic, and all I found was her old diary," she said, handing a worn leather-bound book to Erik. "It's locked."

Erik turned the book over in his hands. On the front there was an emblem carved into the leather. An eagle with its wings spread wide, carrying something in its talons. "What's it carrying?" Erik showed the book to Becka.

"Looks like an apple," she said.

"Odd thing for an Eagle to be carrying."

"Let me see, said Brian."

"I wish I had an apple to eat right now," said Adam.

"They're not quite ripe yet," said Aimee, glancing across the field to the orchard on the west side of the property.

"Sure will be nice when we can make apple pie," said Adam.

"Apple pie with sweet cream," said Kami, rubbing her belly.

"Not really something we should think about right now, is it?" Brian snapped. "We have to get to the bottom of all of this."

Erik put a hand on Brian's shoulder. Brian swiped it away.

"Stop it boys!" Becka yelled. "We can't get into the cave. We can't open this diary."

Erik walked closer to the tree. He started pressing on the bark all around it. The old oak was full of knotholes. He put his hand into one, and suddenly he was inside the cave.

"Erik!"

"Where'd you go?"

Erik banged on the other side of the door and called to his brothers and sisters. "There's a knothole, I just put my hand inside and it transported me inside."

The others all reached their hands around in the holes that covered the tree.

"Nothing is happening," said Brian.

"Which hole was it?" asked Aimee.

"Backside of the tree, about four feet up, I just stuck my hand in there."

"I've got my hand in there right now," said Becka. "Is there a lever? Or something to push?"

"No." said Erik's muffled voice from within the tree.

Adam stood back from the tree; his tummy was growling even though he had just eaten a good meal. Suddenly Adam was inside the cave standing next to his brother.

"Whoa! Little brother! Good job. Did you find the knot? Put your hand inside?"

"I wasn't even near that knot," said Adam. "I was just standing on the front side of the tree. All the other kids have their hands in the knots, and I can't reach very many. I was just standing there watching them."

"That's crazy," said Erik. "Were you doing anything else?"

"Nope. Just standing there thinking and trying to clear my mind of all evil."

"What were you thinking about?" Erik asked.

"I was thinking about how we're never going to figure this out so we all should just go inside and make some apple pie," said Adam, licking his lips.

"With sweet cream?" Erik asked.

"Of course, with sweet cream," said Adam. "Isn't that the only way...."

Erik started yelling at the others. "You have to think about apple pie, with sweet cream."

"What?" yelled the others.

"We can hear you telling us to think about something, but we can't hear what you're saying to think about..." Aimee yelled.

Erik stopped yelling and closed his eyes. He envisioned his mother in her blue and white apron baking in the kitchen. He saw the smile on her face as she pulled the aromatic pie out of the oven, cut a slice for him, and poured sweet cream on top. When he opened his eyes, he was outside of the cave again.

The others jumped.

"How'd you do that?" they all asked together.

"I don't think I can say it out loud," said Erik. "It seems to be some kind of spell where you think about something, and you get transported in. Each of you will have to think of it for yourself to enter."

"Hey! Where'd you go!" They heard Adam's voice from deep within the tree.

"So, what do we think about?"

"It's almost everyone's favorite dessert. So, it shouldn't be too hard."

Aimee held Kami's hand. "We'll do this together," she said. "Just think of our favorite dessert. Picking the fruit, cutting them up with Mama. Rolling out the crust."

"That's my favorite part!"

"Tossing the apples in cinnamon and sugar."

"Don't forget the pats of butter on top!"

"Cutting a nice big slice and pouring on the sweet cream."

Before they knew it, the girls were on the inside of the cave.

Still on the outside, Erik stood with Becka and Brian.

"I know it's not your favorite dessert, Becka," said Erik. "But you know what we're talking about right?"

"Yes." Becka tried to clear her mind of all evil, but the dessert they were talking about tasted bitter to her, so it was evil.

"You can do this Becka," said Brian. "I know you don't like to eat this dessert, but I've seen you laughing with Kami, Aimee, and Mama when you make it together."

"I can only imagine some evil beast trying to use that Think charm to get into the cave," said Erik, smiling. "Can you just picture an ogre or troll standing here...."

Becka closed her eyes. The thought of a monstrous ogre standing in front of the great oak and trying hard to think about apple pie and sweet cream made her smile. She grinned and thought of the last time she had churned butter and skimmed the cream off the top. Adam had squealed with joy when she let him have the first taste. She had gathered apples with Kami earlier that week. Her smile broadened as she remembered Kami's basket, which usually carried flowers, completely full of apples. Kami had cried that it was too heavy, and Becka said, "I'll tell you what, you carry the basket and I'll carry you." They laughed all the way home. Becka had stood singing in the kitchen as she peeled the apples. She opened her eyes and Kami rushed into her arms. "Good job, Becka," said Kami. "And you don't even like apple pie!"

"I don't like it for myself," she said, smiling at the blue eyes beaming up at her. "But I love how you and Adam like it when we make it together."

Still on the outside of the old oak tree, Erik stood with Brian. "Will it help if I go on ahead?" he asked.

"It would help if you weren't here at all."

"I know you're thinking of all the times I picked on you... Brian... What if you think of a time that we worked together?"

"We have never worked together on anything, Erik. I did all the chores before you would even wake up in the morning."

Erik's eyes searched the countryside. We planted all those apple trees with Father. We built that playhouse for Kami. Remember playing on the edge of the Forbidden Forest together?

Erik closed his eyes and thought of apple pie with sweet cream. Soon he was inside the cave.

Brian thought about everything Erik had said. There were some good times. While they were building the playhouse for Kami, Erik had complimented Brian on his work. "I always thought Erik just wanted me to do all the work." The thought entered his mind that maybe Erik knew Brian was more skilled at woodworking than he was.

Brian thought of the family, sitting around the kitchen table, and having dessert together. The girls really made a tasty apple pie with sweet cream. He took a deep breath and could almost smell the cinnamon and apples. When he opened his eyes, he was in the cave.

Erik put an arm around him. "I knew you could do it little brother. Look."

Before their eyes was a vast cave full of amazing sculptures. It was quite a mess, with bits of clay and tools lying everywhere. They were all mesmerized as they looked at their mother's creations.

"Why didn't she show us these before?" Kami stood staring in wonder at a magnificent life-sized sculpture of herself.

"She has to finish them," said Aimee. "I'm reading about it in her diary. It opened when we entered here."

"What do you mean?" Brian exclaimed. "Look at this awesome dragon. He is perfect. What could she possibly do to make it better?"

"Mama is very particular about her work, as is any artist Brian," said Aimee, placing herself in front of the magnificent sculpture. "We would never see a flaw, but she would."

"He's missing his mail," said Adam.

"See, young children are honest. He's not perfect, is he Adam?"

"Oh, that's only because he's seen a dragon in his dream," said Becka. "I think they are all completely phenomenal."

Aimee sat down to read more of the diary.

Each of the other children walked around the room and stood before the sculpture that was instantly their favorite.

Kami loved one of her as a baby riding on Brian's back. Jaynea had sculpted Brian into the form of a centaur. She had formed beautiful flowers in Kami's hair and placed fairy wings on her back.

Brian found one of himself as a baby too. He was being held by Erik who had a look of sheer joy on his face. "Erik loves you very much," Becka said, quietly.

"Maybe he did, then." Brian didn't look at her. His tone was angry, but she knew he had a tear in his eye, though he would never let her see it.

Adam jumped up and down in front of a magnificent sculpture of himself on the back of a centaur. "That's me and Didean," he yelled, ecstatically.

Erik found one of himself in full wizard's dress. "This is wonderful," he said. "But how could she sculpt it so perfectly? All the others are of us as children."

"This is not you, Erik, though you look so much like Father, when he was young," Becka stared at the uncanny likeness.

"This is Papa?" asked Brian.

"Must be," said Becka. Look at this clothing. He was a wizard.

"Look at the books in his hand!" said Kami.

"School books. Magic books," said Erik. He reached out and took a book titled *Spells and Charms* out of the statue's hand. "It's a proper book," he said, astonished.

Brian and Adam peered over his shoulder as he read some spells. "This will come in handy," said Brian.

Becka took a book titled *The Origin of Magic* and flipped through it. "Why would she stop using magic?"

"She gave it up for me." Aimee was holding the diary. "It's all in here, and it's terrible. Something terrible happened right after I was born."

Aimee read. "'It is the winter solstice and soon Athena will marry Guelder. My gift, the magnificent dragon sculpture, is almost ready. I hesitate to use the dust, but I can't imagine any harm will come from it. Clare and Matilda are as mild-mannered as can be, so I'm sure the dragon will be a pet, a lovely pet for Athena. She does love creatures so much.' As I flipped through the pages, I came upon the horrible thing that happened. The dragon attacked Guelder and our grandfather and killed them."

"Oh Aimee! That's horrible," said Becka, hugging her sister.

"So, she gave up magic because it's dangerous..." Erik started.

"She says later that she had to give it up to protect me."

"And our father gave it up too?" Brian asked. "I mean it seems he could have gone after the dragon. Defeated him."

"She says they made the decision together."

Erik thought about the view he had of their property, and how it seemed so remote, and so like a fortress. He looked through more of the spells in the book. "I wonder if there are protective spells around our house, and our lands?" He said aloud.

Adam peered over Aimee's shoulder at the diary. There was a sketch of the dragon on the page. A fierce beast... "So, now we know who has our father and who killed our grandfather, and Athena's boyfriend," said Aimee.

"Now, it's up to us to save our father," said Adam.

"And avenge their deaths," said Brian.

"You are all children," said Erik.

Aimee and Becka exchanged looks. "We are older than you!" they exclaimed together.

"I am not much younger than you!" shouted Brian.

"I am happy to be a child. I'll stay back here with Mama and Adam while you all fight the nasty beast." said Kami. She had sat down by her favorite sculpture and her eyes started drooping, and her head started nodding.

"I can fight!" said Adam.

"We can't be sure that it's this dragon that has our father. We can't even be sure the dragons have him. Adam had dreams; Mama has had dreams. For now, we need to get back to her, and make sure she's okay," said Aimee.

"You are right, Aimee," said Erik. "Everyone, use the Think charm and let's go check on her. Then we need to make a plan."

When the children got back to the cottage, Jaynea was still asleep. She was tossing and turning and yelling out that the dragons were coming, and that someone must save her Denis.

Erik put a hand on her shoulder and whispered, "Mama we need you to wake up."

Jaynea opened her eyes and looked up at her son. "Where am I?" She asked. "Where's your father?"

"Mama, you're here at home with us. The dragons may have captured Father. We need your help to figure out what's going on," said Becka.

"We've been to the cave," said Brian.

Jaynea was suddenly wide awake as reality hit her. "Let's get the little ones to bed, and then I'll tell you older children my plan."

Kami was quick to fall asleep once she had a bit of the herbal tea.

Adam had finally stopped climbing all over Erik and no sooner did his head touch the pillow, then he too was sound asleep with a smile on his face.

Erik stood by as Jaynea tucked Adam in, singing his favorite lullaby.

Good night precious one.
May angels guide you through your dreams.
Sleep tight little son.
This nighttime rest from all your schemes
When angels hide and brightness shines
Your rest will be complete.
Good night little son.
Til on the morrow again we meet.

"He is such a little dear when he sleeps," she said.

"And a mischievous monkey when awake," Erik said, leading his mother out of the room.

Aimee, Becka, and Brian were sitting at the kitchen table sipping tea and talking. Aimee looked up at the frail little woman, amazed at the toll this mysterious illness had taken. "Mother, you haven't fully recovered, sit and have some tea with us."

"I will," said Jaynea, as Erik helped her to her chair. Now that the young ones were to bed, he could see the burden in Jaynea's eyes. "Mama, you can sip a cup of this miraculous tea, but our curiosity will wait until morning, you need your rest."

Aimee knew Erik was right, but she didn't think it would hurt to ask a few questions. "I promise I won't let her stay up much longer," she said, knowing that Erik's comment had been as much to silence them as it had been to show his concern to their mother. "Mama," she began, holding up the diary. "I read all about what happened."

"Then you know it was my magic, my foolish mistake that brought the dragon to life. The dragon who killed your grandfather, and Athena's betrothed."

"And now he has our father," said Brian.

"Yes!" said Erik. "How do we find him, Mama?"

"I'm not sure, but I'm hoping Athena will know. The boys must leave first thing in the morning and go speak to my old friend. She'll know what to do." With that Jaynea laid her head down on the table and started crying. "I hope she knows what to do," she said.

{ 5 }

Of Plans and Schemes

Erik and Brian were up before the sun. Brian mounted Thunder as Erik strapped on his father's magical boots.

"We will arrive at Athena's by this morning if my calculations are correct," said Erik, "It's hard to tell but I'm pretty sure Athena lives in the center of the forest."

"You're really going to run along next to Thunder; our fastest stallion?" Brian asked, looking down at the worn boots.

"I'll have to regulate my speed, so I don't run faster than Thunder."

"Erik! Brian!" Adam came running out of the cottage in his nightclothes, a pack hanging from his right shoulder as he tried to pull it up on his left. "I'm coming too."

"You can't come," said Brian. "You'll just slow us down and get in the way."

Becka came out of the cottage, "It might be nice for Mama if you boys took him along," she said. Without even looking at Adam she took his pack, removed his night shirt, handed him some shorts, and pulled a shirt over his head. "That way she could really get some rest."

"You mean it would be nice for you," said Brian. "Let's go Erik."

Erik looked at his baby brother. He was beaming from ear to ear at the prospect of traveling with the big boys. "You know Adam; you have grown tall while I was away. I think you are big enough to come along on our journey."

Adam cheered.

Brian rode away.

"I'll tell Mama that you took him," said Becka, "Just take good care of him."

"Here you go Little Warrior, just climb right up here on my back."

"Do those boots make you strong?" asked Adam.

"No, but they'll help me catch up to Brian; and you can ride with him on Thunder."

As the brothers entered the forest, the trees seemed to close in around them. Thunder's ears twitched as his gate slowed.

"Don't worry boys," said Erik. "Athena does like to play practical jokes, anything she throws at us will be merely for fun."

"I'm not worried," said Brian, leaning forward in his saddle.

"Me either," said Adam, hanging on to Brian for dear life.

"You never know --"

A magnificent dragon rose before them. "It's just an illusion," said Erik, brandishing his sword.

"Doesn't feel like an illusion!" Brian yelled as he pulled up on the reins to keep Thunder from getting singed by the flames that suddenly filled the path before them.

"Oh boy," said Adam. Jumping down from Thunder's back, he grabbed his knapsack and ran behind a tree.

"That's right, you keep hidden while we fight the nasty beast," said Brian. Unstrapping his crossbow, he loaded an arrow. Just as he was about to shoot, he heard Adam yell; "Fire!"

The arrow caught fire and whizzed through the sky; the flame catching a low branch afire.

"How'd you do that?" Brian asked, loading another arrow into his bow.

"Aimee was up early studying this book of spells, I crept into her lap and paid close attention as she turned each page and described them to me — ohhh, here it comes."

The first arrow had bounced off the dragon's chest landing next to Erik and sending him flying into the forest near the other boys. "I think these boots are making me move so fast he can't see me or something. He almost got me with his humongous tail."

"Here's a spell you could use," said Adam. "Just load an arrow and yell—what's this word?"

Erik looked over his brother's shoulder. "Centum scindo!"

Brian had just released an arrow, yelling "Fire!" as Adam had done. The single flaming arrow split into a hundred that soared into the chest and underbelly of the giant beast. As the dragon flew away above the trees, the brothers heard a screaming cry of agonizing pain.

All three boys fell to the earth, catching their breath. "Guess it's a good thing we brought you along after all," said Brian, taking the book from Adam. "This sure came in handy."

"But how did you know which spells to use?" asked Erik, grabbing the book from Brian. "You don't read very well yet."

"There are lots of pictures," said Adam. "I just found a page that showed someone using a crossbow like Brian and I could read the word 'fire' so I just yelled it and then I saw this picture --" He turned to a sketch of an arrow splitting into a hundred, "and showed it to you."

"Nice work, Little Warrior," said Erik, patting his brother on the back with the vigor deserving of a valiant soldier.

Adam pulled a loaf of bread and three apples out of his knapsack. "Becka packed this for us," he said, handing the food to his brothers.

"I suppose this would be a good time for a snack," said Brian. "So, that dragon definitely wasn't an illusion?"

"No," said Erik, "but it would be nice if these burns on my arm were."

"I think I saw a healing spell in here," said Brian, flipping pages. "Here it is, but you need to gather these herbs and things."

"Athena will probably have something," said Erik.

"Too bad we don't have time to explore these woods," said Adam. "I've always wanted to look around in here."

"We can go slower," said Erik. "We need to pay close attention to the path now."

Soon enough Erik spotted Athena's cottage up ahead.

"I'm surprised no boulders or flaming branches have loomed across our path," said Erik. "I hope nothing's wrong."

Erik knocked on Athena's door. "Come in, come in," said the sorceress as she practically pulled all three boys through the door.

"Athena, is everything okay?" Erik asked.

"I've lived in these woods for sixteen years now, young Erik. No one knew I was here. And now, after you left, goblins accompanied by a dragon guard stopped by, and it wasn't for a spot of tea. They are looking for someone, Erik, or more than just one someone."

"We met a dragon along the path," Brian remarked.

"Our little brother Adam had a spell book with him, or we never would have --"

Athena looked at the boys. She sat down. She stood back up. She rang her hands. "Erik, you're injured," she said, and she pulled a jar off a shelf, absentmindedly rubbed the poultice on Erik's burned arm and began to rummage around the cottage looking for who knows what. "You must have told me there were six of you when we first met," she said.

"Yes, there are the three of us and we have three sisters."

"I'm Adam and this is Brian," said Adam, holding out his chest. "Can I help you find something?" And without permission he climbed up on a chair and began pulling things off a shelf.

"I think your friend's gone mad," Brian whispered to Erik.

"Here it is, here it is," she said, producing a cobweb covered scroll.

"Wow, what happened to this?" Adam asked, as he reached behind a clutter of jars on the shelf, pulled out an old, chipped clay mug, and handed it to Brian.

Brian held it up to the light coming in from the window. The front had a distorted face of an old woman sculpted onto it.

"That's Matilda," said Athena looking up from the scroll. "Your mother sculpted her for me," she said.

"Wow, I never knew our mother could sculpt something so hideous," said Brian.

"I'd be careful, Matilda might hear you." Athena spread the scroll out onto the table in front of them.

Erik read.

Three fair maidens,
Three valiant sons
Six shards of mountain flesh
Placed by the chosen ones.

"What does it mean?" he asked.

"It's a prophecy," said Athena.

"Well, just because we have three sisters, doesn't mean it's about us," said Brian. "I mean they're not exactly fair."

"That's right," said Adam, still searching through Athena's things. "They make me do their chores for them and --"

"That's not what --"

"Brian! Adam! This is serious. We need to tell Athena what we came here for. Maybe it has something to do with this so-called prophecy."

Adam jumped down from the chair and landed right in front of Athena. "We came here because the dragons have our father," he said.

Athena's shoulders straightened then hunched. She stood up and then sat down again. "Sit here and tell me all about it," she said, patting the chair next to her.

"All we know is that our father is missing," said Brian.

"I had a dream. The dragons have captured Father." Adam sat up straight.

"Mama tried some detection thing," said Erik. "She couldn't sense him anywhere. She sent us here because she thought you might help us find him."

Athena put her head in her hands. "I haven't used real magic—wait! Adam, you said you had a dream."

"Yes, I did. But I don't remember all of it --"

Athena stood up. She began searching around the cottage again, this time under a bed in the corner. "Adam, can you try to find the other old lady mug? I've a feeling Clare and Matilda will be able to help your father more than I can."

Adam jumped back up on the chair and began searching. Brian looked around the room too. Erik stared at the scroll.

"Here it is!" said Athena, producing an intricately carved wooden box. "The Dreamcaster." She placed the box on the table. "I don't know if it will work after all these years."

Erik ran his fingers along the carvings of dragons, clouds, pixies, and flowers.

"I found the other mug," said Adam, jumping down right in front of Athena again.

"Good job," she said, patting the little boy on the head. "Now Brian, you sit here, across from Erik." She handed each of the older boys a mug. "Now you must recite a charm, it's a kind of ritual, let me see if I can remember, umm. Oh, wait, first we must fill them with tea. Adam, can you get down that green sack?"

Adam jumped back up on the chair, "This one?" He asked.

"Yes, now bring the teapot."

Adam placed a few tea leaves in each mug. Athena poured the hot water. "Now each of you must say, at precisely the same time, 'a fine long life to you my friend'."

"I want to do it!" Adam jumped up and down like a kangaroo.

"You're going to get to use this," said Athena, opening the wooden box.

"Wow," said Adam, "it looks like the spyglass Father brought back from one of his trips to Greece, except for this contraption on top." Adam reached out his hand, then drew it back and looked at Athena.

"You may hold it," she said, "but be careful."

"Of course, be careful," said Adam, taking the Dreamcaster from its velvet lined case and holding it up to his eye.

"Now, back to you boys," said Athena. "Just click the mugs together and say: 'A fine long life to you my friend'."

"But he's not my friend," said Brian, "he's my brother."

"He's probably the best friend you'll ever have," said Athena. "Just give it a try."

The boys raised the mugs and clicked them together. "A fine long life to you my friend," they said simultaneously.

Suddenly the mugs shook. Tea dripped over onto Erik's burned hand. The eyes of both old ladies popped open, and they spoke simultaneously.

"It's about time someone woke me from that fitful sleep," said Erik's mug.

Brian's mug was speaking through one long yawn. "You—really should — have warned—me, Matilda. If I had known, we were going to have—company — I'd have put the tea on." Upon the word 'tea' she let out a startled little gasp as she had just noticed the face of a blonde-haired, blue-eyed boy staring back at her. "Clare, where are Jaynea and Athena? I'm being held by a young man."

"Oh, you are at that," said Matilda. "Looks like I've got me own fine young gent over here."

"Nice to meet you Matilda, I'm Erik," he said, relieved that she hadn't spit in his face.

Brian had almost dropped his mug, "I'm Brian, Jaynea is my mother," he said, turning Clare so she could see Athena who was beaming in the corner.

"I thought you might like to meet the sons of Jaynea," she said. "And we need your help."

"Of course; always coming to us for advice, but wait, how long has it been?"

"Sixteen years," said Athena.

"Sixteen years!" exclaimed Matilda. "It seems like yesterday two giggling maidens first came to us asking all sorts of questions,"

"Yes, they asked us everything from which dress to wear to the town picnic, to how to get rid of a bothersome younger brother. Remember when Jaynea came to us for advice about young Denis of Caraigdun?"

"She had fallen head over heels for him," remembered Athena. "When, all the time we were growing up, she referred to him as 'that stinky boy'."

"I told her not to waste her time getting involved with that one," said Matilda.

"Our mother married 'that stinky boy'," said Brian.

"Oh, Matilda," said Clare. "You were always advising the girls to be so cautious, they had to get married sometime. And look at them now; Jaynea with three fine young sons."

"We have three sisters at home," said Erik.

"Oh, Matilda, three more giggling girls for us to sit and chat with," Clare was excited.

"She's a bit too excited for a clay mug," whispered Brian.

"And how about Athena, then," Clare began.

"Yes, did you marry that fool Guelder?" asked Matilda.

Athena turned away; it had been so long since she had heard his name. "Guelder was killed – by -- well that doesn't matter now. Guelder died sixteen years ago on the eve before our marriage day."

The mugs were silent for the first time since they had woken.

"I'm so sorry," said Clare.

"I'm very sorry to hear that too," said Matilda, sincerely. "What soulless creature could have done such a thing?"

"Yes, you must tell us dear," said Clare, turning to Athena. "It wasn't Maldeminthir!"

Brian could see ripples in the tea as the mug shook.

"No Clare, he is in prison, safely locked away on the Ilse of Spectarum. It was a creature of whom you have never heard," said Athena, trying to smile. "I think the creature who killed Guelder has something to do with this." And she held up the scroll.

"The prophecy," said Clare.

"Our prophecy," said Matilda.

"Yes," Athena said. "I wrote it down many years ago."

"These old lady mugs made the prophecy?" Brian asked.

"What does it mean?" asked Erik, shooting a disapproving glance at Brian.

"We don't know," said Matilda. "We make predictions and sometimes they come true. Mostly it's just because we've been alive for so long."

"That's right," said Clare. "We've seen so many things that we can predict the outcome just by the choices people make."

"We would have predicted that your mother would marry your father even though we advised her against it."

"But when we made this prophecy, we didn't have any reason for it."

"I think there is a reason now," said Erik. "There's me and my brothers and Aimee and Becka and Kami. We are three valiant sons, and three fair maidens."

"But what is the mountain flesh?"

"I think I know," said Athena. "It is the mountain where the dragon lives; the dragon that your mother sculpted sixteen years ago, the one that killed Guelder."

"That's what she was talking about," said Erik.

"The reason they gave up magic," said Brian.

"I saw a dead mountain in my dream," said Adam.

"I thought so," said Athena. "Matilda and Clare, we need your help to interpret Adam's dream; to see if the events that have been happening to the children of Jaynea have anything to do with this prophecy." Athena took the Dreamcaster from Adam. Her fingers fell upon a set of three small dials just below the mirrors. "When did you dream about your father?"

"I had that dream for three nights. It was last week; I don't know my days very well, but I think one was Wednesday."

"Wednesday," said Athena. "The moon was at 3/4, Venus was low. And the stars were just so." Having set the dials, she handed the contraption back to Adam.

Adam looked in the eyepiece and pushed the button; the mirrors started spinning, and then halted. A moving picture flashed upon the wall; an image that looked like Denis. A man dressed in tattered old clothing, and he was old, too old to be Denis. The man was moving swiftly through a thick dead forest. One other man was with him. When the first man turned to speak, they could see the other man clearly.

Athena uttered his name, "Guelder."

"Look," said Brian, pointing to a figure climbing just out of sight.

Adam focused the Dreamcaster on that part of the dream.

"It looks like Father," said Erik. "He's trying to reach them."

Guelder and the old man came to the edge of a cliff. Behind them a magnificent castle stood at the top of a cliff faced hill. They stopped only for an instant. Their lips moved, and they jumped. Suddenly out of the clouds above the castle appeared two small black dragons. They swooped down upon the men, snatched them in their powerful claws and returned them to an unseen place inside the hill. A third dragon grabbed Denis carrying him in through a different entrance. The dream faded as Adam brought the Dreamcaster down. He had heard Athena gasp at the sight of the men but held his hand steady.

"Who were they?" asked Erik. "The old man looks like Father, but he is so much older."

"The old man is your grandfather," said Athena, a tear in her eye. "He was traveling with Guelder many years ago when the dragon attacked."

"It is true then," said Adam. "The dragons have captured Papa."

"It looks like he may have attempted to rescue Grandfather," said Erik.

"And Guelder," said Athena. "Could it be that Guelder and Marcus live?"

"Well, they definitely aged in the dream. It was as if Adam saw them as they would be now, when he has never seen them at all," said Clare.

"It can be the only explanation," said Matilda. "It seems they have been captive somewhere in Mount Ceo'ban' all these years."

"Yes, that's it," said Clare excitedly. "In your dream it was clear they had escaped and almost got away."

"And those filthy black beasts stopped them," said Erik.

"Then Father is safe," said Brian. "We just need to free them."

"Yes, we brave warriors will go and set them free," said Adam.

"And slay the odious dragons," said Brian.

"Yes, and slay the smelly old things," said Erik.

"Whoa, boys," said Matilda.

"This is not some little hunting trip for an elusive Tom Turkey," said Athena, winking at Brian. "These creatures are fierce and cunning. Somehow, they have kept Guelder and Marcus hidden in this mountain. Sixteen years ago, many of the wisest wizards came here and cast strong detection spells. None could detect the spirits of Guelder and Marcus anywhere on this earth. We all believed they were dead. There were traces of dragon blood mixed with the blood of the victims found on the trail from Cathair. We knew they had put up a valiant effort, but all evidence showed that they could not have survived. Gwandoya was and still is the fiercest dragon ever known to exist in these times."

"How is it we have never heard of this Gwandoya?" Matilda asked. "We were aware of all evil on the earth. Are you telling me that this Gwandoya creature was born after I went to sleep sixteen years ago and immediately grew to full height and strength overnight?"

"As Athena said, our mother sculpted him," said Erik.

"Ahha, so he gained life just as me and Matilda did," said Clare.

"With the stardust," said Matilda.

"*Stardust?!*" Adam couldn't believe his ears.

"It was a gift to your mother from your father. He had the help of a great wizard, his father Marcus. They worked together and figured out a way to travel to the closest star. Marcus believed that the power of the stars was the greatest power in the universe. Your father accompanied him on his only trip. They returned with six tiny seeds and a pouch of stardust. Marcus wasn't sure how to use these two amazing discoveries, but he knew they would be powerful. He insisted on keeping them safe. Your father agreed but took some of the dust without Marcus knowing. He gave it to your mother and explained what it was. She experimented with tiny bits of the dust and found out that she could use it to make her sculptures come to life."

"That's how Matilda and I were born," said Clare. "Your mother is our creator."

"That is amazing," said Erik.

Matilda was fidgeting. The tea that sat cold in her cup was spilling over the sides. "She's not really our creator," she argued.

"What do you mean? She formed us and put life into us."

"Yes, but something we never told her is that our spirits already existed," Matilda wrinkled up her nose. Cold tea was dripping down her face.

"Your spirits already existed?" Athena looked into the old woman's eyes.

"That's right," said Clare. "Matilda, and I had been floating around on earth for years."

"How else do you think we gained all that wisdom?" asked Matilda's muffled voice. Brian had taken a cloth and was wiping the tea from her face.

"Why didn't you ever tell us this before?" asked Athena.

"Never seemed like you needed to know; you thought Jaynea had created us and well, in a way she had. She gave us a place to settle while we waited out our sentences."

Erik stood and began walking around the room. His brain was going over all the information of the last few days. "Okay, so let me get this straight, our mother sculpts a dragon and, when it comes to life as an evil being, she thinks it's her fault because she was angry at our father."

"But now," Brian interjected. "We have just found out that the dragon took on a spirit that must have been evil to begin with. A spirit that probably was floating in limbo for years, stewing over his fate, and now he's taking it out on people in the form so graciously made for him by our mother."

"Right, this dragon captures our grandfather and Athena's fiancé. Everyone thinks they are dead and now we've found out they are alive but guarded by this same dragon."

"We found out because of my dream," said Adam, his smile gobbling up his face.

"But we have no idea who this evil creature really is," said Brian.

"I might," said Clare. "I have been thinking about all the evil creatures I have come upon through the ages."

"Yes, good idea," said Matilda. "That has been part of our restitution, you know, to protect the innocent from the wicked."

"Matilda, do you remember about three hundred years ago, a loathsome creature called Foltzbane?" Clare asked.

"Yes. I guess I do if I must. Was he that wicked ogre who went around pillaging all the villages?"

"Yes," said Clare, gravely. "He is the one who killed many wee children. He was beyond the powers of good. His heinous crimes against the innocent were unforgivable."

"He wasn't repentant anyway," said Matilda. "As a matter of fact, he was so untrustworthy even the underworld refused to let him in."

"Sentenced to remain in limbo for all eternity," said Clare, "a bodiless form with no place to hide. Good and evil spirits tormented him in the place between."

"Could it be possible that this Foltzbane is now the dragon my mother named Gwandoya?" asked Erik. "I suddenly have a terrible feeling about leaving the women home alone."

"Mama is in danger," said Adam.

"We must return immediately," said Brian.

***

Back at the cottage Jaynea slept soundly. The girls decided this would be a good time to explore her cave. Aimee and Becka wanted to find something that would tell them more about magic. Kami found a wonderful cave that was full of all kinds of discarded junk.

"It's a pirate's treasure," she said, running into the room.

"I always wondered what Mom did with all that stuff Father brought back from his trips," said Aimee.

"Look, here's that wonderful silk dress from India," said Becka, as she brought the dress up and rubbed it against her cheek.

"Look at this dress," said Kami, as she held up a beautiful blue Kimono. "Can I try it on?"

"I don't know," began Becka.

Aimee stopped her, "Sure you can Kami," she said, glancing at Becka. "Why don't you stay here and play with the pirate treasure for a while."

"Yeah," said Becka, catching on. "You have fun, there's even a mirror over here."

"We'll just be exploring the boring parts of the cave."

Aimee and Becka walked slowly through the dark tunnel lighting the torches that lined the walls.

"My insides feel all knotted," said Aimee. "I fear something ominous may jump out at us at any minute."

"I'm sure our mother, who has kept the fact that she is a powerful witch from us for all these years, has protections on these caves," said Becka.

"She has kept the most ominous creatures we know of out for all these years," said Aimee.

Becka smiled. "Our brothers," she said.

Aimee laughed. "That had to take some powerful magic."

"Well, I'm hoping we come upon some magical things," said Becka.

The next cave they came upon was magical indeed. It wasn't like a cave at all. Furnished with beautiful furniture from the Orient it was perfectly clean and set up just so.

"This must be where Mama comes when she's had enough of our messy house," said Becka.

"Yes, look at this writing desk, everything laid out so neatly," Aimee said, opening a drawer. "Oh, look," she said to Becka who was lounging on a chaise lounge.

In the drawer Aimee found a little book bound in leather. "Becka, look. My name is engraved on the front." A small rosebud adorned the upper right corner. She slowly opened the cover and saw a beautiful pencil drawing of herself as a baby. She flipped the pages to find that her mother had written many wonderful memories and with each year had drawn a new rendition of her daughter.

"I've never seen anything so wonderful," said Becka. "Do you think there's one for me?"

She opened the next drawer on the left side of the desk. "Oh, it's beautiful," she said, slowly taking the book into her hands. Her book was also bound in leather and engraved with her name but in the top left corner there was a caterpillar hanging from a leaf. She opened and started reading. Aimee was reading her book when she looked up and said quietly in amazement, "Becka, the caterpillar."

Becka turned the book over and saw that the caterpillar was crawling around on the leaf. "That's fantastic," she said. "Let me see your rose."

Aimee opened her book and started reading again. "It is so beautiful Aimee; your rose is slowly opening."

Aimee tried to jump to the end of the book to see what would happen, but the rose went back to being just a bud. "Must have to read from the beginning to make the magic work."

The girls were enjoying themselves reading their books when they heard a loud bang. Becka ran from the main cavern and down a tunnel to the treasure room.

Kami met her in the passageway.

"I—was — and."

"Calm down Kami, just tell me what happened," said Becka, bending down to Kami's height.

"I found this; it was long and straight so I thought it would make a good baton. I was spinning around dancing and singing, and all the clothing started dancing with me. I was having loads of fun when suddenly there was a great flash of light and a loud explosion, I ran out and --"

"What were you singing about?" Becka asked, taking the 'baton' from Kami.

"Umm, the usual things, you know flowers and rainbows and, well some unusual things, like um dragons --"

"Dragons," said Becka, pushing Kami behind her and looking toward the billowing smoke. They made their way slowly down the corridor. Becka stopped when she thought she had reached the entrance to the room. There was still a lot of smoke from the explosion. As the smoke cleared an amazing sight appeared. A small dragon was milling around in the room. He must have been a baby because he wasn't too steady on his feet. He wouldn't have been too intimidating except that he seemed to be frantically practicing his fire breathing skills. Little bursts of flame came out of his open mouth and flaring nostrils. He had already caught some of the old clothes on fire.

Thinking quickly, Becka waved the 'baton' at the dragon. "Dragon, go home to your mother," she ordered. Suddenly there was another flash of light. When the smoke cleared the dragon was gone, but the fire was still there. Becka picked up an old rug and tried to put out the fire. "Go get Aimee," she yelled.

Aimee was already on her way, and the two girls put the fire out quickly. They decided it would be best to get Kami out of the cave for now and get some fresh air. Becka carried the wand that had conjured the dragon, her journal, and several other things inside her cloak. She was a bit worried that some magic would not allow her to leave the caves with these things. Aimee went first, tucking her journal inside her own cloak. "I guess it's no problem taking these things out of here," she said, seeming to read Becka's thoughts.

Kami raced up the hill. "Adam!" She yelled. "You are home."

"Come quick," he yelled. "Mama is sick again."

The girls raced up the hill into the cottage. Jaynea was tossing and turning in her sleep, beads of sweat dripping from her forehead.

"How could you leave her like this?" Brian demanded.

"She was sleeping soundly when --"

"One of you should have stayed with her." Erik picked up the teacup that sat on her bedside table still full of the healing tonic.

Becka took it from him. "It's not our fault," she said.

"Denis. ... I told you not to --"Jaynea spoke in a whisper.

"Be quiet. Mama is speaking." Adam laid down next to his mother and put his ear next to her mouth. "What is it Mama?"

"Dragons ... dragons have him," Jaynea said.

"Mama, you must wake up," said Adam gently, shaking his mother.

"She's dreaming," said Brian. "Maybe we can see her dreams with this." He placed the Dreamcaster in front of her eyes; an image appeared on the wall and then disappeared as Jaynea rolled to and fro.

"Mama, you must wake up," said Kami. "You're just having a nightmare, Papa is fine."

"Denis," said Jaynea. Her eyes opened slowly, and she stared into Kami's face. "The dragons have your father."

"Mama, we've brought the Dreamcaster from Athena's cottage," said Brian. "It will help us see where he is."

Jaynea didn't say a word. She motioned for Brian to bring the contraption to her. He held it while she peered into the eyepieces. An image appeared on the wall. It was an extension of Adam's dream. The dragons took Marcus and Guelder from the cliff and then Denis came running up behind them. A goblin arrow pierced his side; a dragon swooped down, grabbed him and flew back toward the mountain.

Kami hid her face in her hands. "Oh, Father," she cried.

"We will save him!" said Adam.

"I hope it's not too late," said Becka.

"Mother, does this contraption show what really happened? I mean, dreams aren't real." Aimee handed a teacup to her mother.

Jaynea took the tea but set it down on her bedside table. "Since I haven't been able to contact your father, I believe the Dreamcaster is showing the truth. Adam and I had the same dream, so that confirms my worst fears. Yet, it is amazing that Guelder and Marcus are alive...." She motioned for Adam to hand her the book of spells that rested next to her tea. After flipping to a page with a drawing of a ray of magic entering a cloaked figure, she handed the book to Aimee. "You must direct your attention and all the energy in your soul to yourself and each of your brothers and sisters, Aimee."

Aimee ran her finger across the words under the drawing. "These words, Mama?"

"Yes, my Aimee. Say them now."

Aimee read the words to herself and then recited them out loud. The incantation came out strong, but nothing happened. "Let's all say it together," said Aimee.

The six children gathered around the book. Aimee helped Adam and Kami with the pronunciation of the strange words. Jaynea smiled as she saw her children band together. "That's a good idea, Aimee."

And together they said: "*Magicae intensio!*" Each of the children of Denis and Jaynea of Caraigdun stumbled as a ray of energy entered their bodies. A faint smile flickered across Jaynea's face. "Now the magic will be strong in you." She said and then fell back into her bed. Unconscious again.

"We have to get her to the caves," said Erik.

"I'll carry her," said Brian.

{ 6 }

Dragons!

As the group walked across the yard to the old twisted oak tree, Adam was the first to notice them. "Dragons!" he yelled.

Spiraling out of a perfectly clear sky seven dragons the color of flames came swooping down with the speed of an eagle targeting prey.

Brian laid Jaynea in the tall grass and covered her with the invisibility cloak. *I wish I had another,* he thought. Amazingly a cloak appeared neatly folded over his arm. He wrapped it around his shoulders just in time to hear Erik yell:

"Take cover!" But Erik did not take cover fast enough; the sharp talons of an auburn colored scaly beast snatched him off the ground.

In an instant, Brian sent an arrow flying to the breast of the dragon that carried Erik. The slight wound distracted the dragon enough that Erik could shake free just as they rose above the top of the forest. Falling into the trees he grabbed a limb and caught his breath. He winced at the pain in his ribs but found his footing on a low branch.

Adam was not so easily captured. The first dragon out of the sky did not bother with him. When the last dragon flew down, Adam had found a hiding place. A plan formed in his brain as he watched Erik rise into the air.

Devastated and almost frozen to her spot, Kami dove into the tall grass and the dragon missed her on his first pass. She had little time to think before the second. What can I do? What can I do? She thought.

"I am usually a friendly person," she said. "I don't want to make friends with you, mean old dragon."

She closed her eyes tight, fully expecting to be carried high into the air at any second. Suddenly she heard a loud clunk just over her head. Her heart pounding, she turned her head and opened one eye.

The dragon was flying at her but kept smacking his paws on some unseen barrier. She buried her head and said over and over, "I don't want to be friends with you, mean old dragon."

Aimee and Becka had flung themselves into the woods. The old oak seemed so close, yet so far, and they knew they couldn't find refuge there and leave their brothers and sister to fend for themselves against six fire-breathing flying lizards.

"Now what?" asked Aimee.

"Stay together," said Becka.

"Split up," said Aimee.

The dragon swooped down as the girls ducked behind a tree. "He can't get in too close as long as we stay by this tree," said Aimee. "The branches are so low."

"Did you feel the heat from the flames he was throwing our way?" Becka asked.

"They won't burn us up," said Aimee.

"I suppose you think they'll just hold us for ransom," said Becka.

"No roasted maidens today," said a manly voice.

The girls looked around.

"Up here."

Looking into the branches of the tree they could see shiny armor with a handsome head poking out. "Sir Kebin Dante Bruin at your service," said the man.

"Where did you come from?" asked Becka, as she snuck around the tree and started pulling things out of her satchel.

"I believe your sister has summoned me. Something about being held ransom by a fierce dragon."

"Summoned you?" Becka looked at Aimee.

"When you mentioned we were to be held ransom I had a quick thought of the brave knight who would have the honor of rescuing me from the tower."

"Aimee, there is no tower, it's a dark dreary cave and we aren't even there yet."

"Here come two of the nasty beasts now," shouted Sir Bruin, jumping out of the tree and landing in front of the two girls.

"They will have no second thoughts about roasting your brave knight," said Becka. Her hand grasped a long handle, and she pulled the object from the bag.

"My brave knight will conquer," said Aimee, with a swooning sigh.

Sir Bruin held off one dragon, but the other slipped by and grabbed Becka from behind the tree. "Lot of good he did me," she said, as the nasty beast carried her into the clouds. Looking down, she saw a strange sight. There was a crossbow floating in the air and aimed at her. "Someone must be using a levitating spell," she said. "Hope they don't try --"

Sure enough an arrow released, barely missed her shoulder, and pierced the dragon's claw causing him to lose his grip. Falling into the pond, Becka came up and got captured again. This time the dragon flew swiftly out of reach of the bowman, away into the clouds.

Adam had made his way into the house by hiding inside a barrel and moving forward as the dragon looked elsewhere for him. The rules for hide-and-go-seek say that you cannot take your hiding place with you. Good thing Adam doesn't have to follow the rules. Once inside the house, he went to the room he shared with Brian. There were all kinds of creatures carved from wood but mostly small knights and horses that had never been ridden or were doomed to have the weight of a man upon their backs for eternity. Taking the carvings to the edge of the door, Adam watched as the dragon circled around. He waited until he was spotted and then looked down at the wooden figures. "The day you have been waiting for has arrived, Sir Elmwood," he said, as he looked at a strong-looking knight who rode on a valiant steed. "Live! And...umm...grow! And fight the dragons!"

The dragon came swooping down as the army rose between him and the little boy. Adam hopped on a horse and sounded the attack. "Forward to battle!" he yelled. Charging, he held a sword out in front of him.

Sir Elmwood swung at the dragon with his sword. The dragon breathed his heavy breath, sending flames across the top of the army.

Adam looked at Sir Elmwood, who was rubbing his head, "Singed a bit, lad. Well worth it though. Well worth it."

"He may send you all up in flames if he gets closer on his next pass," said Adam.

"Have to find some way to extinguish his flame for a moment," said Sir Elmwood.

Adam climbed off his horse and grabbed a bucket. The dragon was high in the sky. Clearly surprised by this army, he must have been planning his strategy.

Adam ran to the water barrel and filled the bucket. Just then the dragon swooped down and snatched him by the shoulders. "Ouch, that hurts," he said.

"What do you expect?" asked the dragon. "These aren't kitten paws I've got here."

"You can speak!" Adam exclaimed.

"Of course," said the dragon.

"Can you sing too?"

"Sing? Well, no one's asked me to sing in years, but it used to be known far and wide that the great Ferlawn could sing like a dove." The dragon opened his mouth wide and let out a bellow that sounded like a dying cow.

Adam flipped the water over his head and into the gaping mouth of the dragon. Steam rose as the fire went out and the dragon dropped the boy. The loyal horse caught Adam and rode back to join the army.

"Nice work," said Sir Elmwood. "Now we will conquer."

Three of the dragons focused their attention on the floating bow in the center of the field. Arrows flew out of the bow with speed, but not quickly enough to ward off three dragons. Erik, who had been fighting his dragon from the tree, climbed down and came running across the field carrying a bow and one long arrow. Erik fitted the arrow to the bow. Barely able to raise it from the injuries he sustained, he closed his eyes and mumbled "centum scindo," as he pulled back the string. As four dragons swooped to capture their victims, the arrow split into one-hundred shining lines and rose into the sky. Each arrow made its mark and pierced the dragons several times. They retreated behind the pond licking their wounds. As they did, the evil dragon Gwandoya appeared on the edge of the pond. He clapped as he walked forward.

"My congratulations," he said, smiling his wicked grimace of a smile. "I am highly impressed with the children of Denis and Jaynea. Their parents have trained them well in the ways of magic." His giant tail swished, and his eyes lit with fire. "I have gained my purpose here. We go."

They heard a muffled groan from behind the oak tree.

Sir Bruin had lassoed the dragon's mouth and tied him to the tree. Gwandoya flew to the creature's side. "Fend for yourself, Denwen. You couldn't even defeat this imaginary knight fighting for his lady. If you can get yourself out of this predicament and return home, you may have a place in my army. Or you may not. We shall see."

He did not say another word but took off into the sky. The other four dragons followed.

"You're not really imaginary, are you?" Aimee asked, still entranced by the gaze of the brave Sir Bruin.

Sir Bruin leaned over and kissed Aimee smack on the lips. Kami, who had just gotten free of her bubble shield and was walking past, giggled.

"Did that feel imaginary?" asked Sir Bruin.

"Didn't look imaginary to me," said Kami, still giggling.

Aimee was in a swoon, floating in the clouds. "Didn't feel imaginary to me," she said.

Brian ran to where he'd laid his mother. As he reached out his hand to touch the invisibility cloak, the one around his shoulders disappeared. "Mother!" Brian searched frantically in the tall grass.

"What's going on?" Erik asked. "Where did you put her?"

"She was right here. I covered her with the invisibility cloak. They couldn't have found her."

"They got Mama?!" Adam yelled. They all got down on their knees and searched the grass.

"Gwandoya takes her to do his bidding," said the dragon Denwen as his wretched laugh filled the darkening sky.

Sir Bruin snapped his fingers, and the beast disappeared. "Where have you sent the foul beast? My brave and magical knight," asked Aimee.

"To a place where he shan't be able to harm you fair maiden," said Sir Bruin.

The group gathered in the middle of the field.

"Becka is gone too," said Kami. "I saw the dragon fly away with her, but I was too afraid to come out of my bubble and save her."

"She is not gone," said Aimee. "Look."

They all looked toward the pond where Becka had fallen. A large clear bubble was rising out of the water. Kami ran to the pond. The bubble floated over to where Kami was standing and popped on the shore. "Becka," Kami ran to her sister and threw her arms around her. "I thought the dragon took you away."

"I thought so too," said Erik. "I saw him fly over the trees with you in his claws."

"It saw it too," said Adam.

"We must let him think he has me," said Becka. "The girl that the dragon flew away with is merely a reflection. But she can reflect back to me what she sees in the dungeons of the dragon."

"Very ingenious," said Brian. "But if you are out here in the open much longer Gwandoya's spies will let him know the girl is but an image. We must hide you in the cave and use this spy to our advantage."

{ 7 }

Inside the Cave of Jaynea

Once inside the cave the children scoured the rooms for anything that might help them find their mother and father. Erik, Brian, and Adam gathered weapons and gadgets. After they had amassed more weapons than they could carry, the boys searched through the spell book of Adam's.

"There must be something in here that will give us some clue how to get into the mountain and slay the dragon," said Erik.

As the boys perused the spell book, Aimee read her journal and Kami searched through the junk room. Becka sat in a quiet corner of the caves gazing into the mirror. She watched in horror through the eyes of her reflection as a dragon dropped her unconscious mother upon the cold stone ground of the dank and dreary caved prison. "You must get help," she whispered, hoping the girl could hear her. Suddenly Becka heard the faint sounds of a melodious harp. "Help!" she willed her reflection to yell. "Is someone playing a harp?"

The harp playing continued. "Ha-ll-o-o!" she yelled at the top of her lungs. She listened as the sound of her voice became clearer and echoed through the caverns.

The sound of the harp stopped, and then she heard chattering. "Must finish, must finish today. Can't get distracted now, can we? The Master doesn't like it when we get distracted. Put us down in this dungeon because we get distracted. But it's almost finished."

"He-ll-o!" yelled Becka again more loudly.

The chattering stopped. "No, distractions!" yelled the voice.

Becka's reflection turned around. She had thought the voice was coming from a different cell far down the tunnel. Now she listened carefully for a minute. The chattering started again. It was behind her. She couldn't see very well. Even though she was sure it was day by now there was little light in her place of confinement. She walked toward the sound. The voice continued to chatter wildly. She heard something fall on the hard grown.

"Confounded!" yelled the voice. "Now I shall need to ask for more red paint. This will never do. This will never — ah-ha! The voices. The voices. The music. Play the song. Must play."

The harp music started again. The reflection that was Becka came to a narrow passageway. Getting down on her hands and knees she crawled along the ground. The passage became narrower and narrower but as it wound around more light shone through. The passage widened again and soon Becka could stand. She came into an enormous cave. The man had left the harp and was now working out a tune on a long wooden instrument. "Must finish, must finish," he said as he put the flute down and started painting.

Becka stood and watched him for a minute. Easels surrounded him, each holding a partially finished work of art. There were writings all over the walls. One wall of stone had a large piece of slate. The man had used chalk to write music.

"Finish and he will let me go," said the man.

Becka was afraid to disturb him. She didn't want to startle him. But she knew she had to get help for her mother. She cleared her throat softly. The man looked up at her.

"Finally, the master has sent a model," he said. He motioned for her to wait there as he cleared painting supplies off a wooden stool. He looked up at her as if she should know what he wanted of her without him saying. "Well come on then," he said. "Sit here."

When Becka sat on the stool, the man grabbed her hand and yanked her off. "That will never do," he said, placing her firmly in a standing position next to the stool. "No, no," he said, taking her arm and practically dragging her across the room. When they had finished dodging easels, knocking a few over, Becka let out a gasp as a running waterfall appeared before her. "How could this be?" She asked.

"Stand here," said the man. "No, no. That will never do. Sit here." Then seeming to notice the tattered, muddy clothes she wore for the first time. "We'll have to remedy that," he said, waving his hand.

A beautiful, full-length gown of gold replaced Becka's peasant clothes. Putting her hands to her head, she felt that her hair was all piled on top with tendril curls dangling and flowers throughout.

The real Becka called her sisters. "Aimee, Kami, come see this!" The old man was still chattering away about the setting and conditions when he turned and looked at her. "Who are you calling?" he asked.

"My sisters."

"There is more than one beautiful maiden confined in these horrible chambers?" he asked.

"I'm not here," she said.

The old man reached out and touched the reflection that was Becka. "I can feel your skin. Do you feel this?" he asked, pinching her.

Aimee and Kami gasped as they saw their sister dressed in the beautiful golden gown. "What--?" Aimee stammered.

"Shhh," said Becka. "I'm talking to a madman in the dungeons of Gwandoya, trying to get help for Mama."

"Yes, I felt that," she said. "But what you see is my reflection; I am sitting in a cave very far away from you. But your magic crossed over, you've transformed my clothing into a golden gown."

"My magic reached outside of this dungeon. Impossible."

"My magic reached in and yours reached out,"

"So, I've finally really gone mad," he said, stroking his long white beard.

"Tell him to take care of Mama," said Kami.

"Let me talk to him," said Aimee, grabbing the mirror. But as soon as she took the mirror from Becka's sight the man disappeared.

Becka took the mirror back, "Aimee and Kami, I want you to see this, but the mirror has to stay just so or the magic will not work." And then she whispered. "I think he's crazy and I'm not sure he can or will help Mama, I must proceed carefully."

Aimee and Kami looked over their sister's shoulder. "Okay, we won't move," said Kami.

"Stuck like glue," said Aimee.

"What is your name?" Becka willed her reflection to ask the man.

"Name—name—William is name, was name."

The old man started painting but didn't get very far when a tune started whistling from his lips as if it had a mind of its own.

"Confounded!" exclaimed the old man. Then, seeming to remember that he was in the presence of a lady of royalty he bowed. "Your radiant beauty inspires me in so many ways," he said.

Suddenly a pianoforte appeared. The old man sat down and picked out a tune. He played the pianoforte for a minute, came back to the painting, went over to the slate, rubbed out the writing with his shirt-sleeve and scribbled something new.

Becka watched with much interest. *This man is very talented, she thought. If he could just focus on one thing long enough, he would have a masterpiece.*

"Yes, a masterpiece," said the old man.

"You read my thoughts," said Becka.

The old man stopped. "Was that your voice then?" he asked, looking at her. "Finally, a voice that understands me." He put down the flute and stared at Becka. "You have not been sent by Gwandoya to model for the queen's statue, have you?"

"I'm afraid not," she said.

The old man gazed intently at her. "You would have made a grand model in that dress," he said. "I am William," and he bowed and extended a wrinkled hand. "To whom do I have the pleasure of making an acquaintance?"

"I am Becka, daughter of Denis and Jaynea of Caraigdun," said Becka, curtseying low.

"Daughter of Denis and Jaynea of Caraigdun," he said, freezing.

And then what she heard were no longer his words but his thoughts. *Denis of Caraigdun is your father?*

Yes. Becka thought. *He is being held captive in the dungeons right now.*

Yes, my son is here, he tried to rescue us but was injured...

"Why'd you stop talking?" Aimee asked.

Becka turned away from the mirror, "We're talking to each other in our minds," she said, "But it's our grandfather!" she exclaimed.

"Grandfather! Grandfather!" Kami called. "Can you hear me?"

"What is that melodious sound I hear?" he asked, cuffing an ear with his hand.

"We don't have time to get to know each other right now, Grandfather," said Aimee. "Our mother is there with you, she is unconscious--"

A rather large goblin had appeared, covered head to foot in full armor. He was hauling a large portion of clay.

"Gwicksped," said William, who they now knew must be their grandfather Marcus.

"You will sculpt a body for the bride of Gwandoya, and a new human form for him," demanded Gwicksped, opening the iron bars and shoving the mound of clay into the cave at Becka's feet.

Becka heard Marcus' thoughts. *He must think you are Jaynea. Gwandoya brought her here to sculpt the bodies, just as she sculpted his form years ago.*

"I will not," said Becka.

"You will or your friends will die," said Gwicksped.

"We're all going to die anyway," said Becka, trying to get through the gate before it closed.

"Feisty little thing isn't she," said Gwicksped. "Better use a bit of that energy on this clay. Gwandoya's wedding is planned for sunset on the eve of the full moon."

"The eve of the full moon is only ten days away," said Becka. "Anything that my moth — I could sculpt by then would be half finished at best."

Gwicksped took her by the hair, crushing the flowers as he pulled out the bun. You are to sculpt small models by the morning of the eve of the full moon," he said, yanking on her head. "Gwandoya will take care of the rest." Shoving the reflection of Becka away, he closed the bars with a bang. "As far as your meals are concerned Gwandoya wants you to be strong while you finish the work. This madman can conjure anything you want to eat."

Marcus was still working at an easel. He had quieted down for a minute but when the goblin said, 'madman' he started screeching loudly, "More red paint! More red paint! Can't finish me picture without more red paint!"

Gwicksped covered his ears, "I'll have some sent down to you, old man. Just stop that racket."

Marcus laughed hysterically as Gwicksped ran away from the bars. "He hates the sound of my voice," he said, winking.

Marcus backed up slowly. He chattered wildly again but motioned for Becka to follow.

"No way out, no way out," Marcus chanted. But as he chanted, he lifted a tapestry that covered one long wall revealing a drawing and writings scratched into the wall.

To one side was a small picture of Mount Ceo'ban and the castle of Gwandoya. Marcus had drawn a dome around the entire area. He pointed with his finger as he changed the tune of his chant. "Magic too strong, magic too strong," he said. But as he said these words, he pointed to the shield, then to the spell and then to two transparent forms on broomsticks just to the inside of the dome.

Becka was trying to take it all in. She read the spell and looked closely at the figures. She could tell by the way Marcus acted that he was worried that someone was listening.

"It's us," said Aimee, and she hastily pulled a charcoal out of her pocket and started to copy the drawing.

"Two children to break through the magic," said Marcus. He pointed to the drawings again. This time he pointed to three different places on the drawing. Three figures stood around the base of the mountain.

"The boys," said Kami.

"Yes," said Marcus. "I have seen this picture change as each of you were born. It's how I know about each of you. It's how I know about the prophecy. My grandchildren will save me."

Becka pulled away from the mirror. Her mind ached.

"Wait, you have to tell him about Mama," said Aimee. "Do you even know where she is?"

"I saw her dropped in the cave next to our grandfather," said Becka. "Here, I'll tell him. Grandfather, our mother is in the cave through that tunnel. My reflection will show you, but I must go for a while. Tell Mama that we are making a plan to come and save her, and you and father."

The old man looked directly into the reflection that was Becka's eyes and smiled. "I knew you'd save me one day," he said. "I've been dreaming about it for years and now it will come true, and I will finally get to meet my grandchildren! And don't worry girls; I will keep your mother safe. Oh—and your father is in the cave next to me, he is recovering from his wound. Guelder is with him and Gwandoya's evil guard doesn't know but I can get to them through this other tunnel."

"I feel much better knowing you are there," said Becka. "I will check in with you again soon."

{ **8** }

Enchantments

After the girls told the boys about their conversation with Marcus, the older children got Kami and Adam fed and put to bed so they could make some decisions about how to proceed. Aimee and Becka walked the two young ones to a couple of special rooms.

"Mama would want them to experience this," said Aimee.

"Yes, in case we never return," Becka whispered.

In each room there was a bed covered with several soft feather mattresses. Fit for a princess, Kami's bed had pink silk curtains hanging from the bedposts all around. There was a beautiful white nightgown lying across the bed.

"Oh, it's all so beautiful," said Kami, "but I can't sleep there. I'm filthy from fighting the dragons; and besides, Mama doesn't get to be comfortable tonight."

"You know what Kami," said Aimee. "I'd bet she is comfortable; I'd bet Grandfather conjured a nice bed for her."

"That's right," said Becka. "You saw how he set up his cave. He conjured that settee for my reflection to sit on and the guard even said he had permission to conjure as much food as they wanted. I'd bet Father and Mother are sleeping soundly right now, dreaming about us coming to rescue them."

"Yes," said Aimee. "And you know Mama would want you to get a good night's rest after fighting dragons today."

Kami walked slowly over to the bed and ran her hand across the silk curtains. Then she picked up the nightgown --"

"But don't put that on yet," said Becka.

"Look what happens when you walk into this little chamber over here," said Aimee, as she drew back a silk curtain to reveal a narrow doorway.

Kami gazed into the small room; it was dark and looked rather empty. "I don't see any--" Just as Kami crossed the threshold a large tub appeared overflowing with bubbles. Candles floated just above her, and the scent of lilacs filled the air.

"Now you be careful not to slip under," said Becka.

"We'll check on you after we get Adam all set," said Aimee.

When Aimee and Becka turned around Adam was nowhere in sight. They ran down the corridor calling for him. When they came upon the main chamber Erik and Brian were sparring with swords.

"Have you seen Adam?" Becka asked.

"Can't say I have," said Erik, taking three quick steps forward.

"Nope, been keeping my eye on Erik's sword," said Brian, taking three quick steps backward and one step to the left.

"Can you stop and help us—" Aimee lunged for a curtain that was swinging slightly. Adam ran past grabbing her skirt and spinning her around. "Get him!" she yelled.

The boys stopped long enough to laugh.

"Don't let them put me in that horrible place," yelled Adam.

"Must be some kind of horrible torture," said Erik.

"Sounds menacing," said Brian.

"It's just a bath," said Becka.

"A bath!" Erik caught Adam under the armpits.

Brian grabbed him at the ankles. "Show us the way," he said.

Adam kicked and screamed as the boys raced toward his fate. Both stopped when they saw the overflowing tub of bubbles.

"The soap has exploded," said Erik laughing, as he and Brian started swinging their little brother.

"One — two — three!" They yelled, tossing him into the billowing foam.

Adam came up sputtering. "This isn't so bad," he said, calming down, as he blew the light fluffy stuff off his mouth.

"Don't worry, they'll have to take one too," said Aimee, stifling her laughter.

"You're not getting me in a tub full of exploded soap," said Brian.

"I think you'll want to be clean once you see what we've found for each of you," said Becka.

"As soon as you've finished your bath, go ahead and get into your nightclothes," said Aimee, to Adam who was now making shapes out of the foaming white stuff.

"Yes, and go right to sleep then, you'll need your rest Little Warrior," said Erik.

The older children gathered back in the main cave. Eric and Brian brought weapons, Becka brought scrolls and books, Aimee brought all six journals. The emblem on Brian's journal was a dragon growing from egg to young dragon. Erik's was a lion, Kami's a dandelion, and Adam's a frog.

"I'm going to take Adam and Kami's journal into them," said Becka. "It'll give them something to take their mind off thinking about Mama and Papa in the cold dark dungeons."

When Becka got back the others were already discussing the situation. "Well, Becka," said Erik. "We've decided that it would be best if you stay back with the young ones."

Becka didn't glare at him or even put her hands on her hips; she just bent over and started laughing. "Great joke," she said. "Now let's get serious. Marc — Grandfather pointed to six figures on the map, so we have to bring Kami and Adam with us."

"She's got us there," said Brian.

"Okay, well our plan of action will have to include them," said Erik. "Now did anyone find anything that gives us some idea of how we might get to Mount Ceo'ban?"

"Well, Gwandoya's dragon guards will certainly be out looking for us, so we have to find some way to get there without being seen."

"Brian has an invisibility cloak," said Erik.

"And it split into two when we were fighting the dragons. I covered Mama with the other half --"

"Well, they found her, so somehow --" Becka began.

"Yeah, I was wondering if maybe Gwandoya could see her since he was invisible himself," said Aimee.

"That makes sense," said Erik.

Becka picked up one of the books and started flipping through it. "Maybe we can find a spell that will transport us to the mountain."

"Great idea," said Brian.

They all began looking through the piles of books and scrolls. After a while Erik said, "Aimee, how did you conjure that knight, who came to your rescue during the battle with the dragons?"

"I just thought about him and wished for him," said Aimee.

"So, maybe we can just wish ourselves over there," said Brian.

"Wait," said Becka. "Look at this."

In front of her was a very large leather-bound book full of old torn pages. The others gathered around, and Becka pointed to an area on the page. "Doesn't this look like it could be Mama's cave?"

"Yes," said Erik, "and these are tunnels leading all over the place."

Their eyes followed the winding tunnels past the labels that said; Lair of Prestwick, Den of Orif the Ogre, Dwelling of Tibolt the Troll, with things scribbled across the page like "temporary," "only on a good day," and "use the changing spell."

"This looks really familiar," said Brian, pointing to a section on the map the farthest corner away from the caves of Jaynea.

"That's what I thought," said Erik. "I think it's Athena's place."

"Yes," said Brian. "See this torn corner? I'd bet it said 'Athena.'"

"So, maybe Mama or Athena constructed these tunnels between their secret places," said Becka.

"Or they were already there, and that is why they chose these locations," said Aimee.

"This looks like it said, 'Realm of Hidden Magic,'" said Brian.

"Mama said these caves are protected, so maybe this entire underground system of tunnels is protected," said Erik, turning the page. "And look, it goes on and on all over Caraigdun, and under the Forbidden Forest."

"All the way to Cathair to the west," said Brian.

"And Mount Ceo'ban to the Northeast," said Aimee.

"So, we can follow this system of tunnels undetected by Gwandoya's evil spies," said Becka.

"It's worth a try," said Erik. "At the very least we can follow this route to Athena's cottage, let her know what's happening, and ask her if these tunnels still exist."

"And will lead us to our parents," said Brian.

"Should we tell them our plan?" Becka asked, pulling the mirror from her cloak.

"I'd like to check on Mama," said Erik.

"Yes, make sure they are okay," said Aimee.

"But don't tell them too much," said Brian. "They'll just try to nix our plan."

Erik sidled up to his sister. "You can really see them and talk to them?" he asked.

"Have a look," she replied.

"Tell them I said 'hello'," said Aimee. "I'm going to check on the young ones."

Erik and Brian peered over Becka's shoulders. "Wow," they both said at once. Through the mirror they saw a half-eaten turkey carcass, fruits and vegetables of every kind, an assortment of breads, and a choice of desserts they had never laid eyes on or imagined. Marcus was sitting back, rubbing his great belly. "You must eat, to get your strength up," he said, as he leaned forward and handed a turkey leg to Jaynea. "I can't eat not knowing what my chil --"

"Mother, we are here," said Erik.

"Can you hear us?" Brian asked.

Jaynea looked into the reflection's brown-green eyes. "Boys are you —but how?"

"Yes, Mother, we are here," said Becka. "Now listen to Grandfather and eat."

Jaynea stood, suddenly filled with frantic energy. "You must all promise me you will not come near this horrible place," she said, as her face filled the mirror.

"Told you," Brian said.

"Mama, do you think any of us will rest until you are safe?" Erik asked. "We can feel the magic you released in us."

"I only did that so you could protect yourselves. If I could, I'd take it back and hide you all away again. I am safe here," she said, faking a smile. "Look, your grandfather has treated our wounds, and you wouldn't believe the beds --"

A hand took Jaynea by the shoulder. "Hello children."

"Hello Father."

"Jaynea, they must come. It's part of the prophecy --"

"Do you think I care about some old --"

Jaynea ranted about it being all her fault for conjuring the dragon. Marcus pulled her aside as gently as possible.

Denis spoke. "Erik, Brian, I'm not sure how long Becka's magic will last. Very nice job Becka," said Denis. "But your grandfather is one of the most powerful wizards of all time and he's been locked up in these dungeons for sixteen years because we did not detect that he was here. They have cast some spell that allows him to conjure the necessities of life."

"More than just the necessities" — Brian interjected.

"He can even heal but cannot break the shield --"

They could barely hear their father over their mother's loud protests.

"You'd better deal with her," said Marcus, putting Jaynea's hand in Denis's. "Boys, listen carefully, there is a spell. I used it once when I was in Gwandoya's chamber, my bat friend Chalta flew out, but the opening only lasted for a few seconds. Gwandoya stopped me from escaping. My powers alone were not enough… The words are *Contego Distraho*, but you must chant them, and it needs to be all of you. … She is fading!"

Their father's face appeared before them. "Becka, you are fading, we probably… ."

Becka bowed her head. She could feel her own energy draining away. Brian grabbed the mirror. "Father! Mother!"

"It's no use," said Erik.

"Did you at least catch the words for the spell?" Brian asked.

"*Contego Distraho*," said Becka. "*Contego Distraho*."

Brian found the map and wrote the words down next to the base of Mount Ceo'ban.

"I'll never get that image out of my mind," said Becka.

"What image?" Aimee had returned from tucking in the young ones.

"The image of Mama screaming like that," said Brian.

"Were they torturing her?" Aimee asked, grabbing the mirror from Becka's limp hand.

"Nothing like that," said Becka. "She was just insisting that we not come to rescue them, and then they pulled her away and she was struggling to get free --"

"She was screaming in the background to us while Grandfather tried to tell us the spell that will bring down Gwandoya's shield around the mountain." Said Brian.

"So, they know we have to come," said Aimee.

"Yes, they know we are the ones. They know it is our destiny to conquer the dragon." Erik added.

Everyone was quiet for a moment. The caves seemed somehow darker, somehow danker. Brian started loading supplies into his knapsack. Erik searched through the pile of weapons. "I guess we can't take them all," he said.

"Better choose the one that's most likely to kill the dragon," said Becka, who had dumped out the contents of her satchel and was deciding which items to bring. "How are we supposed to know what we'll need?" she questioned, throwing her hands in the air.

"I think we need to get some sleep," said Aimee. "Boys, Becka and I found something for each of you. I put it on your bed. We wanted to make a real presentation of it --"

"Come on," said Becka. "We can't let seeing Mama like that get us all down and depressed! Boys, we have a surprise for you."

"Exploding soap," said Erik.

"I'll pass --" Brian started, but Aimee yanked him by the hand and began dragging him through the passageway. "Becka's right, come with me."

When Brian and Aimee got to his room, Brian stood in amazement. "Wow, this is better than Adam's room."

Relief sculptures of knights jousting, wizards dueling, and warriors fighting dragons adorned the walls. Some sculptures showed dragons fighting dragons; some were of creatures that Brian had never seen before. "I'll have to ask Mama about these," he said, as he ran his fingers along the walls.

"This is the surprise," said Aimee, holding up a shiny chain-mail suit. "We thought you might like to bathe before you wore something so amazing."

"Maybe." Brian took the suit from his sister and let the chains drift across his hand. "I've never seen anything like it."

"We hadn't either," said Aimee. "It must be magical to be so light and yet it looks so strong. I'll let you decide if you'd like to bathe, little brother. The tub appears behind that curtain if you need it. I'm going to take a quick bath and get some sleep."

Brian put a hand on Aimee's shoulder. Then, uncharacteristically, he threw his arms around her and gave her a huge hug.

"Thanks," she said. "I needed that."

That night, as the boys lay clean and fresh in their feather beds, they spoke to each other through adjoining rooms. "Do you see what I see?" Adam asked.

"I see the back of my eyelids, Adam," said Brian.

"Me too," said Erik. "And so should you, Little Warrior. We have a...." Erik had opened his eyes. "Brian, you have to see this."

Brian was lying on his back. When he opened his eyes, he felt like he was outside, staring at the night sky. The stars were brighter than he had ever seen before.

"It's like we are at the top of the world. The stars seem so close," said Erik.

"Or like we are out in the far reaches of space among the stars," said Brian.

The boys lay quietly, gazing at the expanse, until finally they all fell asleep. The dreams they dreamed that night are fit for another tale that may be told upon this tale or saved for another time.

{ 9 }

Into the Hidden Realm of Magic

When Adam woke up, the ceiling was back to normal. "I'm having so much fun with this magic," he said, as he bounced from room to room waking everyone up.

"If only there were a spell to make you sleep longer," said Aimee as she yawned and stretched out her arm accidentally on purpose, knocking Adam onto the floor.

"I'm ready to get up, Adam," said Kami. "I'll help you wake up the others."

"I thought you'd be the last one to wake up and get started on our quest," said Becka, groggily.

"I'm more confident after the dreams I had last night, Grandfather was in them, and we went on marvelous adventures with him. In others he told us stories of his adventures and his life and all about our grandmother who died many years ago." said Kami.

"I believe our dreams will make for some good stories to pass the time on our journey," said Aimee, beaming as she thought of her own comforting night vision, that included a certain brave night. "I can't wait to hear about yours, Kami."

When all were awake, they gathered in the main cave for a hearty breakfast.

"Everyone, eat quickly," said Brian, who'd barely touched a bite.

"So, you made a plan," said Kami.

"They found a map of tunnels in these caves," said Adam.

"Then we don't have to go outside," said Kami.

"We shall stay hidden at least for a while," said Becka.

"We've packed supplies in a knapsack for each of you to carry," said Erik. "Do you think you can handle this, Little Warrior?" He asked Adam as he placed the pack on his shoulders.

"I have some things I want to bring," said Adam, taking the pack off and dumping out the contents.

Becka threw up her hands. "All my hard work," she said.

"I'll put it all back," said Adam. "I just need to fit these other things in here."

Becka let out a sigh and walked over to where Aimee stood peering into the depths of pitch darkness. "I wonder what's in there."

"According to the map there is a troll, an ogre, and a dragon this way; this is the way to Prestwick's Lair. Mama wrote 'friend' here and then crossed it out and then wrote it again, so I've a feeling he can be in a bad mood sometimes." Aimee said.

"Prestwick? Is that a troll or a dragon?" asked Kami. "Wait, wait, it's the dragon! I know because he was in my dream last night and we were having a picnic with him. He will be in a good mood. I am going to get to make friends with a dragon after all and my new friend is going to help us conquer Gwandoya!"

"That would be nice," said Erik, tousling Kami's curly locks. "But we will have to be ready for battle, just in case. Better clip those long nails of yours Aimee."

"Clip them?" asked Brian, "they'll be impressive weapons in hand to hand combat."

"As far as I can tell from Mama's scribblings the creatures in the tunnels between Athena's and here are friendly sorts, just trying to keep a place where they can get away from the troubles of the world, you know. Wouldn't hurt to be on guard though," said Aimee.

Each of the travelers threw a pack over his shoulder, and the group began the journey. Adam and Kami held their torches out in front of them and ran ahead through the winding tunnel. Kami seemed surprisingly comfortable in the dark dreary caves.

"Don't get too far ahead," yelled Becka.

"You never know what might be lurking around a corner," said Erik.

A few steps more and it was Erik who jumped. But it was Kami and Adam that scared him as they hopped out from behind a rock formation.

Brian laughed. "You never know what might be lurking around the corner," he said in a mocking tone.

"We found a door," said Kami.

"Can we knock?" Adam asked, jumping up and down in front of Aimee.

Aimee held the map up for Becka to see. "What do you think?" She asked.

Becka took a long hard look at the wall. It was smooth, with no doorknob and had a few markings scratched crudely along one edge. After glancing back at the map, she said, "Let's let Erik knock."

Erik didn't hesitate. He walked right up to the door and laid his fist down hard. His knuckles barely reached the door the third time when the slab flew open. Erik was immediately turned into a toad and the door closed.

Brian quickly picked up the toad. "You never know what's lurking behind a door either," he said, looking the toad in the eye.

Aimee and Becka were laughing but Kami didn't like this at all. "Turn him back," she said, taking the toad from Brian's hands and shoving it at her older sisters.

"Let me try," said Adam.

"No, no, you might turn him into a… something too big for us to hang on to; then we will lose him forever," Kami warned.

"And this is bad, how?" asked Brian.

"We need to stop playing around and get to Mama!" Kami added.

Aimee bent down to hug her sister. "Mama and Papa are fine," said Aimee. She positioned Becka in front of the door but a little to the side. "Now hold up the mirror."

Becka pulled the mirror out of her cloak and held it in front of her face. Aimee glanced at a page in the book then took Becka's hand and turned the mirror around to face the door.

"Stay just so," said Aimee. She reached out her hand to knock. Before the third knock she jumped back as the door opened. They all got a glimpse of a hideous troll just as it turned into a bunny and the door closed.

The group hurried away down the corridor.

Then Kami screamed. "Erik is changing," she yelled.

Aimee and Becka turned just as the toad sprouted arms and legs. Soon a befuddled Erik stood before them shaking his head.

"I've just had the strangest dream. I was green, and I kept sticking my tongue out to eat flies," he said, looking around at the faces staring at him. "It wasn't a dream, was it?"

Aimee and Becka exchanged glances. Adam snickered.

"I didn't like the trick they pulled on you," said Kami, hugging her big brother.

"It says here that the spell always took about a half an hour to wear off," said Becka.

"But Erik has already changed," said Aimee. "That means --"

"The troll!"

"Run!" yelled Adam, as the group followed him down the dark passageway.

A loud sound, sort of a growl, sort of a roar, more like the loud yawn of a monster awakening came barreling down the passage.

Erik threw Adam up on his back. Becka grabbed Kami's hand.

"There is no place to hide," said Aimee, who was bringing up the rear and could feel the breath of the troll on her neck.

Brian let her pass and pulled his sword. "Back, vile beast," he said as he jabbed at the monster.

Suddenly a door opened. Aimee pulled Brian in just in time. The door closed and disappeared.

"I could have taken him," said Brian.

"He is three times your size," said Aimee.

"He has a brain the size of a pea," said Brian.

"Well, you've got him there," said Erik. "Yours must be the size of a peanut."

The group was out of breath, but Adam started laughing. Aimee and Becka were smiling but with knitted brows. "That was a close one," said Kami.

"The troll's power must have weakened since the last time Mama pulled that trick on him," said Becka, catching her breath.

"That was quick thinking, making that door, Aimee," said Becka.

"It's a good thing I couldn't sleep the last few nights," said Aimee. "I remember some spells from studying the books."

The group started down the only passageway in sight. The torches cast eerie shadows on the dark gray walls. It was a long walk before they came to a spot where they had to make a choice. Erik took the map from Becka. The older children studied it long and hard by torchlight.

Kami could see by the looks on their faces that they thought they were lost. "It is the same as in my dream," she said, taking Erik by the hand. "Follow me."

Kami led the way down the passage to the right. "The door will be just about — here." Kami held up a torch. The group could see the faint outline of a door in the rock wall.

"This isn't the home of Prestwick," said Erik, pulling Kami back.

"Let her knock," said Aimee. "Maybe it's a back door."

Kami knocked and didn't even stand back. The door opened and revealed a magnificent gray-green dragon. Diamonds adorned the mail on his chest, and he wore rings on all his pointy fingers and toes.

"I have been expecting you," he said, bowing to Kami.

"It is very good to see you, Prestwick the Magnificent," she said, curtseying.

"But they have never met," said Brian.

"Better be polite," said Aimee.

"Yes, I'd just go along," said Erik. "He seems to be in good spirits and if he says he's met Kami before well he probably has."

"That was a splendiferous dream we had together last night then, wasn't it?" asked the dragon, extending his arm to Kami.

Kami giggled. "Splendiferous for sure," she said. "I wish we could share our dreams more often."

"I'm afraid it is a rare thing that we get to cross over in the realm of dreams," said Prestwick. "I am just glad that it was you and not that wretched troll, or --" Prestwick stopped and looked at the group. His ears twitched, as his eyes fell on the three boys, "or — one of these detestable creatures."

"These are my brothers," said Kami. "They are only detestable sometimes, and I promise they will be on their best behavior if you let them in."

"I would rather they stay in the passageway, but I will make an exception for the daughter of Jaynea. Are you sure you don't want me to shove them out my front door? They are likely to run into a nasty troll. He has been running up and down the passage for some time now screaming about someone turning him into a bunny." Prestwick grinned at Aimee and Becka, "Like mother like daughters, I presume."

Becka and Aimee curtseyed. They decided it best to let Kami dominate the conversation. Prestwick seemed to be a one-on-one kind of dragon.

"I know you're only joking about my brothers," said Kami. And then she whispered, "I know you have a kind heart even if you don't let on to anyone else."

Prestwick showed Kami to a soft chair covered in red velvet. "You may sit here," he said.

He pointed to two more soft chairs, "Ladies."

Prestwick did not speak to the boys. Adam started to ask where he should sit. Becka put a finger to her mouth and motioned for him to sit on the stone floor.

All three boys obeyed but when the dragon waved his hand and filled a table with fruit and sweetbreads along with the tea, Adam could no longer contain himself. He jumped up and ran to the dragon's side. "I know I'm a boy," he said tugging at the dragon's arm. "But I'm not de-taste-able."

Prestwick turned to face Adam. Aimee tried to pull him back; sure that the dragon would burn him up with one swift breath.

Prestwick gave the girls a look that told them he would not hurt the little boy. "I can see that this little dragon slayer is hungry. And I suppose these other vile creatures would like to sample some of these delectable morsels. I'll be glad to share and give you all the advice you need on how to conquer Gwandoya, as your beautiful sister asked in our shared dream, but this boy will have to do me a favor first." When he said the word 'boy,' Prestwick's eyes narrowed, his brow furrowed, and his nose wrinkled.

"Tell me what you want, and I will decide," said Adam.

"You must agree before I tell you." The dragon said.

"I agree," said Adam, before the girls could stop him.

"You must promise," said Prestwick.

"Cross my heart," said Adam, waving his hand each way across his chest.

Prestwick looked Adam up and down. Then his big green eyes settled their gaze on Adam's deep blue ones.

"You must light the flame," said Prestwick.

"That's easy," said Brian, "I'll do it for him."

"He's not allowed to play with fire," said Erik.

"That's one rule I do have to follow," said Adam, looking at Aimee.

"I... think ... it will be okay this once," she said, turning to Becka for approval.

"I think it's the only way he'll help us," Becka whispered.

"It will require the shrinking spell," said Prestwick.

Everyone looked at the dragon.

"Where is this flame that needs to be lit?" Becka queried.

Prestwick did not say a word. He just opened his mouth very wide. A sheepish and embarrassed grin showed through his eyes.

Erik and Brian laughed.

"So, your fire has gone out then?" Brian asked.

"It's been out for seven years now," said Prestwick. "It was the witch, what was her name, she had long blonde hair?"

"Here in this book," said Becka, as she pulled a spell book from her satchel and flipped through the pages. "Grezelda?"

"Yes, that's her," said Prestwick glaring at the picture of a plain-looking witch with a full head of flowing blonde tresses.

"What did you do?" Erik asked.

"It was an accident really," said Prestwick, "While performing the illustrious task of lighting the bonfire on the eve of the Festival of Spring.... I was aiming for the wood, really I was."

"You didn't light her hair on fire?" asked Becka, with a gasp.

"It was an accident," he said, looking down at the floor.

"I believe you," said Kami, throwing her arms around the dragon's neck. "And I'd like to light the flame for you."

"Much too dangerous," said Prestwick, "all the gas that's built up down there these seven years; wouldn't want a pulchritudinous thing like you to go up in flames."

"Pul-ki-what?" asked Adam. "Watch what you're calling my sister!"

"It means beautiful," whispered Aimee.

"Why didn't he say so?" asked Adam in a whisper. "Everybody is always using big words. Could have just said, 'pretty.'"

"Wouldn't mind at all if Adam gets charred to ashes, though, would you?" asked Brian, drawing his sword.

"No need to get your knickers in a twist, young dragon slayer," said Prestwick. "The little warrior will wear this."

Prestwick turned around and pulled a suit of armor out of a trunk. "I chose Adam for a practical reason. He is the smallest, is he not? He will fit into the armor and then I can shrink him."

"Do I have to climb into your mouth?" Adam asked.

"Deep in my throat," said Prestwick.

"Sounds like fun," said Adam, holding his arms up as Prestwick pulled the armor over his head.

"I don't know about this," said Brian. "This armor will become an oven if the flame explodes."

"Adam will be roasted alive," said Becka. She removed the armor from her little brother. "I'm sure Brian will fit into it, or we can conjure up a larger suit."

"Do you think you can conjure up anything and everything? The resources must exist within the reaches of your magic girl. I had this armor created especially for this purpose," said Prestwick. "This metal is rare, hence the smallness of the suit."

Erik took a stick out of the fire and held it up to the outside of the armor. The metal glowed immediately, but the inside remained cool, "Seems safe to me," he said. "We need the information you have about Gwandoya. If this is the only way you will give it — so, be it." He took the armor from Becka and placed it over Adam's head.

When they had the rest of the pieces fitted to his small frame, they each gave him a hug.

Prestwick placed a very long stick in Adam's hand. "This is the eternal dragon flame, Adam." The end of the stick was not burning but there was a faint glow emanating from it. "It took me five years to find it and another two until you arrived to help me. I don't know why the witch felt the need to punish me so severely, her hair grew back the next day. You will find the wick to the left side of my throat down the farthest left passageway. The passage in the middle leads to my stomach and the one just to the right leads to my lungs. Please don't confuse the passageways."

"We wouldn't want you to be digested, Little Warrior," said Erik, patting Adam on the back.

Adam put his hands to his ears. "That echoes," he said.

Aimee kissed him on the cheek and lowered the mask over his face. "Light the flame and get out of there as quickly as you can," she said.

Prestwick gazed at Adam and concentrated hard. He stopped for just a minute and said, "think small everyone."

All the minds in the room focused on making Adam about one inch tall.

"Mediocritous," said Prestwick, with a flick of his tail.

Suddenly Adam disappeared. They all searched the floor.

"I think we thought too small," said Kami.

"No one move," said Brian. "Here he is," and he bent down and scooped up the tiny figure that was waving his arms frantically; trying to get someone's attention. He placed him on Prestwick's outstretched tongue. "Be careful," He whispered.

The whisper was as loud as an ocean wave in Adam's ears. He held the dragon flame in front of him as he walked slowly on the tongue. *Squish, squash.* He covered his face with his free hand as an odious stench rose to his nostrils. "It really stinks down here," he said.

It wasn't long before he reached the three passageways. He held up his hands. "I write with this hand," he said, looking at the hand which held the dragon flame. "So, this is my right hand." He held up the other hand. "This is my left."

Starting down the left passageway, Adam could smell the gas rising. He turned back to the opening and took a deep breath. Holding his breath, he ran down the passage and touched the flame to the wick. A split second later he was running out onto the tongue, the fire swift upon his heels. He didn't stop to see if anyone was there to catch him. He just jumped right off the end.

Erik caught his little brother, but the outside of the armor was scalding hot. He tossed Adam in the air. Like a hot potato, they passed him from person to person until he came to Becka who had thought to put oven mitts on. She placed him down on the table. Prestwick had turned and was aiming the uncontrollable flame at the fireplace. The room was quickly filling with smoke.

"Probably should have gone outside," said Aimee, opening the door.

The group ran down the passageway until they came to a ladder. It was wooden and rickety, but they had to have fresh air. Erik carried Adam in his pocket. One by one they climbed the ladder. The smoke was rising with them as if they were climbing a chimney, but once they reached the top there was plenty of fresh air for all.

"Where is Prestwick?" Kami asked. "He can't fit through this hole. How will he get out?"

The group looked up to see that the dragon had found a way out. He was flying over their heads, flames still coming from his open mouth.

"It will be a few minutes before he has control of that," said Brian.

It was only a short while when Prestwick landed nearby. Looking at Adam he said, "think big everyone! Megatonious!" and the tiny Adam was back to normal.

"That was so much fun," said Adam. "You really should gargle with peppermint water though," he said to Prestwick.

"Can't do that," said Prestwick. "Wouldn't want my flame to go out again, would you?"

"Well, you can at least eat some peppermint," said Adam.

"If I come upon some in my travels, I promise I will eat some," said Prestwick. "Now for that feast!"

Roast mutton and broiled turkey legs, pies of all sorts, fruits and vegetables appeared on a blanket in front of them.

"Now, what would you like to know about Gwandoya and his band of misfit dragons?"

"We need to know everything you know about Mount Ceo'ban," said Erik. "How many entrances are there? How many guards at certain times of day? What special powers does Gwandoya have within his own magical realm?"

"I haven't ventured out of the protective cave in seven years," said Prestwick, "too dangerous to go out without my flame. But there have been whisperings. I will tell you what I know, and since I lived in the depths of Mount Ceo'ban for a thousand years before Gwandoya took it over, I shall draw you a map."

"A thousand years," said Kami. "You don't look that old."

"Not a day over nine hundred," said Brian.

The dragon ignored Brian. "Thank-you," he said to Kami with a bow. "I am actually two-thousand, seven hundred, and thirty-three years old by your standards."

"You must have a lot of good stories to tell," said Adam.

Prestwick was gaining respect for a boy for the first time in his life. "That I do," he said, smiling at Adam.

"We will have plenty of time for stories when we get this mess cleaned up," said Erik.

{ **10** }

The Magnificent Garden of Athena

Once they had all the information they could get from Prestwick, the dragon told them a safe route to follow to Athena's cave, hugged Kami profusely, and bid them farewell. He had given Kami a special gift, but she was to tell no one of it.

The group arrived at the entrance to Athena's cave at nightfall.

"Is there a special charm we need to get in?" Kami asked.

"Let me guess," said Adam. He stood in front of the door and didn't say a word but closed his eyes and scrunched up his face. "Well, it's not roasted turkey with dressing," he said, frowning.

Aimee and Becka checked the map.

"Mama scribbled something here," said Aimee.

"Looks like we have to do these actions," said Becka.

"Okay everyone, first you pinch your nose with your right hand," said Aimee, demonstrating.

"Then you put your left hand behind your head like this," said Becka.

"Now stand on one foot and spin around three times," said Aimee, attempting to perform the actions while explaining them but falling over in the process.

Erik and Brian began to laugh.

"It won't work if we don't all do the actions," said Aimee, glaring at her brothers.

"Now everyone, together," said Becka.

The group did the actions and when they got to the standing-on-one-foot-and-spinning-around part, the sound of laughter echoed throughout the tunnels.

"It's not us," said Erik and Brian looking at each other.

Suddenly Athena appeared behind them in the tunnel, holding her stomach, and bent over laughing. "I haven't seen anyone attempt that silly spell in years," she said. "Your mother and I made it up so we could have a good laugh at your father's and Guelder's expense many years ago. Here, here, I don't think that spell will even still work." Then she turned and looked at the girls. "Jaynea's daughters," she said. "It's very nice to meet you all."

Aimee and Becka curtseyed, and Kami ran forward and hugged their mother's old friend.

"I've got a regular old key here somewhere." Athena reached into her pockets and began pulling out all sorts of things. There was a small leather-bound book, small glass bottles, some empty and missing their corks and some half full of interesting looking liquids. There were feathers, pebbles, diamonds, and gold coins. She tossed all these things on the floor as if they had no value whatsoever.

Adam snatched up several of the gold pieces. Aimee picked up a diamond. Becka went for the small glass bottles.

"Here it is," said Athena, pulling a rather large brass key from deep in her cloak. As she placed the key in an invisible keyhole, the great stone door turned on hidden hinges. Athena passed through the door motioning her friends to come along.

"Don't you want these things?" Aimee asked, admiring the large perfect diamond in her hand.

"I've been meaning to clean out my pockets for a while now," she said. "It is nothing of worth. You may keep whatever you like."

The children filled their own pockets with Athena's interesting discards and then followed her into the garden. Everyone stopped and stared at the amazing sight before them. It was as if they had just stepped into a different world all together. They had entered a vast open space filled with plants of all types. To the right was an open field overflowing with wildflowers. The sunflowers were taller than Erik. The sun shone brightly in the enchanted cave sky; yet it was night in the real world outside.

"I thought the cave was underground," said Erik.

Athena seemed to forget that she had guests at all. She ran from plant to plant talking to each as she went. She had a watering can in her hand and was giving them each a drink.

Kami saw that there were other watering cans beside an old shed. She took Adam's hand, and they raced to help their friend.

The watering cans were empty. Kami picked one up. "I wonder where we find water to fill them."

As she said the word 'fill' the can became heavy. Adam noticed it was full of water. "How did you do that?" he asked.

"I think I said 'fill' and it filled," she said.

Adam put his hand on a can, "Fill," he said. He tried to lift the can, but it was too heavy. "Brian, can you help me over here?" he asked.

All six children watered the flowers and strange plants.

Kami had just given a long drink to a rather large daisy. "Ah, that is so nice of you," said a voice. Kami looked around. Athena was just behind her watering something that looked like weeds. Must have been her voice I heard. Kami thought.

Adam came running over. "I think the plants can talk," he said to Kami. "That one over there just told me that the water was fine but what he really wanted was a nice scratch behind the ears."

"That's silly," she said.

"You're silly," said a fierce-looking plant from across the path, "silly for not bringing me any water yet."

Kami and Adam ran to where Erik and Brian were talking to a tall, strange plant that had small daggers for its leaves.

The dagger plant spoke to the two small children. "You don't want to give that menace any water," he said. "Best let Athena tend to him."

Kami tried to smile at the dagger plant.

"You look pretty dangerous yourself," said Adam, sticking a finger out to a dagger leaf.

"They are not ready to harvest," said the plant. "They will be sharper than the daggers wielded in the forge of the dwarves of Mt. Pyrrhus."

"When will they be ready?" Brian asked.

Athena had just come up behind them, "In about three years," she said.

"I wish they were ready now," said Adam. "I would like to have one to fight Gwandoya."

Kami had gone back to the daisy plant. "You spoke to me, didn't you?" she asked.

"I always speak when there is someone nice to speak to," said the daisy. "I am surrounded by wicked plants here and have no one with whom I may have a civil conversation."

"I shall move you close to the roses," said Kami.

"They are so vain," said the daisy.

"You are my mother's favorite flower," said Kami. "The roses are not more beautiful."

"No, but they think they are. Better put me over there near the dandelions. I have always wanted to speak with them. Many unfairly label them a weed, but they are so beautiful when yellow and have given many wishes to the pure in heart."

Kami started moving the large pot. "Erik, please come and help me move this flower."

"I am sorry Kami," said Athena. "Daisy must stay here between the dagger plant and the vampire plant."

"Vampire plant," Kami looked up to see that the fierce-looking plant in the corner was smiling and showing two long fangs.

"But she is so beautiful and wishes to have a pleasant conversation with the dandelions."

Athena looked at the daisy. She had a pleading look on her face. "I suppose it will be okay, for today," she said.

Erik and Brian moved Daisy next to the dandelions. They chatted excessively. "You see, I cannot stand the chatter for too long," said Athena. "And you will see tomorrow why I use Daisy to separate Dagger from Vampire."

After they had attended to all the plants, Athena called everyone over. "Sorry, I've been away and needed to care for my friends. I suppose you are attempting to make the prophecy come true. But where is your mother?"

"The dragons have captured our mother," Kami blurted out.

"We are on a quest to save her," said Adam.

"Not Jaynea too." Putting her head in her hands, Athena sat down on a bench that appeared out of nowhere.

It was then that the children noticed how weary she looked. "I've been trying to find a way to rescue the men," she said, "but it seems hopeless. I know there is a prophecy, and you children are involved but you've had no training as wizards and Matilda and Clare couldn't have figured that in when they made the prophecy so long ago."

"Well, we've already proved smart enough to gain information about the dragon and his lair," said Erik.

"And we even have a map," said Aimee.

Kami pulled the map out of her pocket and unrolled it on a table.

"Ahh, yes," said Athena. "This could be the work of only one dragon. Prestwick."

The group gathered around amazed to see that Prestwick had written the map on black parchment, in shimmering silver ink. "How could he make silver ink?" Kami asked.

Athena took Kami's hand and ran it across the surface of the map. Kami's fingers felt the raised writings and drawings. "How wonderful," she said. "Adam, feel this."

Adam ran his hand over the map and smiled. "What kind of ink is that?" He asked.

"It's not ink," said Athena. "Prestwick uses silkworms to do all his drawing and writing. After all, they are cousins of his, he is just a large worm you know."

"Ahh, a thread of silk," said Aimee, running her hand over the map, "a lovely way to make a map."

"Who cares what it's made of as long as it's accurate," said Brian.

"Prestwick never does anything without a bit of flair, Brian. Such things add spice to life," said Athena. "Now children of Jaynea and Denis, I want you all to take a good look at this map. We don't really have time to make copies, so you'll have to get as much of it into your heads as possible."

Erik pointed to a large space in the center of the map. "This is the lair of the hideous Gwandoya. You can see that there is no entrance to this area. Gwandoya has enchanted it so that he is the only one who can enter. The walls are three times thicker than the other walls of the castle. Now here is where the dungeons are. They are rather large and there are many cells and chambers throughout each of these caves. Prestwick himself doesn't know how many."

"Our parents, Guelder, and Grandfather are in one of these cells," said Adam.

"That's right," said Brian and we really have no way of knowing which cell."

"There must be some way to find out," said Aimee.

"Right," said Becka. "I'm not too keen on the fact that this is going to be a long, long journey in the first place. Then we must find a way into an impenetrable fortress and then spend days trying to stay undetected as we search for three men and our mother."

"And, what's worse," said Kami. "Prestwick says that those tunnels have a stench the likes you have never before encountered."

"Couldn't be any worse than that stench rising in the throat of Prestwick," said Adam.

"I'm sure that was really wretched," said Athena, grinning at the way Adam twisted up his face and held his nose when he finished his sentence. "This odor is not unlike that odor."

"Then I shall lead the way," said Adam, putting his chest out.

"But this odor is mixed with the repugnant stench of death," said Athena.

"And not just any death, I suppose," said Brian, playing into her dramatic demeanor.

Athena looked around the garden as if she suspected ears to be listening. The flowers all seemed to be asleep.

"Not just any death," she said, "the death of children."

"I hate that," said Adam.

"He goes for the small ones first," said Brian, narrowing his eyes at Kami and Adam.

Aimee frowned at Brian, "there is a time to joke and a time to be serious," she said.

"That's right," said Athena. "Gwandoya has always been hungry for the blood of children. He has murdered hundreds, and he will not think twice when it comes to devouring all of you."

Kami had been quiet. Her innocent little voice broke into the conversation. "The spirits of the children are happy in heaven now, right Aimee?"

Aimee hugged her little sister. "Of course, dear," she said. "Oh, Kami, I wish you didn't have to go on this quest. I wish we could just send our brave big brothers to save Father."

"It's okay, Aimee," said Kami. "I'm not afraid. And if I die, I will get to meet our grandmother. Grandfather told me in a dream that I look like her."

"That's a brave girl," said Becka. "But you must do everything you can to not die, my sweet little Kami, for I would miss you so." The three sisters hugged each other tightly.

Erik and Brian glanced at each other. "We can't let them go," said Brian. "There must be some way we can conquer the dragon without them."

"You must not trifle with a prophecy of this magnitude," said Athena. She waved her arms, and the garden transformed into a dining hall. Each of the children was standing individually outside the hall. Each in front of a separate door, a threshold that opened into the room. Athena sat at a long table full of serving trays, goblets, pitchers, and dessert platters. A delightful aroma, the smell of delectable foods wafted from the room.

"We have no time for tricks, Athena," said Brian.

"Brian is right!" said Erik. "It is ridiculous to ask the girls and young Adam to go on this quest! Brian and I can conquer the dragon on our own."

Athena didn't say a word but nodded to Adam to enter the room. As soon as he did, a tray filled with fresh fruit. She motioned to him to retreat, and the tray sat empty again. Kami entered the room, and the vases filled with flowers. Kami started backing out of the room to let someone else have a turn, but Athena motioned for her to stay. Aimee entered the room, and nothing appeared. Becka came forward and an apple pie appeared.

"All three of us work together to make apple pie," said Aimee.

"I get the idea..." Brian started. "This is a waste...."

Aimee motioned for Brian to hush, as Athena bade him to enter. A turkey dressed and accompanied by savory dressing appeared. Erik entered the room and two roasted pheasants appeared on either side of the giant turkey. Adam re-entered the room and the fresh fruit, along with a loaf of hot crusty bread appeared. "Wow, that's cool," he said.

"The meal is only complete if we are all in the room," said Kami.

"Yes," said Athena, "but notice that the goblets and pitchers remain empty. It is your mother who brings in fresh water each day."

"We would die without water," Becka commented gravely.

"You will die without each other," said Athena.

"I could survive on just the turkey," said Brian.

"I survived without my family for a full year during my apprenticeship," said Erik.

"Sure," said Aimee. "You...we all could survive on less, but Athena is just trying to show us that we are all needed."

"Yes," said Kami. "We are all important to the quest. No matter how much I don't want to go, if I don't come something will be missing. I don't know what I can contribute. Flowers don't seem to...."

"But you will contribute," said Becka, wrapping her arms around her younger sister. "We all will participate in the task of rescuing our parents."

"Maybe, maybe... you'll rescue the captives and Brian and I will destroy the evil dragon," said Erik, giving Brian a knowing glance.

"Everyone will have to do their part," said Athena. "Now, sit down and eat. I believe this will be your last full meal before your journey's end."

Kami leaned over to Aimee. "I hope that doesn't mean we're going to be separated," she said.

No one in the group seemed to have much of an appetite. "It's not the same feast without Mama here," said Kami.

"No water to wash it down," said Adam.

"Come on all of you," said Athena. "We must figure out a way to find the captives in the many caverns of Mount Ceo'ban. There was this contraption called the Detectrol. I think I still have it in the trunk in the cottage."

"It's an old contraption your mother, and I used years ago to find the boys during hide-and-go-seek. If it's still set to their readings, it should still be able to detect Denis and Guelder."

"But that was such a long time ago," said Aimee.

"They are grown men now," said Erik.

"There shouldn't be any reason it won't work," said Athena. "You'll just need to get past the invisible magic wall that Gwandoya has around the mountain, and into the dungeons."

"The Detectrol will keep you turning in the right direction in all those tunnels and caverns. It will glow brighter and brighter as you get closer and closer to the men."

"So, you girls cheated at hide-and-go-seek," said Becka smiling.

"All right everyone, don't get all excited," said Athena. "It has been years; I'll have to go look and see if it's even still up there."

"But that means you will have to leave the protection of the cave," said Kami.

"Remember that my cottage lies in the enchanted forest," said Athena. "The dragons will detect a simple peasant woman in the forest if I go up. But none of you must follow me. My spell right now is only for me. I never expected to have visitors of such great importance."

Athena walked over to the wall. Turning to say, "I'll be right back," she vanished before their eyes.

"So that's just the entrance to the outside world," said Brian, whispering to Erik.

"I've a feeling she wants us to think that." Erik said, leaning close. "She clearly tends this garden often, so those vines shouldn't be so overgrown.""I see what you mean," said Brian. "At the very least there should be a clear path."

"That's right, now if we could just figure out how to get over that wall."

"Shouldn't be too hard to climb," said Brian.

"You boys can explore in the briars and brambles. Let's go look at all the beautiful and interesting plants," said Becka, motioning to Aimee and Kami to follow. Kami gazed into a large ball that seemed to be made of glass. Adam balanced on a high marble wall. Aimee and Becka sat by a pond full of lily pads and floating candles.

Erik and Brian were pulling away a tangling of half dead thorny vines. They could just make out the appearance of a stone wall. Suddenly Athena was behind them. "One more step and you would have entered the forbidden part of the garden," she said.

Erik was sure she would let them enter wherever they wanted, but when the boys turned, they saw that Athena's face was angry. She motioned for them to leave the path and go back to the others. She stayed by the wall and seemed to be checking an invisible lock.

"What's behind those walls that she is so worried about us encountering?" Erik asked.

"Maybe it's a hideous beast that she keeps hidden and lets out only when a traveler of The Forbidden Forest comes along that she really wants to scare," said Brian.

"I don't think so," said Erik. "Athena told me it is the travelers' own imaginations that frighten them more than anything else." He leaned closer to his brother, "I think she's protecting something behind that wall Brian."

"Well, it wouldn't surprise me if Athena had a treasure hidden away."

Everyone, gather around!" Athena motioned for the group to sit on benches in front of the rose bushes. "I've gathered a few things from my cottage; something for each of you. Kami, this basket is for you."

"Thank-you Athena," said Kami, "I'm sure it will come in handy for gathering berries along the trail."

"I'm sure it will be magical in your hands, Kami," said Becka.

"Of course, Becka has the mirror. Let's see. Oh, here are the things for the boys, just a couple of old keys. Don't know how they can help you. I don't even remember what they open. Matilda said you'd know what to do with them."

Athena pulled the last thing out of the bag. "This is for you Aimee," she said, placing the stone around Aimee's neck.

"Athena, it's beau --" she cut herself off as she glanced down at the plain gray stone tied to a string of leather.

"Guelder gave it to me many years ago. No time to tell the story now. I must leave you all to a good night's rest as I venture on my journey."

"Can't you wait and begin with us in the morning?" asked Kami.

"I wish I could," said Athena, leaning down to hug the little girl. "But I've decided I'll need to round up an army of creatures who will fight on the side of good. Doing that in secret will be no simple task. The sooner I get the word out the better."

Adam joined Kami in hugging their friend. "I will miss you," he said.

Athena walked to the place where she had entered and, turning to look at the children one last time, she waved her hands and was gone.

{ 11 }

The Quest Begins

Brian could not sleep at all that night. He was wide awake when he noticed Erik, eyes open, staring at the ceiling. "What good is magic if we can't get to our mother without going through all this effort? How do we know she'll be alive when we reach the caves?"

"Go to sleep," said Erik. "Maybe she'll visit us in our dreams."

The next morning the others woke to the sounds of their little brother racing around the garden.

"I saw Mama in my dreams!" Adam said.

"I saw her too," said Brian, rubbing the sleep out of his eyes.

"She sang to me, and I saw our grandfather again," said Kami.

Erik turned over in his bed and hid his head under his pillow. He closed his eyes tight but couldn't get the images of battle out of his mind. Their mother hadn't visited him. All he saw in his dreams was devastation.

Becka called everyone over to a breakfast of luscious apples and a kind of orange fruit they had never seen before.

"*Mmm*," said Adam, licking his fingers. "This is so juicy."

Aimee had bitten into her orange fruit as if it were an apple, eating the skin and all.

"Athena told me about this special fruit that comes from very warm lands," said Becka.

"This is an amazing discovery," said Aimee, taking another bite.

Becka cringed at the sight of Aimee eating the tough outside skin of the fruit. "Athena said you are supposed to take this outside layer off," she said, taking the fruit. "And you aren't supposed to eat the seeds."

"It's all delicious to me," said Aimee, taking the orange fruit back from her sister.

"Remember, she eats melon rinds too," said Erik.

"Yuck," said Kami.

"Whatever you eat, just hurry. You're all eating like snails chasing sloths," said Brian. "We're already getting a late start."

"Normal people are grumpy if they've woken up *too* early," said Aimee.

"Yeah, Brian," said Becka. "You'd think you'd be happy that you got to sleep in a bit before this long journey."

"Well," said Erik, smacking his brother hard on the back. "This one never could be called normal then could he."

Brian didn't say a word. He stood up and threw a knapsack over his shoulder then began pacing in front of the entrance back into the caves. A few minutes later Adam was struggling to put his own knapsack over his shoulder. Brian rushed over and grabbed the bag from the little boy. "Can you please hurry," he said. "Don't you care about our mother?"

Adam crossed his arms over his chest and looked up at Brian, a hurt scowl on his face.

"You'd better pull your head together, Brian," said Erik, taking the knapsack and placing it on Adam's back, "if you want to get her back."

"Yeah," said Adam, adjusting his load. "Pull your head together."

When all were ready the group stood by the exit into the caves. Becka pulled Athena's key out of her pocket. Kami ran back to get some of the orange fruit. As she ran back toward the others, she caught a glimpse of the glass ball. Thinking she saw an image in the ball she stopped to have a look; her own image peered back at her. "Could have sworn, that was Becka's reflection just then," she mumbled.

"Everybody got everything, now?" asked Becka, holding the key in the lock.

"Yes, we all have everything," said Brian putting his hand on the key and turning it. "Let's go."

The first few hours of the journey were quiet. They were in a pitch-black part of the tunnels. They each carried a small torch that Athena had given them.

"According to this, we should come upon a group of caves soon." Erik held his torch close to the map. "This says that a couple of creatures named --"

Suddenly Erik was hanging upside down by his ankles, held in the grasp of an enormous hand. Adam ran forward beating at the enemy and soon was dangling next to his brother.

"Let go of my brothers," Brian yelled, holding his sword high.

A very large finger came down and knocked the sword out of Brian's hand. The next thing they knew, all three boys were dangling side by side.

"Nice of ye all to come along just now when I'm in need of a snack with me tea." The voice echoed through the caves as if a hundred giants surrounded them. As the giant raised the boys to his mouth Adam's torch lit up the hideous face.

"I'll burn you with this torch," said Adam, frantically swinging it in front of the giant's eyes.

"Ahh, a feisty one is it?" Roared the giant. "Ye'll be puttin' me eye out then will ye?"

With a blast of his rank breath, the giant blew out the small flame.

"You can't eat my brothers!" Kami screamed.

"Give me one good reason why not," said the giant. Lowering the boys a bit, he bent down to get a closer look at the person who belonged to the voice. "Looks like we've got a sweet little girl for dessert here."

The giant reached out to pick Kami up in his other hand. Becka and Aimee came forth out of the shadows, their torches lighting their faces. "Put them down!" Becka yelled.

The giant stopped and looked hard at Becka for a very long time. Then surprised them all by saying, "Jaynea is that you?"

"We are the daughters of Jaynea," said Becka.

"Yes, that's it, a daughter of Jaynea. Ye have the same flowing brown hair and brown-green eyes. A bit taller ye are, but the smitten image, the smitten image."

The giant looked at the boys still hanging in his firm grasp.

"Sounds like you are friends with our mother," said Erik, his voice cracking.

"Aye," said the giant. "We go way back, way back we do. And ye have the privilege of calling her *mother*?" The giant glared hard at the boys and then looked back at the girls.

"Does she like them?" He asked. "I mean, maybe I'd be doing me old friend a favor gettin' them out of her hair. Which one of these scoundrels should I eat first?"

"Our mother wouldn't like you anymore, if you eat any of us," said Adam trying to get at the giant with his fists.

Just then another loud voice came from behind the giant and the tunnel was lit by a large torch. "I smell the blood of children," he said, sniffing the air. "Caoimhin, ye were goin' ta save a bite for Grog, weren't ya?"

"These three little men are barely a bite at all," said Caoimhin.

The second giant glanced around at the girls, "I'll have a bit of dessert then," he said, stepping forward.

"I think Jaynea will be disappointed with ya if ye eat her daughters," said Caoimhin.

The giant named Grog stopped. He peered closer into the girls' faces. His big, bearded one came down to their level. "Daughters of Jaynea, and just as beautiful," he said, "but if these boys are anything like her, we'd better eat 'em quick. Crafty they'll be, Caoimhin, with a wicked streak as long as me arm."

"Our mother, crafty and wicked?" said Aimee, putting her hands on her hips.

"You'd better watch what you're saying," said Erik.

The giant turned to look at the son of Jaynea. "I'd wager she's had to be extra crafty to deal with the likes of ye, lad," he said.

"Well, if you have to eat one of us it may as well be Erik," said Brian, who had decided that there was no way any friend of their mother's would actually eat them.

"Let's let the girls be the judge of that," said Caoimhin. "Which one gives yer mother the most trouble young ladies?"

Caoimhin winked at Kami. She went along with the game. "That would definitely be Erik," she said, trying to sound serious. "He's always playing jokes on her and getting into mischief."

"That's right," said Aimee, "and he was always knocking over my wooden block towers when he was a baby."

"And pulling off the heads of my dolls," said Becka, trying not to smile.

"Troublemaker from the start," said Caoimhin, taking Erik in his other hand and slowly raising him toward his mouth.

"Girls, what are you doing?" yelled Erik, his voice cracking wildly.

"Ah, Caoimhin, don't just pop 'im in yer mouth and swallow 'im whole. If 'e's been givin' our Jaynea trouble 'e deserves a slow, painful death. Let me string 'im up by his toes and poke a 'ole in 'is 'ead. I could use a bit o' blood to mix with that brew I'm distillin'. Then we could cut 'im up into little bits and put 'is parts in a nice stew."

"But wait. Maybe it's Adam you should eat," said Kami.

"Maybe you're right," said Becka, "he has been getting into a lot of mischief lately."

"Yes," said Kami, "he's the one who pulls the heads off *my* dolls."

"I'll just pull their heads off and eat them all," said Caoimhin. Putting all the boys in one hand again he reached out with the other to pinch off their heads.

Seeing the color drain from Adam's face was more than Kami could handle. "I didn't mean it," she said, running forward. "Our mother loves them."

A thunderous rumble filled the tunnels as Grog let out a great guffaw. Kami put her hands over her ears and looked up as Caoimhin turned her brothers right side up in his hand.

Grog picked Kami up gently and held her in his hand. "Well, if she loves them," he said.

"He wouldn't really have eaten them, anyway, would he?" asked Kami.

"He's partial to chicken," said Grog. "And I haven't actually had a child for supper since yer mother taught me years ago that they were good for something else. Can't really remember what that something else is right now though," he said, glaring at the boys.

"I don't know about them," said Kami, warming up to the giant. "But I can sing you a lullaby."

Grog smiled and placed Kami gently on his shoulder.

"Did you really know our mother when she was young?" Adam asked.

"When we were all younger," said Caoimhin, with a faraway look in his eye. "Follow us; we've got a chicken and potato stew for lunch, and a large crusty bread I baked myself. Can't let the children of Jaynea continue their journey without something hot and tasty to warm their bellies."

"We've got a few good stories to tell about yer mother too," said Grog, trudging through the tunnel with his hands in his pockets. "I'm surprised yer mother would let you come."

"The evil Gwandoya has captured our mother," said Adam. "We are on our way to save her and our father."

Caoimhin and Grog both stopped in their tracks.

"Jaynea captured?" Caoimhin's brow furrowed. "But she gave up magic many years ago just to avoid that very thing. What interest does that evil creature have in our sweet Jaynea?"

"It's a long story," said Aimee, not really knowing where to begin.

"We didn't know we were wizards and then our father found our grandfather and Athena's boyfriend Guelder in Mount Ceo'ban. Our father was injured trying to get to them to help them escape." Kami was talking fast as the two giants stared at her. "Mama showed us the cave that she has all of her sculptures in and taught us we are wizards, but she was still ill from the horrible disease…"

"And then the dragons came."

"The yellow-bellied coward brought an army to do his dirty work, then," said Grog, with a snarl.

"I made the wooden soldiers real," said Adam.

"I protected myself with a dome shield," said Kami.

"We all helped," said Becka.

"Ye defeated the dragons," said Caoimhin, "with no help from the adults."

"We didn't need them," said Erik.

"Most fun I've had in a long time," said Brian.

"Wish I could have seen that," said Caoimhin.

"Ye are the children of Jaynea," said Grog, rubbing his thick black-gray speckled beard. "Fierce and cunning, she is that one."

"But while we were fighting, they captured Mama," continued Kami.

"So, we are using these tunnels to get close to Mount Ceo'ban without the dragons finding us," said Aimee.

"Then we met that funny troll," said Adam.

"You daughters of Jaynea didn't play that old trick on him, did you?" Caoimhin asked.

"Turned him into a bunny they did," said Erik.

"Got ye first, I'll wager," said Grog, with a smirk.

"Then we met Prestwick," said Kami.

"That old dragon would have to get in on all the fun," said Caoimhin.

"I got to light his flame," said Adam.

"E's full of enough 'ot air without 'is flame lit," said Grog, groaning.

"Next we got to see Athena's garden," said Kami.

"I 'aven't visited 'er in years," said Caoimhin. "Wonder if she still 'as that cocoa plant?"

As the children told the long story, Caoimhin walked forward again, "Keep talking," he said, as he beckoned them to follow, "I'm listening."

"What's happening to you?" asked Kami, gasping.

Caoimhin was shrinking, his clothes changing from the overalls of a giant to the long glowing black robes of a sorcerer.

"Ya could 'ave warned them before ya just changed like that," said Grog, almost stepping on the wizard.

"It's much more fun to see the looks on their faces," said Caoimhin, barely glancing back to witness those looks, as he hurried past the others.

"Why'd you get small if you're in such a hurry?" asked Becka, keeping stride. "I do like your cloak, though."

"Yes," said Aimee, running to keep up. "When do we get our wizard clothing?"

"Wizard clothing, bah!" said Grog. "It's what's inside ye that counts."

"Well, but it is fun to dress up," said Kami.

"I could fill my pockets with all kinds of stuff," said Adam.

"Well, we need to get you on your journey quickly, but Grog and I can provide you with a few items of clothing. To keep you camouflaged once you come out of these enchanted caves, mind you."

"Right, not so you can look good," said Grog.

Soon they arrived at a huge wooden door, so large that Grog didn't even have to duck to enter. He reached out his pudgy hand, ready to turn the knob that only a giant could reach, but Caoimhin waved his hand and the door disappeared.

"No time to wait for that heavy old thing to swing open," he said. Hurrying into the room he began rummaging through old trunks. There must have been a hundred of them stacked around the room. Shelves carved out of the stone cave walls were full of crates, bottles, and leather bags.

Caoimhin moved swiftly from trunk to trunk opening lids with a wave of his hand. "Grog, I need you to get that crate off the top shelf," he said, as he threw an old cauldron, something that looked like a compass, and a large roll of brown paper, on the floor.

Grog pulled crates off the top shelf. He held seven crates in his hands and brought them down to Caoimhin's level. "Which one?" he asked.

"Ah, here it is," said Caoimhin, pulling two small velvet pouches from the bottom of a large crate.

"Here Kami and Adam, here is a prize for having the best startled look on your wee faces when I changed from giant to wizard."

"You best not be givin' away me gold," said Grog.

"Just a little treat to save fer later," said Caoimhin.

Adam was dying to look in the bag. He hoped it was some of Grog's gold. He had always wanted real gold.

Kami gave Caoimhin a hug, "Now that you are smaller, I can hug you properly,"

"When's he going to change?" asked Adam, pointing up at Grog.

"E's always going to be that way," said Caoimhin.

"Some wicked witch put an ugly spell on him, eh," said Brian.

"Watch it there lad," said Grog, piercing Brian with his eyes. "Don't know 'ow any son of Jaynea could 'ave as ugly of a mug as ye."

"Don't know how anyone so big as you could have such beady eyes," said Brian.

"Now, now, lad," said Caoimhin. "Ya don't want to be getting on 'is bad side."

"That's right," said Grog, speaking slowly and carefully, his voice seeming to get deeper than humanly possible. "Son of Jaynea or not I'll be breakin' yer bones and spreadin' the marrow on me bread."

Brian started to speak but felt a strong hand on his shoulder. Caoimhin whispered in his ear. "Friend or enemy he will be loyal," he said.

How can an enemy be loyal, thought Brian, but he decided not to ask any questions. The breath of Grog was in his face. "Any friend of my mother's is a friend of mine," he said, reaching out to shake the giant's enormous…finger.

"This remains to be seen," said Grog, a questioning smirk crossing his bearded face.

"Grog, stop messing around and go stir the stew," said Caoimhin, still pulling things out of the trunks and crates.

Kami and Adam dug through the piles. "Look at this," said Kami, throwing a purple velvet hooded cloak around her shoulders.

"This one's perfect for you," said Adam, as he ran to Aimee, handing her a royal purple cloak trimmed in white fur.

Aimee reached out and took the cloak slowly in her hands. She rubbed the fur against her cheek.

"What do you have for us?" Brian asked, cringing at Aimee's dramatic performance.

"Actually," said Erik, taking the cloak from Aimee. "None of us will be able to wear these bright colors in the woods."

"That's true," said Brian, picking up a dull brown cloak. "This is more like it."

The three girls were standing in front of a giant-sized mirror.

"A bit vain aren't you then?" Brian asked Grog.

"It's not me mirror," said Grog, "Caoimhin uses it when he makes himself big like me."

"I can see that," said Erik.

"I'm not giving up my gorgeous white cloak," said Becka.

"White?" queried Brian.

"White?" questioned Erik, as he pulled a dull green cloak around his shoulders and admired himself in the mirror. "We're wizards not snow queens."

"Or fairy princesses," said Brian.

Caoimhin waved his hand, and suddenly each cloak turned the muted green and brown colors of the forest.

"Ugh, my beautiful purple cape is now the color of a horny toad," said Aimee.

"Mine's not," said Kami, who was still looking in the mirror.

"Yes, it is," started Becka, "ohhh --" When they all looked in the mirror their cloaks were still gorgeous shining fabrics that sparkled and shimmered, but when they looked down, they were the drab camouflage colors of the forest.

"Neat trick," said Brian. "The girls can keep their vanity when they look in the mirror."

"But stay camouflaged in the real world," said Erik.

"Well everyone, I'm sorry we won't have time to tell ya stories of yer mother," said Caoimhin. "I suggest ye all eat up quickly and be on yer way, to save yer mother and father."

"We'll go with 'em," Grog said, "to save Jaynea."

Caoimhin looked at Grog, "It is not our place," he said.

The children expected Grog to argue. They all would have liked to have the giant on their side. Grog walked over to the enormous cauldron and stirred the stew. Each of the children brought a bowl to him which he filled to the brim, but he didn't look up again until it was time for them to leave.

"The stew and bread were yummy," said Adam.

Caoimhin was helping the little boy put his knapsack on his shoulders. He put something into the bag. "Just a loaf of crusty bread," he said. "You'll be needin' yer strength fer this long journey."

"You'd think being a wizard would make it so we could always have everything easier," said Becka, heaving her own pack onto her back.

"Right," said Aimee. "You'd think we could just use our magic to conjure ourselves into the mountain."

"Or at least conjure up a brave knight to carry it for us," said Erik in a mocking tone.

"Special gifts require a lot of the holder," said Caoimhin, helping Kami with her pack. "The more magic I learn the harder it gets, really; harder to know when and what to use. And the more ye know the more the forces of evil will want you for that knowledge. Enough profound wisdom for one day, ya'd better get going."

Kami turned around and hugged the tall wizard, "I hope I get to see you again," she said.

Adam and Kami ran to hug the giant Grog "Don't be sad that you don't get to come," said Adam. "We will save Jaynea for you and then we can come back and hear some stories."

"I'll wager ye'll have a few more tales of yer own," said Grog, finally smiling. "Ya can't stop me from walking them to the clearing," he said, turning to Caoimhin.

Picking up the group and putting the lot on his shoulders, Grog took several long strides down the tunnel until they came to an underground wood. "This is The Buried Enchanted Forest," he said. "I can't go past 'ere." He placed them all gently on the ground.

The giant reached his large hand into a deep pocket and pulled out an old piece of faded, folded paper. He rolled it up and tied it to the back of Brian's pack. "I don't 'ave much magic," he said. "This is all I've got really, but I'm giving it to ye, lad. I used it once before to save Jaynea. Suppose it might come in 'andy again." Turning to Adam he said, "Lad, I know ya want some of me gold and I don't 'and it out to just anyone, but 'ere's what ye'll get if ya bring Jaynea back to see me."

Adam's eyes grew as large as saucers when he saw the huge shiny coin that the giant pulled out of his pocket. "I'd give it to ya now as a bit of incentive, probably'd weigh ya down on the journey though."

"I'll be back for it," said Adam. And then he did something that no child had ever thought to do before. He grew to just the right size of a giant child and threw his arms around Grog's neck. Kami did the same and soon the giant was struggling to keep his balance as he got the best hugs he'd ever had.

Laughing and laughing all three fell over and rolled out into the clearing, "We'll be rollin' over yer brothers and sisters if ya don't watch it," said Grog, squeezing the children one last time. "Best shrink down now and be on yer way."

As the children crossed the field of wildflowers, Kami stopped to look back. The giant stood smiling at them, little daisies and forget-me-nots stuck in his beard. Waving goodbye to her new giant friend she blew him a kiss and ran to catch up with the others.

$$\{\ 12\ \}$$

Through Thick and Thin

By the time the children had made their way to the other side of the field, Kami had gathered a nice basket full of beauteous wildflowers.

"These—ahhh—ahh — ahchoo, things make me sneeze," said Adam, rubbing his eyes.

"Oh, didn't you pack a hanky?" Aimee asked, as she turned to see that the sneeze had covered the boy's upper lip with wet yellow ooze. "Use mine," she said, pulling a clean white hanky out of her skirt pocket.

Adam wiped his nose smearing the ooze all over one cheek and handed it back to her. "No, no, that's quite all right," she said, pointing to the initials. "Look, you're in luck, 'AV.,' Now you have a monogrammed hanky all your own."

Adam wadded up the hanky and shoved it into his cloak pocket.

"This is real fun making all these new friends," said Kami. "I wonder who we'll meet next."

The children stopped and peered into the thick forest that was ahead of them. "Do you think it's called the enchanted underground forest just because it's underground?" Kami asked, her voice shaking.

"I'm sure there's nothing to be afraid of," said Aimee, peering into the dark wood. "I'll tell you what though. Just to be safe, why don't we send Erik and Brian up ahead to scout things out."

"Great idea," said Becka, smiling crookedly at the boys.

"I'll go too," said Adam, marching ahead.

Erik pulled the little boy back by his pack and held him dangling off the ground.

"Put me down," said Adam, his arms flailing and legs kicking at the air.

"We'll let you come, Little Warrior," said Erik, still holding on. "But you'll have to bring up the rear." He put the little boy down behind him.

"The rear isn't any better than the front," said Becka, placing the little boy between the other boys. "Both have unprotected sides."

"Good thinking," said Brian stepping to the front and shoving Erik behind. "And in the front, you can see what's coming."

"Alright then," said Erik. "I'll bring up the rear. No time to waste; girls, if we don't return in an hour, best turn back and see if you can't get the giant to help."

"Be careful," said Becka. "Look for spiders and snakes; I'm not going in there if there are spiders and snakes."

"I'm not afraid of spiders and snakes," said Adam. "I see spiders and snakes on the farm all the time."

"I think it's just full of pixies and faeries and probably unicorns and that's why it's called the Enchanted Forest," said Kami, always looking at the positive possibilities. "I'd love to meet a unicorn."

"That would be nice, wouldn't it," said Becka.

"Don't think there's any chance of that," said Brian, reconsidering his decision to take up the lead.

Before they knew it, pitch black surrounded them. They all lit their torches and walked side by side. "I have a feeling that if we're going to be attacked it will be from out there," said Brian.

"Or there," said Erik, pointing to his side of the barely visible wood.

"I can't imagine anything could live in here," said Brian as the air grew thick around them. "I think it's called the 'Buried Enchanted Forest' because anyone who goes in here gets buried alive."

"Don't say that," said Adam. "I'm not scared of creepy crawly things like the girls but buried alive doesn't sound like fun."

"Well, that's quite far enough. Don't you think," said Brian, "no snakes or spiders in here, eh?"

"Scared, are you?" Erik inquired. "Frightened of what might be out there in the dark?"

"I just don't like how the air feels all thick and thin at the same time," said Brian, "too thick to walk through and too thin to breathe."

Just then the boys' torches went out.

"How could that happen?" asked Brian. "There's not even a small breeze in here."

"Maybe it's because there's no oxygen in the air," said Erik. "Solon told me that all creatures must have oxygen to breathe."

"Fire is a creature?" asked Adam.

"Sort of. I guess," said Erik. "He showed me that when you cover a flame with a snuffer the reason, the flame goes out is that you've stopped the oxygen from getting to it."

"So, the fire can't breathe anymore, and it smothers."

All the boys were struggling to breathe, as they kept walking in a direction that they thought was forward in the dark.

"But it really just goes to sleep," said Adam, yawning. "I mean it will wake up as soon as you get some oxygen to it, right?" Adam lay down on the cold ground.

"You have to have some way to relight the flame," said Erik, trying to get a spark with his flint and steel as he walked past the other two.

"I'm feeling tired," said Brian. "Maybe we should rest for a minute."

"Wait," said Erik, "We've lost Adam."

Erik turned back to find Adam and tripped over Brian who had laid down in the path. "Get up, Brian," he said.

"I can't go another step," he said. "I'll just rest here while you go for Adam."

Brian's voice drifted off.

"This is no time for a nap you blunderhead," said Erik, who would have kicked him if he could see him.

Erik got down on all fours and crawled back to the place where Adam was. "Amazing how I can kind of see better when I'm down here on the ground like this," he said. "Dark must rise just like hot air. I think it was hot air that Solon said rises, but it doesn't feel like it's rising in here though."

Erik's hand reached out and found Adam's warm body; his chest heaved as he took long shallow breaths. "Maybe a nap isn't such a bad idea after all," he said, placing Adam's head on his chest and closing his eyes. "Wow, I never thought there could be more light behind my eyelids than there is out there." Erik barely finished his sentence, as he drifted off to a deep sleep.

Back at the edge of the forest, Aimee was tired of waiting. "We should have gone in with them," she said.

"It was your idea to send them ahead," said Becka.

"I was really just fooling around," said Aimee, "but when you mentioned spiders and snakes."

"Let's just go in and have a look," said Kami, lighting her torch with a piece of flint and steel. "I'm pretty sure we're going to meet something pleasant and make another friend."

"Don't really see why anything pleasant or friendly would like to live in this place," said Becka, with a huff.

The girls plodded along the path huddled together so closely they could hear the beating of each other's hearts. The torches dimmed and soon went out.

"Well, that's just great," said Aimee, pulling out her flint and steel. When she struck them together a small spark pierced the darkness for a split second and was gone. "Ugh, I should have looked up a spell to make light or fire before we ventured in here," she said.

"I'm not sure if magic will even work in here," said Becka, drawing her sisters close.

"I don't know," said Aimee. "Look at Kami's basket."

The little girl had been carrying her wildflower-filled basket at her side the entire time. With the light from the torches out, the flowers in the basket glowed.

"Mama always said that I brought sunshine into the house every time I gave her wildflowers."

Aimee and Becka almost crushed the little girl between them as they hugged her closely. Soon they were breathing in the fresh scent of daisies and buttercups as they walked along the path.

"What's that up ahead?" asked Becka.

"It's our brothers," said Kami, running ahead still holding the basket. "And I think they are dead."

Aimee and Becka didn't enjoy being left without light and the air seemed to grow very heavy as soon as Kami left their side, they followed their little sister quickly, gasping for breath as they went.

"I don't think they are breathing," said Kami, holding the basket up to their faces.

"They're breathing," said Aimee, putting her hand to the boys' noses. "Just barely."

Becka had a hunch, "Kami, you stay here and keep these flowers close to Aimee and the boys." She took half the flowers and used them to light her way to find Brian. He wasn't far down the path. Becka brought the flowers close to Brian's face. She could see a huge smile and knew he was in a deep sleep and seemed to be having comforting dreams. She shoved the flowers closer to his face. "Brian, wake up," she said. "What are you thinking, lying down on the job when our mother's being held captive?" She shook him hard, worried that he'd never wake up. Luckily, his smile changed to a grimace, and he sat up with a start.

"I was fighting the dragon," he said, looking around. "Where's Mother?"

"We haven't even gotten to the dragon, yet," she said. "You wouldn't have woken up if it hadn't been for Kami and some magic trick, she pulled with these sunshine flowers of hers. Not only do they cast off light, but they seem to help us breathe while in this thick air."

Brian got up and stretched and yawned. His eyes were wild like he still wasn't sure who or where he was yet.

Aimee and Kami came walking up the path. Each sister allowed one brother to lean on them.

"Aimee's height makes her just the right size for me to use her as a crutch," said Erik.

Aimee pulled her weight away from her brother and took great joy in the fact that he was still weak enough that he fell flat on his butt.

"I was just having a bit of fun," he said, "just trying to lighten things up a bit."

"Oh, things are much lighter now without your big smelly body leaning on me," she said laughing.

The group walked on, each carrying some of Kami's flowers in front of them. "Looks like we might be coming to the end," said Erik, who had regained his strength and was out in the lead.

"There's definitely a light up there," said Brian.

"Kind of a strangely shaped opening, though," said Becka.

"Almost looks like a horse," said Aimee.

"An extremely bright horse," said Erik as they got closer.

The light that had been standing still suddenly rushed at them full speed. A breeze blew past them as Adam's flowers were snatched out of his hands. They heard the trotting of hooves and a distant whinny as the creature galloped away.

"It was a unicorn," said Kami. "Did you see it Adam? Did you see the horn?"

"Was kinda hard to see anything," said Adam, standing with his hand still in flower-holding position.

"He must not get very much fresh food in here," said Becka, handing some of her flowers to Adam.

"Did you see how he was all lit up?" Aimee was still staring in the direction of the unicorn's departure, hoping to get another glimpse.

"I wish he'd come back," said Kami. "I'll give him my flowers."

"The flowers are wilting," said Brian. "I think we'd better hurry if we're going to make it out of here alive."

The group pressed forward, moving as swiftly down the path as possible. Suddenly there was no path. The light from the flowers showed that the forest had grown up over it. Briars and vines obstructed the way.

Adam sat down on the ground. "I'm getting hungry, how about some of Caoimhin's crusty bread?"

Becka pulled him back onto his feet. "I don't think we have time to eat, but soon."

Aimee whispered to Erik and Brian. "We need to get Adam to safety soon."

Brian pulled out his knife and started hacking away. As he moved forward, the vines closed in behind him. Soon the others couldn't see or hear him.

"We have to go after him," said Kami. Taking a long sword from Erik's pack she started hacking at the vines.

Soon she was gone too.

"Now we're out of things to hack with," said Becka.

"I've got this," said Adam, pulling an ax out of his pack that seemed way too long to fit.

"Stay close," said Erik, chopping at the vines. "I think you'll all have to hold on to me to make it through."

When they reached the other side, they didn't see Brian or Kami anywhere. The knife and the sword were lying far ahead on the path. The good thing was that there was plenty of light and the air was cool and fresh.

"I can breathe," said Adam, taking a big dose of fresh air into his lungs.

Erik ran ahead to retrieve the sword and knife. Before he reached the place where they lay, he fell into an unseen pit. Adam heard him yell as he fell, his voice echoing up and fading away. The ax flew forward and landed next to the other weapons.

Adam ran to see what happened to his brother. "Wait," said Aimee, following him. "We don't know what's down there."

"My brothers and my Kami are down there," said Adam.

"You have no fear, do you?" asked Becka.

"Nope, no fear," said Adam, jumping into the spot that somehow concealed a well-hidden hole. "Look out below!" They heard him yell, as he disappeared from sight.

"After you," said Aimee.

"No, that's quite all right," said Becka. "Age before beauty."

"Let's go together," said Aimee, taking her sister's arm.

"I hope we both fiiiiii --" Becka's voice trailed off as the two girls threw themselves into the unknown.

{ 13 }

A Pair of Grumpy Wizards

Becka and Aimee slid down a long spiraling tunnel that went on and on, deeper and deeper into the earth.

"It's beginning to feel a bit damp in here!" yelled Aimee as they slid faster and faster.

"It's feeling rather wet," yelled Becka.

Suddenly a rush of water came over them carrying them even faster through an ever-widening tunnel of barreling water. The girls sputtered and held on to each other as they came out of the dark and into a very large and open pool. The warmth of the bright sun hit them in the face as they pulled themselves out of the water, dripping wet.

The others were standing by, wet and muddy.

"You look like a couple of drowned rats," said Erik.

"We've been looking around while we waited for you," said Brian.

The group was standing to the side of a beautiful river of clear water. To the left were large rock walls with several places where underground streams gushed out into the river. To the right was a beautiful forest. Not thick, and full of briars like the forbidden forest. This wood was full of tall pine trees and very little undergrowth.

"According to this we have found a shortcut," said Brian.

"Are we still protected?" asked Kami.

Brian held up the map. "The Hidden Realm of Wisdom is what it says here."

Becka took the map from her brother, "Yes we are certainly still concealed from detection," she said. "See this ring drawn around the caves. This hidden realm is within the ring. Though it appears as if we have left the caves altogether."

"Which way do we go now?" Adam asked.

"Into the woods," said Brian. "It shouldn't be more than another day's journey to the place where we are to meet Athena."

Walking toward the woods, Aimee kept feeling like someone was breathing down her neck. "Don't walk so close," she said, thinking Erik was trying to annoy her. But when she turned around Adam was the closest behind her.

Erik felt someone tap him on the shoulder but turned around to see no one.

Suddenly just in front of them there appeared a cloaked wizard. He had a dingy gray hood pulled over his head concealing his face. "Looks like we've got some live ones," he said.

No sooner had he disappeared than another wizard appeared wearing a brown cloak. "Fine specimens, these are indeed," said the second wizard and then vanished.

"Time, we had a bit of fun, eh?" asked the voice of the hidden gray wizard. "You will have — how many tasks should we give them?"

"I don't know," said the brown wizard's voice. "I'm not prepared for visitors, especially not six visitors."

"Certainly not six all at once," said the gray wizard's voice. "Shall we do the standard three?"

"I think several more, since there are so many of them."

"Well, four then, but not more. It's not really very entertaining once we get past four."

"I think six, one for each of them." As the voices continued to quarrel, the children heard a clattering sound, like the wizards were rummaging through a pile of junk.

"Are you prepared for six?"

"Here, we'll start them out with this. We'll have time to come up with more as they go along."

"Right then," said the voice of the gray wizard. "You start, but I get to tell them the rules."

The gray wizard lowered his voice. "Those who dare to enter the Hidden Realm of Magic must accomplish—umm — as many tasks as we see fit to give you. There are three rules to follow. Not more. Not less. Listen well, as the rules I tell. The first rule is, no magic. The second rule is you cannot speak in words to each other. And --"

There was a long pause as the children heard the whispering of the wizards. They could just make out the brown wizard saying, "Time limit, time limit."

"And you must complete the tasks before time runs out."

Suddenly a large hourglass appeared before them. "How much time do we have?" Kami asked.

"The sands of time run out in one hour," said the gray wizard. "Now, begin."

Instantly the ground between the children and the woods began to crack and spread. Aimee and Brian were bound in ropes and lowered to a cliff below. On the same cliff was a beautiful maiden with long flowing blonde hair. The brown wizard appeared and waving his arms caused a fire to burn below the cliff. "This task is for the brown eyed, arrogant tall lad," he said. "Save these three from the horrible, painful death of being consumed in the smoldering heat of this flaming chasm. As the hot molten lava oozes closer and closer to their feet, you must use this amazing flying contraption, (designed and built by the greatest aero wizard of all time), with which to perform the rescue."

"That would be him," said the gray wizard who was floating high above them getting a regular bird's-eye view.

"Remember this," continued the brown wizard. "You can fly with only one passenger at a time. The fair maiden cannot be alone with your brother. Wouldn't want them to be left without a chaperone, then would we?" he said, winking and nudging Erik in the ribs. "Your sister can not be alone with the fair maiden. Wouldn't want her to tell stories about you then, now would you?" he said, with another wink and a nudge. "Good luck."

The brown wizard joined the gray wizard in the air. "Wait," said Erik, "How do I fly this thing?"

"Eh, eh --" said the gray wizard. "No talking."

"You said no talking to each other," said Kami.

"That's right," said Adam.

"Oh right," said the gray wizard, looking at the brown wizard. "He will help you this time but then you will have to follow the other rule of not asking for help from us."

"Or anyone that passes by," said the brown wizard.

"Can you tell us your names?" said Kami. She noticed that when the wizards spoke the fire died down in the chasm.

"Right," said the gray wizard. "I am the amazing and terrible Mathius, and this is Mikos."

"There you go with that amazing and terrible thing again," said Mikos. "You can't just throw adjectives out there like that. What's so amazing and terrible, anyway? As if you're going to eat these children for supper."

"I am terrible."

"You're a wimp," said Mikos. As his concentration failed, the fire started dying down in the chasm. "You don't hear me going around calling myself Mikos the Great and Horrible, do you? I mean if you really were terrible, you wouldn't want everyone to know right up front like that. You would have to be sneaky about it. And actually, if you were terrible, you'd probably have eaten these children for supper already. And if you were amazing, you wouldn't just come right out and say, 'I'm amazing'. That just shows that you are full of yourself. If you want people to know that you are amazing, you have to do something amazing."

"Are you finished?" asked Mathius, glaring at Mikos.

"It's very nice to meet you, Mathius the Terrible and Amazing and Mikos the Loose Tongue," said Becka curtseying.

Kami curtseyed too. "Very nice to meet you," she said, smiling.

"Hey, can we get on with this," said Aimee on the cliff below. "The flame died out, but we are still stuck down here!!"

"That's Aimee down there, and Brian, and I am Kami, and this is Adam and Becka," she said, pointing to her siblings. "We are from Caraigdun."

Mathius and Mikos glanced at each other.

Erik noticed the look. The same look that Athena had when he told her about his parents.

"Hey!" yelled Brian, "The fire started up again, can we get going on this!"

"Better get to your task Erik of Caraigdun," said Mikos, coming down out of his seat and standing by Erik. "You just climb in here and put your feet here. You'll have to pedal hard to get this whirligig to turn."

Erik pedaled; the whirligig turned. The wheels rolled.

Mikos returned to his seat. "Are you sure that thing will fly?" asked Mathius.

"We're about to find out," said Mikos, grinning.

Erik was so busy trying to figure out how to fly the contraption he had no time to think about the order in which he would save the victims. When the flying machine fell past them at a disconcerting rate of speed, Aimee let out a sigh of exasperation and Brian yelled, "Hey! We're up here!"

The fair maiden gasped, as only fair maidens in distress can.

"He is so brave and handsome too," she said, placing her clasped hands to her bosom.

"He's a blunderhead," said Brian, cringing at the maiden.

Erik got control of the whirligig just before it plunged into the flaming gorge. "Step in," said Erik, reaching his hand out to Aimee. She reached out her hand and then pulled it back.

"I can't go first," she said.

"Eh, eh, eh, no talking about the problem," said Mathius, from above.

Erik extended his hand to the maiden. "I knew you'd save me first," she said, falling into Erik's lap.

The flying contraption fell swiftly from the weight of the plump girl. Erik pedaled faster. "You'll...need...to sit...back...there," he said, trying to form words with no breath in his lungs. "You—have—to — help me — pedal."

"Pedal?" asked the fair maiden. "I'm sure a strong, handsome, brave warrior like you can pedal for the both of us," she said, looking into his brown eyes.

For an instant, Erik stared back into her blue eyes. The trance didn't last long though. Feeling the heat of the fire, Erik flipped the plump maiden behind him. "Pedal!" he said, as the flames licked his feet. "You can tell me how brave I am later!"

The flying machine rose higher and higher, soon the maiden was on safe ground. "My brave, handsome hero," she said, with the back of her hand on her forehead.

When Erik got level with the cliff again, Aimee quickly jumped into the back seat and began pedaling with all her might. "Get me out of here," she said, the sweat dripping down her back.

When they got to ground level again, Aimee got out and Erik flew the contraption into the chasm once again. "Eh, eh, eh," said Mikos, shouting through a large cone shaped tube, "can't leave those two alone."

Aimee started climbing back into the flying machine. She stopped and looked at Erik. They couldn't speak but he knew what she was thinking. "You'll have to come back with me," said Erik, to the maiden.

"You're not getting me near that heat again," she said.

"I'm dying down here!" Brian yelled.

"Let him die," said the maiden. "I don't want my dress to be singed any further."

Erik reached for the maiden's hand. She pulled her hand away sending the flying machine spinning out of control. Erik brought it back to the two girls; Aimee was frantically trying to hold on to the girl who was much bigger than her and struggling fiercely to get away.

Erik grabbed the maiden's hand. Aimee pushed, and Erik pulled and soon the maiden was in her place. She folded her arms across her chest. Erik pedaled frantically, but the contraption fell swiftly past Brian. "I'd suggest you pedal if you don't want to see more than just your dress singed!" yelled Erik, feeling the energy draining from his legs.

When they reached the cliff, they had another struggle to convince the maiden that she would have to be the last one out when she had been the first. After much pushing and pulling and screaming, the boys had control of the contraption and flew up to safe ground.

"You can clap now," said Erik, looking up at Mikos and Mathius who seemed like they were thoroughly enjoying the show.

From below, they heard the screams of the maiden.

"Seems you've forgotten something," said Mikos.

"Can't I just leave her?" asked Erik.

Mikos shook his head. "She's the prize," he said, grinning broadly.

Erik flew down into the chasm one last time. The flames came kicking up as the maiden climbed into the contraption. "You're not brave at all," she said. "What kind of knight takes their damsel back to the peril? Why, I could have died down there, waiting for you to decide whether you were going to save me. Brave, courageous, heroes don't stand around and decide whether...."

Erik was glad she was angry; his legs were tired, and she seemed to pedal as fast as she was talking.

Once on safe ground, the maiden, who was still chastising Erik for his lack of bravery, disappeared. Mikos, Mathius, Becka, Adam, and Kami clapped and cheered wildly.

"Never thought I'd meet anyone more dramatic than you," said Erik, poking Aimee.

"Oh, Erik, my brave, handsome, courageous, hero," said Brian, batting his eyelashes.

"I'm just glad she wasn't real," said Aimee.

"She's real," said Mathius, smiling. "We just like to borrow her every once in a while."

"That took a long time," said Adam, looking at the hourglass, which was half empty.

"Most entertainment we've had around here in months," said Mikos.

"Better move on to the next task," said Mathius. "The pit."

As soon as Mathius spoke the word, all six children found themselves lying on their backs at the bottom of a round, dry pit. They were in a circle; with their hands and feet tied to the next child with tight ropes that were staked to the ground. No one could move, except to stretch out their fingers and reach the fingers of the person next to them.

"There were rats crawling around in the last pit," said Mikos. "And it was wet."

"I didn't like the last travelers as well," said Mathius. "I wouldn't want the little one, Kami, to think I really was terrible."

Swinging above the group were three large pendulums. Each was sharpened to a gleaming blade and swung dangerously close. "You are terrible," yelled Kami. "This scares me."

"It's just for fun," yelled Mathius. "I won't let *you* get hurt."

"Can we at least talk to each other, this time," asked Adam, who had turned very pale.

"If you promise not to say anything mean about us," said Mathius.

"I promise," said Adam, trying to squirm his way free of the ropes.

"You must escape but you cannot break yourself free," said Mathius. "You can only free the person to your right. Here is your only tool."

A sharp knife appeared in Adam's left hand. The other children spoke at once.

"Use it to free my right hand," said Brian, whose right hand was next to Adam's left.

"Pass it to me," said Erik, who was on Adam's right side.

"The pendulums are moving closer," said Aimee.

"I'm trying to think here," said Adam.

"Oh, my gosh, you would give the knife to the one of us who doesn't even know his right from his left," said Becka.

"Of course, I know my right from my left," said Adam. "I figured it out when I had to go down into Prestwick's smelly old throat didn't I?"

"Get down to business," said Brian, "before we're so chopped up, you'll be able to switch your left and your right!"

Adam thought out loud. "If I toss it to Erik, he can't free me because I'm on his left. But I can't cut Brian's ropes because he is on *my* left."

"You have to get the knife into your right hand," said Becka. "Then you can cut Erik's ropes which are on your right."

"What do you want him to do?" asked Erik. "Flip the knife over his chest with his fingers and expect it to land in his hand. That sharp knife could kill me."

"Quiet, or we're all going to die," said Adam. "I wish I had never asked that we could talk to each other."

Adam spoke his thoughts aloud again. "It's too dangerous to toss the knife to anyone. I can't cut Brian's ropes because he's on my left — that's it." Adam quickly took the knife between two fingers. "Brian can you feel it?"

Brian realized that his little brother was handing the knife to him. He stretched his fingers as far as they would go. "Got it," he said.

Brian turned the knife around in his fingers. "Just tell me if I'm cutting something other than rope," he said, aiming the knife to where he thought Adam's ropes must be.

"Ouch," said Adam.

"Sorry, did I --?"

"Just kidding," said Adam.

"I like this group," said Mathius. "They've got spunk."

"Quit fooling around," said Aimee, "Kami is crying over here."

"I could take her out of there," said Mathius. "But I think you'll need her to finish the task."

"Just be quiet, you mean old wizard," Kami was mad.

"Don't worry Kami," said Adam. "I've almost got one hand free."

Brian had slowly sliced through the ropes, and sure enough Adam's hand was free. "Now I can free Erik," he said.

Adam took the knife in his left hand and reached over to Erik's left.

"Ouch," said Erik. "And I wasn't kidding."

"Sorry, Erik," said Adam, pulling the knife back. "It's still hard to see with my head tied down like this."

"Don't fool around," said Aimee. "This is serious."

"My head's not tied down," said Kami.

"That's good," said Erik. "When the knife gets to you, you'll be able to lean further over and cut more of Aimee's ropes."

"Then I'll cut all of Brian's and we'll be moving fast," said Aimee.

Kami worked quickly when the knife got to her. The pendulums were dangerously close. But it seemed like they had stopped lowering. Maybe Mathius wasn't so terrible after all, she thought. Maybe he had stopped the pendulums to give them more time.

The group passed the knife around the circle. As soon as they were all free, the pendulums disappeared.

"I suppose you just borrowed those too," said Brian, rubbing his rope-burned wrists.

"Now get us out of here," said Kami. "I'm tired of playing your games."

"That's the fun of the pit," said Mathius. "You have to find your way out."

"We never tire of games," said Mikos. "Besides, he's gone easy on all of you. A grotesque beast usually comes out after the pendulums disappear."

"I want to see the beast," said Adam.

Becka clapped her hand over his mouth. "Let's just find our way out before the beast finds his way in," she said.

The children walked around the pit. To one side was a large metal gate.

"That's probably where the beast is," said Kami.

"Anyone got any rope?" Erik asked.

"I do," said Adam, reaching for his pack. "In my pack."

"Up there?" Aimee asked.

"Up there," said Adam.

Brian was examining the gate. "Let's just climb up this," he said.

The others glanced up to the top of the gate. "It doesn't go all the way out," said Aimee.

"I think I could hoist myself up, once I get to the top," said Brian, already climbing up. "Then I'll get the rope and send it down to --"

They heard a loud snarl as sharp claws reached for Brian, knocking him off the gate. Everyone stood back as the hideous creature came into the light.

"Ahh!" Kami screamed and hid behind Aimee.

Aimee and Becka screamed too, but it wasn't only because of the creature. When he appeared, hundreds of huge rats accompanied him. Adam quickly scrambled onto Erik's shoulders.

"Decided to spice things up a bit ay," said Mikos.

"Was getting boring," said Mathius.

Erik was thinking fast. The little boy on his shoulders gave him an idea, "Adam you'll have to get down."

"I hate rats," he said.

"Just get down for a minute," said Erik, setting the little boy on the ground. "Becka, you're the tallest. You'll have to climb on my shoulders."

"I'm too heavy."

"Just do it," he said, as the rats swarmed at their feet.

Becka climbed on Erik's shoulders. "Can you reach the top?"

"We need Brian or Aimee."

"Brian, you go next," said Erik, holding his sister's ankles and bracing himself.

"It will be too much weight," said Aimee, "here Brian, stand here."

Brian stood next to Erik. Becka caught on and positioned herself with one foot on Brian's shoulder and one on Erik's. "Now I'll go," said Aimee.

"Hold me steady," said Becka, helping Aimee up onto her shoulders. "I don't think I can --"

Becka was losing balance, but Aimee was at the top. She grabbed the edge of the pit and dangled for a few seconds, then pulled herself up. Becka, Erik and Brian fell in a heap; the rats took their chance and crawled all over them.

Becka screamed. "It could have worked the other way too you know," she said, jumping up and fighting off the furry creatures. "Then I'd be out of here."

Adam giggled at his sister as she jumped all around pulling rats out of her skirt.

"This is not funny," said Kami, who was keeping a close eye on the gate.

Mathius saw her close watch, he waved his hand, and the gate rose a little and then lowered just as quickly.

"Ugh," said Kami, looking up at the wizard. "That was mean."

"Just having a little fun," said Mathius, smiling.

A long rope dropped into the cave; Adam scurried up quickly, almost pulling Aimee back down. Kami was next. Knots appeared all along the rope, making her climb easier. "I could have done it myself, thank you," she said, with a *humph* and a flip of her head.

The knots disappeared as Becka began her turn. "Hey, I could have used those knots," she said.

Brian made it up with no problem as everyone pulled him out. As Erik grabbed hold of the rope, the gate opened quickly. The monster took one quick swipe at Erik's leg.

"Bravo," said Mathius, clapping slowly.

"You keep helping them," said Mikos.

"I thought letting old Grordog out at the end was a nice touch," said Mathius.

"You shouldn't tease him like that," said Kami.

"Hey, don't give them any ideas," said Erik. "They may throw one of us back in."

"The hourglass!" yelled Adam.

The top chamber was almost empty. "What happens if we can't complete the tasks before time runs out?" Kami asked.

"That just means...," began Mikos.

Mathius cut him off. "It means a horrible fate worse than death awaits you," he said, narrowing his eyes.

"On to the next task," said Mikos.

"Right," said Mathius. "I have just the thing."

"It's my turn," said Mikos.

"But I've got just the thing," said Mathius, and he leaned over and whispered in Mikos ear.

"Well, alright," said Mikos. "But I get to come up with half."

"Half of what?" asked Aimee.

"This monumentally gargantuan task is so arduous, so strenuous that your cerebral cortex will scarcely come out unscathed," said Mathius, moving closer and closer to the smallest children as he spoke.

"You're doing it again," said Mikos.

"Bit too dramatic?" asked Mathius.

"What did he mean?" asked Brian, looking at Mikos.

"Sounds horrifying," said Kami.

"I'm not scared," said Adam, stepping closer to Mathius.

"It's just riddles," said Mikos.

"Riddles?" said Kami, with a sigh. "That's easy."

"Easy, eh?" said Mathius, glaring down at the little girl. "Not these riddles."

"You will have to answer one riddle each," said Mikos.

"Better have them whisper the answers in our ear," said Mathius.

"Why?" Mikos asked. "Not like they're going to get out of here and tell anyone the answers."

Mathius looked around. There was a rustle in the woods. "Never know where listening ears lie," he said.

"I'll go first," said Kami.

"Very well," said Mikos "Here is your riddle:

The sun could search all day.

But she'd never find them.

They come out and play.

When the day's behind them."

Kami repeated the riddle softly to herself. "That could be a lot of things," she said. "But I think I know what it is."

She stepped forward and, pushing the long entanglement of curly white hair away, she whispered into Mikos' ear.

He paused for a moment. "You have spoken correctly," he said. "You may cross to the wood."

Kami clapped her hands and skipped across the bridge. "Told you this would be easy," she said.

"Now, for Adam," said Mathius.

"Two bodies have I.

Though both joined in one.

The stiller I stand,

The faster I run."

"Can you say that again?" Adam asked.

The wizard repeated the riddle.

Adam said it over and over in his head. "This is harder than Kami's," he said.

Then he saw Kami jumping up and down behind the wizards. She was waving her arms and when she caught his eye; she pointed at something.

Adam looked and knew the answer. He almost yelled it out before he remembered to whisper to the wizard.

"How could you know that?" Mathius narrowed his eyes, shooting daggers at the little boy.

"I believe he had a little help," said Mikos.

Mathius turned to see Kami standing just behind him. She had her hand behind her back and was looking down, pointing her toe into the ground. "You were supposed to cross the bridge," he said.

"I want to hear the other riddles," she said.

Mathius pointed and sent Adam along with her.

"Seems we've got a riddle expert in that little girl," said Mikos.

"Our mother --" began Becka.

"Don't tell him," Erik said, poking his sister.

"That's okay," said Mikos. "Your mother doesn't know the answer to this.

The fiddler and his wife,
The piper and his mother,
Between them ate three half-loaves, three whole loaves and
Three-quarters of another
If each had an equal share, how many loaves did each eat?"

Brian turned away.

"Hoping this one isn't for you?" asked Mikos.

"Not good at riddles," said Brian, bowing his head.

"Then this is just the one for you," said Mathius.

Mikos repeated the riddle with a wicked gleam in his eye.

Brian rubbed his head, contorted his face like he was thinking rather hard, and then walked slowly over to Mikos. "I'm not sure but I'll take a guess," he said, and then whispered into the wizard's ear.

Mikos' eyes got big.

"He didn't get it did he?" Mathius asked.

"How could you have known that the piper's mother was the same person as the fiddler's wife?"

Brian shrugged his shoulders. The wizards did not see the big smile on his face as he crossed the bridge to Kami and Adam.

"Next," said Mathius with disgust.

Erik stepped forward. "You don't know our mother," he said.

Mathius said the next riddle slowly as if he were trying to make it more difficult.

"Two brothers are we,
Great burdens we bear,
All day we are bitterly pressed.
Yet this I must say,
We are full all the day,
And empty when we go to rest."

Erik looked at the wizard, "Can't do any better than that?" he asked and whispered the answer into Mathius' ear.

"I've got a superb one," said Mikos.

Becka stepped forward. She hoped he picked one she already knew. She was getting hungry and worried that her mind wouldn't be able to work out anything too difficult.

"I saw a fight the other day.
A damsel did begin the fray,
She with her daily friend did meet,
Then standing in the open street,
She gave such hard and steady blows,
He bled ten gallons at the nose.
Yet seemed to neither faint nor fall,
Nor give her any abuse at all."

Becka had never heard this riddle. She held her stomach as it rumbled with hunger and put a hand to her aching head. She worked over the clues in her mind. A damsel meets her 'daily friend' in the middle of the street. Then she spoke aloud. "Then she punches him in the nose, and he bleeds ten gallons but doesn't faint. This is an impossibility," she said, looking at Mikos.

"The obvious is often impossible to see," he said, smiling.

Becka stood for a long time thinking. "Can Aimee have hers while I think?" she asked.

Mikos looked at Mathius, "How about this," said Mikos. "Aimee has to keep answering correctly until you get yours."

Aimee looked at her sister, "Better think fast," she said.

Mathius looked at Aimee. She didn't like his beady gaze upon her. "Go ahead then," she said.

"Old Mother Twitchett has but one eye,
And a long tail which she can let fly,
And every time she goes over a gap
She leaves a bit of her tail in a trap."

"That's an easy one," yelled Adam who had come back across the bridge to see what was taking so long.

"I know," said Aimee. "Just give me a chance to answer." She walked over to the wizard and whispered in his ear.

Mathius twisted up in a full-face frown.

"Of course, she'd get that one," said Mikos. "That's something she uses every day."

"You gave Becka something she probably uses every day," said Mathius.

Becka looked up from rubbing her head and racking her brain.

"Now you've given her a hint," said Mikos.

"Never mind," said Mathius. "We're giving her more time to think. Here is another riddle for Aimee."

"A water there is I must pass,
A broader water never was,
And yet of all water I ever see,
I pass over with less jeopardy."

At the mention of the word water, Becka started putting the clues together. She looked at her sister who seemed very puzzled at the last riddle. Suddenly the answer to her riddle popped into her brain. "I've got it," said Becka. "It's the town water pump."

Mathius and Mikos frowned. "You had her going there," said Mathius.

"I suppose we're done," said Aimee.

"You have to answer yours," said Mikos.

"You said she only had to answer until I got mine right," said Becka.

"She's got you there," said Mikos.

"But Becka has to answer another question since she yelled out the answer to the last one," said Mathius.

"I'm hungry," said Mikos.

"You're right," said Mathius. "All of this game playing stirs up a good appetite."

"Besides, the sand in the hourglass has run out," said Mikos.

"Right," said Mathius "time for lunch."

"Time for lunch?" asked Becka who was walking behind the wizards as they crossed the bridge.

"Is that all the hourglass was for?" Aimee asked.

"That's right," said Mikos. "You didn't think we were going to eat you for dinner or anything like that did you?"

{ **14** }

A Few Good Tools

Once the group stood together on the other side of the bridge, Mathius and Mikos shook everyone's hand and thanked them for a good show. "Now it's time for a feast," said Mikos.

"Right," said Mathius. "Follow us."

The wizards disappeared without a trace.

"I suppose they think that since we are wizards like them, we should be able to follow them," said Becka.

"Maybe if we all think about it really hard, we will disappear and reappear near them," said Kami.

Adam closed his eyes and scrunched up his face. They all smiled as he opened his eyes. A frown covered his face as he realized he hadn't gone anywhere.

"I think we should just cross the forest," said Brian. "We've wasted enough time."

Just then Mathius appeared behind Brian and waved his hand. They could all hear his voice as they were suddenly in darkness. "I'm sure you won't think this is a waste of time," he said.

In the blink of an eye, the children stood in a large hall. In the center was an enormous round table covered with all kinds of scrumptious food.

"I think you're right there," said Erik, eyeing the huge roasted turkey leg on a plate closest to him.

"Allow me," said Mikos, as he pulled out a chair for Kami and motioned to Erik and Brian to do the same for their sisters.

Becka eyed Erik suspiciously. She had seen how gentlemanly he could be around other girls, but she had her chair pulled out from under her more than once by her scoundrel brother.

She went to sit down, and true to form, Erik jerked out the chair. The entire room had a good laugh as something unseen hit Erik in the back of the legs, his knees buckled, and he fell instead of his sister.

Becka couldn't control her laughter as she stood over her brother, who was rubbing his head.

"Now you know how it feels," she said.

"So, how come you didn't follow us?" Mikos asked, as the group settled down for a magnificent meal.

"I think they were going to scoffer off," said Mathius. "Heard them talking about wasting time."

"We didn't know how to follow," said Adam. "I tried concentrating really hard, but that got me nowhere."

"I can understand the little ones not knowing how to travel by the transport spell, but you older children should have learned that one a long time ago," said Mikos.

"We haven't been wizards for very long," said Kami.

"Rubbish," said Mathius. "Either you are a wizard or you're not."

"With what wizards have each of you apprenticed?" asked Mikos.

"Erik went to a blacksmith to be an 'appentice'," said Adam.

"A blacksmith? Was it old Holcomb the half human?" asked Mathius.

"That would explain the poor training," said Mikos. "Holcomb was always more partial to the ways of humans; more interested in things that were accepted by at least some humans; like astrology and chemistry without spells."

"Chemistry, without spells? That wouldn't work at all," said Mikos.

"Right," said Mathius, looking at Mikos. "Just like those flying contraptions of yours would never get off the ground without a bit of magic."

"He was strictly a human blacksmith," said Erik, cringing at the thought of the smoldering conditions he had but recently escaped.

"Our mother and father didn't tell us," Aimee said.

Mathius looked at Mikos, "Their mother and father didn't --"

"Tell them," Mikos said, with a smile of recognition.

"Who did you say your parents are?" asked Mathius.

"We didn't say," said Brian, with a look of distrust.

"They're harmless," said Aimee, tossing Brian a reassuring glance. "They are Denis and Jaynea of Caraigdun."

Mathius and Mikos smiled broadly at each other. "Jaynea's your mama?" asked Mathius.

"Seems like everyone knows her," said Becka.

"We don't just know her," said Mikos. "We're her baby brothers."

"Baby brothers?!" Adam looked closely at the wrinkled, haggard faces of the wizards and the gray and white hair. "Our mother is younger than you."

"You both look like you are about a thousand years old," said Kami.

"Not a day over nine hundred," said Brian.

"This is just for effect," said Mathius. And the two wizards waved their hands in front of their faces and suddenly appeared to be about thirty years old.

"Her brothers?" asked Aimee. "She would have told us if she had brothers."

"Not if she didn't want you to know what you really are. The last time I saw you, you were a wee bairn," said Mathius, smiling at Aimee.

"You looked like a shriveled faced leprechaun the day you were born," said Mikos, frowning and smiling at once.

The boys were laughing at the wizard's description. "That wasn't very nice," said Kami.

"Wasn't meant to be naughty or nice," said Mikos, "just a fact that is, just a fact."

"People don't get personality until they're about two years old anyway," said Mathius, placing his hand on Aimee's shoulder. "Personality is what matters."

Mikos ran a hand through his tangled hair. "So that explains why they don't know much magic. I thought for sure Jaynea would have given in by now. What's your quest?" he asked.

"So, what's your quest?" asked Mikos.

"Our quest is to save our parents and slay that mean, nasty, Gwandoya," said Adam.

"He's got Jaynea?" Mathius asked, as both wizards stood and put their fists on the table.

"He has Mama and Father and Marcus and Guelder."

"Marcus and Guelder?" asked Mikos. "Mathius, I told you we have to get out more."

"So, you are all equipped with some powerful spells and tools to help you with this quest I assume," said Mathius.

"We really know very little magic," said Becka.

"I know how to leminate," said Adam.

"I know how to make a glass dome around me," said Kami.

"Are you telling me, you are on a quest to fight the most fierce odious, horrific creature to come along since, Mikos here," said Mathius, poking his brother, "and you have nothing but a 4-year-old boy who can 'leminate' and a little girl who is good at a shield spell?"

The wizards exchanged glances, "This could be fun," said Mathius, standing up and walking over to a large wooden chest.

"That looks like a pirate's chest," said Adam.

"Better than that," said Mathius. Rubbing his hands together and raising them in the air as he spoke, "Expositus."

"They said I wouldn't have to know any big words," said Adam.

"The bigger the better," said Mathius, as a light radiated from the slowly opening chest. Mathius reached in and pulled out a long walking stick. There were figures of animals, people, and objects carved all along it.

"The history of my magic," said Mathius, handing the cane to the little boy.

"What do these carvings mean?" asked Brian.

"This one on the bottom shows that I received an award for levitating at my first wizard trials," said Mathius.

Mikos reached into the trunk and pulled out his own carved stick.

"Each carving shows a progression in magical growth," said Mikos. "We had to make at least four carvings a year after we started apprenticing."

"This one is for transportation," said Mikos, pointing to a carving that was there and then disappeared, reappearing somewhere else along the stick.

"We've missed out on a lot," said Becka.

"Years of training," said Brian, running his hand up and down the stick.

"No matter," said Mathius. "We'll remedy that right away."

"So you can teach us spells and charms and give us potions?" Erik asked.

"Better than that," said Mikos, raising his arms. "We have — The book."

"The book," said Mathius, repeating his brother's ominous tone.

"We found a lot of books in Mama's cave," said Kami.

"This is the only copy of this book," said Mathius.

"What book?" asked Adam. "Hope it doesn't have a lot of big words. 'Cause I can't speak 'em and I sure can't read 'em."

"Get the primer for Adam," said Mathius.

"Right," said Mikos, "the primer."

The wizards dug around in the chest, after a moment each turned around. Mathius held a very large dust covered book. On the front was a family coat of arms. A shield divided into four sections, each holding a symbol of the family. A lion stood proud in the center, a whale below, a falcon with spread wings, and a phoenix coming out of flames occupied the top two sections.

"The book," said Mathius. With a bow, he presented it to Erik.

"I'm the firstborn," said Aimee.

Mathius looked at Aimee. He looked at Becka, who stood half a head taller than Aimee. He looked at Erik who stood a few inches taller than Becka. "Are you sure about that?" he asked.

"She looks like she has Halfling blood," said Mikos. "And he looks like he's a half of a half giant."

"Humph," said Aimee, taking the book out of Mathius' hands.

The others gathered around as she opened the first page. "This is better anyway," said Erik, looking over Aimee's shoulder. "She wouldn't have been able to see if I was holding it way up here."

Aimee stomped Erik's foot, "Enough of the short jokes," she said, as she read. "A book to be passed down from generation to generation, familia a familia, to be held with respect and honor as the name of Clerlongernon.

"Clerlongernon?" asked Brian. "I thought our mother's maiden name was Cler."

"Ah, that would be a tale to tell," said Mathius, looking at Mikos.

"We don't want to travel down that path," said Mikos.

"It is long," said Mathius. Pulling his hands through his long red beard, he looked for a minute as if he might be preparing to tell the tale.

Mikos shook his head.

"Another day," said Mathius. "What are you waiting for?" he asked, reaching over and helping Aimee open the book. "Nothing in these pages will bite you." And he led the four older children outside to begin their training.

"Well, I don't know about that," said Mikos, under his breath.

Mikos brought Kami and Adam on his knee and showed them the primer. As he opened it, a yawn exuded from the pages. Kami jumped, as the book said, "Who's — waking — me, from a sound sleep?"

"It talks," said Adam.

"Of course, I talk," said the book. "Unless you'd rather I sing."

"No need for that right now," said Mikos. "I have two new students for you, your majesty."

"Your majesty?" asked Adam, looking at the old haggard face staring back at him from the front page of the book. "You a king or something?"

"I am King Biblion of the Realm of Enchanted Books," said the book.

"He's not really a king," whispered Mikos. "But if you don't call him 'majesty' he won't give you your next lesson."

"A couple of new apprentices," said Biblion, peering out at Kami and Adam. "They don't look young enough for the primer."

"We got started a bit late, because our Mama was protecting us from a mean dragon," said Kami.

"A dragon?" asked Biblion. "And I suppose your mother has slain the dragon and thus decided that it is now safe for you to learn magic?"

"Actually, he captured her," said Kami.

"And we have to save her," said Adam.

"Save their mother from a mean dragon and no one has taught them any magic?!" Biblion's eyes turned to Mikos. "How much time do I have to train these saplings?"

"I thought maybe you could give them a few pointers today," said Mikos. "They really should be on their way early tomorrow."

"Early tomorrow," said Biblion. "Well then, not much time at all."

The pages of the book began flipping back and forth wildly.

"I think he's lost his mind," said Kami.

"I think he's confused," said Adam.

"Here it is," said Biblion as the pages flipped and stopped. "No, no, that's not it," he said, as the pages flipped some more. "Not it," he would say each time a page passed.

A few minutes later the book finally settled down. Before them Kami and Adam saw a magnificent drawing of a dragon. All around the page were scribbles of almost unintelligible handwriting with arrows pointing to different parts of the creature's body. Kami read some of the writings. "This says, 'dragon's mail, impenetrable, harder than the hardest metal. Claws, for scratching mail, climbing, and ripping apart flesh'."

"That's nice," said Adam.

As the children stared at the page, they saw the dragon's head move. When his gaze caught theirs, his nostrils flared, and billowing flames of fire spread across the page.

Adam put his hand out to touch the page, half expecting the dragon to bite off his finger. "Will he bite me?" he asked, pulling his finger back.

"He's harmless," said Biblion. "Hate to see what would happen if he ever escaped though."

"He's real?" Kami asked.

"That's right," said Biblion, "it took years to capture him. The Great Marcus of Caraigdun finally accomplished it about twenty years ago."

"That's our grandfather," said Kami.

"We get to save him from Gwandoya too," said Adam.

"Your grandfather is Marcus of Caraigdun?" asked Biblion, incredulously. "So, you must be the children of his daughter Vandea."

"She's our aunt," said Kami. "She traveled to distant lands many years ago and we have never met her."

"You can't be the children of Denis," said Biblion. "He was my best student and would surely pass on my teaching to his children."

"Denis is our father," said Adam.

"And your mother?"

"Jaynea," said Kami.

"The precocious Jaynea? Never could get that one to sit still; always fluttering from page to page. Never working on one spell or concept long enough to get it right before moving on to the next."

"I'm sure she's settled down a bit, now," said Mikos who had returned from checking on Mathius' progress with the other children. "She's a mother, after all and hasn't used magic in many years."

"Can't imagine eating a meal cooked by that one," said Biblion. "How could she stick to a recipe? The cake would be missing the sugar for sure; the bread would fall from lack of leavening."

"Our Mama is the best cook in Caraigdun," said Kami. "She has taught me to make cakes and she never leaves out the sugar."

"Your majesty, I think you'd better get to work," said Mikos. "The other children are progressing nicely. They will be on their way early in the morning."

"I must ask one more thing before we begin," said Biblion, and he turned the pages of the book until it settled on a picture of an even more fierce looking dragon. "Did I hear them say that Gwandoya captured their mother?"

"Yep, and that's him," said Adam.

"How'd anybody get close enough to draw his picture," said Kami.

"Your mother created this drawing from a wood cut before she sculpted the body," said Biblion.

"Our mother is a good artist," said Adam.

Kami ran her fingers over the page. "We've met him, you know," she said. "He brought six dragons with him to fight us."

"Six dragons to fight two small children," said Biblion. "He must think your parents trained you well in the ways of wizardry."

"There are six of us," said Kami.

"We each had to fight one dragon," said Adam. "You should have seen us."

"We really must get on with the lesson," said Mikos.

"It's good that I have this background," said Biblion. "But Mikos is correct, we have little time, and I would like to aid in the capture of the fierce Gwandoya."

A pointer appeared out of nowhere and pointed at different things on the page. "Gwandoya is equipped with the usual lethal weapons of a dragon. Here you see his claws which of course you know you must stay clear of. His wings are strong and powerful. A blow from them could take the life out of your small frames instantly. His hind legs support his powerful body. You will find these to be grave weapons should you try to sneak up on the dragon. His tail is an even more terrifying tool and can swat you like a fly from any approach. His ears are sharp. They can pick up the approach of an enemy from miles away."

Next the pointer pointed at the eyes of the dragon. "The eyes of Gwandoya are unlike the eyes of any creature on this earth. He has a power in them that comes from the spirit of the being that lives within him. No one knows how to fight this power because an evil witch stole it for him over three hundred years ago. We do not know where she got the power so we cannot send it back to its rightful owner. His eyes glow with this power. There are other dragons that have glowing eyes but not like Gwandoya for although he has taken the form of an ogre and now a dragon, he is neither, but a human who has borrowed these forms."

"What power does he have?" asked Kami.

"It is the circle of fire," said Biblion.

"Ahh, that's nothing," said Adam. "All dragons breathe fire."

"Feisty lad isn't he," said Biblion. "This fire is not in his breath young Adam, it is as I have been trying to tell you, from his eyes. Now sit still and listen for a minute or I won't teach you another thing."

Adam put his hands under him and tried to sit still, his spirit was squirming wildly within his body. "I want to go outside and learn with my brothers," he said.

Kami put a finger to his mouth. "We have our part and they have theirs," she said. "Now sit still, I want to learn about the eyes of the dragon."

"Gwandoya uses his eyes to make a ring of fire around his enemy. If the victim is not freed from the ring within three brief minutes, they will be sent — spirit and body to — The Dimension of Never-ending Torment."

Adam started laughing.

"What's the matter with you?" asked Kami.

"Did you hear how he said that? All scary and stuff?" Adam couldn't stop laughing.

"This is not a laughing matter," said Biblion. "Reports say that this dimension is full of unspeakable terrors."

"You should have seen the way your face got all twisted," Adam was still laughing.

"My choice of dramatics was meant to emphasize the peril of the circle of fire, young man." Biblion was angry.

"I thought you did a marvelous job of just that," said Kami, poking Adam, who had gotten himself so worked up he was practically falling off his chair.

"Let's move on then," said Biblion. "As long as one of you is paying attention." Kami smiled and sat up straight.

Adam noticed this movement and tried to pull himself together. "How do you get free of the ring of fire and keep from going to the Dimension of --" Adam made his voice sound as deep and ominous as possible but couldn't complete his sentence before he broke out in uncontrollable laughter again.

"He dares to mock the teacher," said Biblion.

"Oh, just ignore him," said Kami. "Teach me about the dragon. Is there a way to break free of the circle?"

"Someone on the outside will have to be within three strides of the circle. Close enough to feel the heat but not close enough to get singed. Then, if you will turn to page three-hundred and fifty-three."

The pages flipped on their own and stopped on page three-hundred and fifty-five.

Kami flipped the pages back and forth. "Looks like three-hundred and fifty-three is missing," she said.

"Missing!" exclaimed Biblion. "Wait. Oh right, I remember now. Many years ago, one of my students ripped that page from this book."

"Which student?" asked Kami, "Do you remember?"

"As a matter of fact, it was a student who couldn't seem to remember the spells so he would write down his favorites and carry them around with him. His name was Grog."

"We know Grog," said Adam, finally composed.

"I remember the day he ripped out the spell. He was frantic and his words were incoherent. Rambling about his friend and how he had to save her."

Adam hopped up.

"Get back here," said Biblion, closing his eyes and throwing back his head. (If he'd had a hand, it would have been placed on his forehead just then.) "How can I work like this?"

"What are you doing now?" asked Kami, as her little brother pulled things out of his knapsack and tossed them all over the room.

"Is this it?" he asked, holding up a piece of wrinkled parchment for Biblion to see.

"Well, it is at that," said Biblion.

"Grog said he used it to save our Mama, remember Kami?"

Kami looked at her little brother. "Guess, he pays attention even though he's squirming," she said, smiling.

Kami looked at the words of the spell. "We're going to have to practice these," she said.

"I'll help you with that Kami, my dear," said Biblion. "First there are a few more things I'd like to tell you about the evil Gwandoya. The last time this book was updated, seven years ago, Gwandoya could not disappear like most dragons."

"He learned how," said Adam, remembering when the dragon appeared by the pond after the battle.

"I have a way that you can see him," said Biblion, "even if he is invisible."

The pages started flipping and came to a stop on a page with a picture of plants, and a lot of words. "These are the plants you will need to make an invisibility potion," said Biblion.

"I see these all the time when I pick berries," said Kami, pointing at a large green-leafed plant.

"These grow by the apple tree at home," said Adam.

"You won't find this in the wild," said Biblion and only the best gardeners have been able to grow it in such a moist climate as we have here.

"I've seen this plant somewhere," said Kami.

"In Athena's garden," said Adam.

"Athena has practiced her gardening skills then," said Biblion. "She is another one that wouldn't sit still."

"We can't go all the way back to her house to get this," said Kami.

"Let's plan a strategy," said Biblion, "a plan of attack. Then we will know whether we need this invisibility spell."

"Should we get the others?" asked Kami.

"I've a feeling the two of you will need a plan all of your own," said Biblion.

"We're not going to be separated, are we?" she asked.

"I cannot say," said Biblion. "All I know is that you must be able to stand on your own. They will learn spells and methods that will be useful to each of them."

While Biblion was busy with Kami and Adam, Mathius and Mikos were working with the others in an open area outside. Mathius came in and began pulling things out of the trunk and thrusting them into a leather bag.

"Can't believe that sister of ours didn't train these children; and then when she has the chance, she doesn't even give them so much as an amulet to help them...ahhh here it is."

Mathius walked out of the room quickly. Kami and Adam barely paid attention to him. They were finally learning how to defeat the dragon.

When Mathius came back outside, he was still muttering to himself about the foolishness of his sister Jaynea.

"She just wanted to protect us," said Aimee.

"She knew better than that," said Mathius. "He who sits home to avoid trouble will soon find it creeping in through the cracks in the walls. Before he knows it, it will have destroyed his home from the inside out."

"Enough of your wise sayings," said Mikos, grabbing the bag out of Mathius' hand. "What interesting trifles are we going to pass on to the children of our sister?"

"I'm sure they will find my collection very useful," said Mathius.

Mikos held out the bag for Brian. Brian reached into the bag and pulled out a small gadget that looked like it might fit over someone's nose. "Don't know if you'll need that," said Mikos.

"Of course, they will," said Mathius, taking the object and placing it on Brian's nose.

"Yuck," said Brian as the device heightened his sense of smell dramatically. "A foul stench, that's horrible."

"He will be able to smell Gwandoya from miles away," said Mikos.

"Maybe," said Mathius, "but he won't know what he's smelling." Mathius removed the device from Brian's nose. The word 'skunk' had appeared across the bridge.

Brian heard something rustle in the bushes in front of him. He looked up just in time to see a black-and-white striped tail disappear. "Why did it have to pick up that smell," said Brian. "I'm sure Erik's body odor would have been bad enough,"

"Erik's body odor may have killed you," said Aimee, laughing.

"The Olfactorial is set to detect the most intense smell about twenty feet away. You can set it to detect things as far as one mile away."

Brian handed the Olfactorial to Erik. "I'll pass," said Brian. "What else have you got in that bag?"

"Oh no," said Erik, shoving the nose piece back into Brian's hand and reaching into the bag. "You had your chance."

Mikos leaned over to Brian as Erik was feeling around in the bag. "Just a warning, eat nothing while you have the Olfactorial on."

Brian looked at the Olfactorial. "Right," he said. "Taste and smell are connected."

Mikos nodded and scrunched up his face like he had just bitten into a fermented onion.

"This looks interesting," said Erik, holding up a smooth round ball about the size of a fist. Erik could see himself in the shiny surface.

"The Doublasphere" said Mikos, taking the ball from Erik's hand. "This is one of my favorites; watch."

Mikos threw the ball across the field. It landed about fifty yards away. Immediately there appeared a person. As he turned to look at the group Becka looked at Mikos and said, "It's you."

"How does it work?" asked Aimee.

"It must be the same as the effects of the mirror," said Becka.

"Yes, but with the mirror, your double will appear right in front of you," said Mathius.

"But with this you can send him out ahead to fight for you," said Mikos.

"The perfect decoy," said Brian.

"Then you can sneak in and finish the job," said Erik.

"Sure you don't want to trade?" asked Brian, looking down at the Olfactorial.

"Not a chance," said Erik, running to retrieve the ball.

Becka picked the bag up and reached in, "Guess it's my turn," she said. Her fingers ran across the edges of what felt like a small book. She pulled it out of the bag. Opening it up, she saw it was full of blank pages. "Is this magical?" She asked.

Mikos took the book in his hand. "Not that I know of," he said, glancing at Mathius.

"It was your mother's," said Mathius. "I believe it is a secret diary."

"That's right," said Mikos, remembering. "We stole this from her years ago."

"Never could figure out how to get the writing to come up on the pages."

"How's a girl's diary going to help us fight the dragons?" Brian scoffed.

"You never know," said Mathius, smiling.

Aimee took the bag and reached in. There were still several things in the bag. Her hands moved from thing to thing. "This feels interesting," she said, "but maybe this—no — how about this --"

"Just pick something," said Brian, who was very glad that he had his cloak hidden in his pack, since he got such a stupid object.

"Don't rush me," said Aimee, feeling around even longer just to annoy him. "This might just be the thing," and she pulled out a rather large red scarf.

"I almost chose that one," said Becka, reaching out and touching the scarf. "Silk."

"Not me," said Brian. "Who would want to be stuck with a stupid old scarf?"

"This isn't just any scarf," said Mathius, taking it with a flourish. He passed the scarf in front of his face.

When he pulled the scarf away, his face was that of an old woman. "Now this will take some practice, deary," he said, in a shaky hag voice. "You must have the gift of drama."

"No problem there," said Brian.

"Watch and learn," said Mathius. With another pass of the scarf, he took on the face of Guelder.

"How did you do that?" asked Aimee.

"Just put his image in my head and here he is," said Mathius, smiling.

Aimee took the scarf out of his hand. She passed it quickly over her face. When Aimee lowered the scarf, Brian and Erik started hysterically. "You look like you got up on the wrong side of the bed," said Erik.

"Just a bad makeup job," said Mathius, waving the scarf over Aimee's face. "Before you try again, you'll need to really concentrate on the face of the person you were going for."

"Who were you going for anyway," said Brian, still laughing, "the creature from the forbidden forest?"

"We won't have to fight at all with that face in the lead," said Erik, trying to sound serious without succeeding. "She'll send the dragon screaming into the night."

"You could do that without the scarf," said Becka, smacking her brother playfully in the stomach.

"I can't do this with these silly people distracting me," said Aimee.

"Listen to her," said Brian, straightening up, "silly people, eh? At least we don't look like this." He stretched out his mouth with his pinkies, pushed up his nose, pulled down the skin under his eyes and stuck out his tongue.

"That's enough," said Mikos, trying not to laugh. "This really takes a lot of practice. How about we silly people go to the other side of the field and let Mathius help Aimee?"

"I don't know," said Erik, as they started across the field. "She may be able to get a date with some of those goblin guards with that face."

"Right," said Brian, "We'll have an easy way in."

Becka turned to go back with Aimee and Mathius. "I'll tell her to keep that in mind," said Becka. "I think I'll stay with them. You never know when I may have need of that scarf trick."

"I thought I'd never get you boys alone," said Mikos, when Becka was out of earshot. "I've got this great spell to show you, but it's based on secrecy so only the two of you can know it and it will only remain potent if you keep it a secret between us. It's a spell that all sons learn. It can be used to fool your mother, or to watch over and protect her." They had reached a pool of water. Mikos bent down and scooped some of the water into his hand. "Show mother," he said. Suddenly a beautiful lady with silver hair appeared in the sparkling clear water. Mikos gasped. "I didn't know it would cross over into the great beyond.

Mama? Is that you?" The lady turned for a minute, as if she had heard his voice and then went back to her weaving. "She must be in Heaven," he said. "Weaving was always her favorite pastime, even when she had to do it to earn an income."

"That spell could really come in handy," said Erik.

Mikos was still staring at the image of his own mother. "Yes, yes. It came in handy to pull tricks on her, and...well... sadly though.... It didn't help me save her. But that's neither here nor there. One of you should give it a go. I'd like to get a look at my big sister."

Brian scooped up some water and said, "Show mother." Nothing happened. "Looks like it'll pierce the great beyond but not the magic of Gwandoya."

"Thanks for showing us, Uncle Mikos..."

"Uncle Mikos? Wow. Sounds so formal. Makes me sound so old. I guess I have been an uncle for a long time. Hopefully, you young ones will live through this quest and then, the fun begins."

{ **15** }

Unexpected Abductors

In the morning, the group felt much better equipped to set out on their journey. Kami and Adam had learned plenty about fighting dragons.

"Will you be coming with us?" asked Kami, as the wizards packed a bit of food in each of the children's packs.

"Can't leave here," said Mikos.

"Umm, that's right," said Mathius. "We've been --"

"Enchanted by an evil witch," said Mikos.

"That's right," said Mathius. "Her evil sorcery doomed us to stay in the hidden realm and pass out bits of wisdom to the few travelers that pass our way."

"You mean get your fill of fun playing games with them," said Erik.

"Seems like no adults can travel with us," said Brian, his eyes narrowing.

"I wish you could come," said Adam. "You guys are fun."

Mathius picked up the little boy and hugged him tightly. "This is for you, son of Jaynea," he said, placing a medallion around his neck. "You will know how to use it when the time comes."

Mikos picked Kami up and gave her a big squeeze, "You are a very brave little girl indeed," he said, placing a tiny version of the hourglass around her neck. "This is just a token to remember us by."

The children started down the path. Aimee turned to wave good-bye but the wizards, her uncles, were gone. "I wonder if we'll ever see them again," she said.

The group kept a good pace as they walked along the path. "Adam!" yelled Becka, to the little boy who was running way ahead. "Don't get so far ahead that we can't see you."

As soon as she said these words, Adam was out of sight. "Who knows what might be out there ready to eat up a little boy," said Aimee, peering out into the tall brush that surrounded them on both sides.

Erik ran to catch up with his little brother. He was out of sight of the others when Adam leaped out from behind a tree and yelled, "*Bulah, bulah, bulah!*"

Erik jumped.

"You thought I was a monster," said Adam, laughing hysterically.

Erik picked Adam up and flipped him upside down. "You have met the odious monster, Erik. I shall break your bones and spread the marrow on me bread."

Adam tried to be serious between the laughter, "Oh, I'm so afraid," he said. "Please don't eat me."

Erik put Adam down, "Quick, let's hide and scare the others."

The boys ducked into the bushes just as Brian was coming around the corner. He was running past when Erik and Adam jumped out in front of him.

"Hilarious," he said. "As if I didn't know you'd be hiding here."

"You can't let on to the girls," said Adam, pulling Brian into the bushes.

Brian squatted in the bushes reluctantly. It seemed like a very long time had passed and no sign of the girls.

"I'm sure they have us figured out," said Brian, getting up. "Let's go back."

Erik pulled his brother down by his shirttail. "They're probably waiting for us to do just that," he said. "It's the turkey hunt trick. If we can wait them out, they'll get impatient and come along."

The boys waited and waited but no sign of the girls. "How far back on the path did you leave them?" asked Erik.

"Maybe they stopped to have a picnic," said Adam.

"That's it," said Brian. "They are probably eating the lunch Mathius packed for us."

"Let's eat too then," said Adam.

"I'm going back," said Brian, pulling his pack onto his shoulders. "I've a feeling something is wrong."

Erik followed. Adam came reluctantly after. "Wait for me," he yelled, as he ran down the winding path.

About one hundred yards back along the path, Brian stopped. When Erik and Adam caught up, he showed them that the tracks of the girls had stopped at this point. "It looks like they've gone off this way," he said.

A few steps off the path, and Adam found a clue. "Look, it's one of Kami's ribbons," he said, pulling a long piece of pink satin from a weed.

"Good," said Erik, "It'll be hard to pick up their tracks in all this brush. Wait! Listen."

The boys heard a loud scream up ahead.

"It's Kami," said Brian. "She sounds hurt."

The boys raced quickly through the brush. Adam was slow.

"You've got the shoes, Erik," said Brian. "Go, save her."

Erik ran ahead. Adam scrambled onto Brian's back, and they tried to catch up.

Up ahead Aimee and Becka were frantically trying to reach Kami. She was high in the air above the weeds and wildflowers, held by a hundred little pixies. They fluttered their wings faster and faster as they flew, holding the little girl by her clothes and hair.

"Ouch," said Kami, beginning to cry. "You are hurting me."

The pixies let go of Kami's hair. "Where are you taking me?" She asked a pixie that was flying in front of her.

The pixie either didn't understand or was outright ignoring Kami. She motioned to the other pixies to hurry.

"If you can understand me," said Kami, looking down. "Please don't drop me."

Soon Kami saw a clearing below with a large sawed-off tree trunk in the middle. The pixies put her down. She gasped as she saw a pixie lying on the tree trunk. A long object that looked like a needle stuck in her side.

"Poor thing," said Kami, her lip quivering. "Is she dead?"

The head pixie pulled at the hourglass around Kami's neck. Kami fought with her and the chain broke, sending the pixie whirling backwards. "Ouch," said Kami, rubbing her neck. "That really hurt."

The pixie banged the hourglass against a nearby tree. When the hourglass wouldn't break, the pixie put her head in her hands and cried.

"Don't cry, little pixie," said Kami. "Do you need the sand?"

The pixie looked up at Kami. She gave her a quizzical look. Then looked at the hourglass and began to point and shake her head wildly.

Kami took the hourglass and carefully removed the top. The pixie grabbed the hourglass out of Kami's hand. She flew back to the stump and made a circle of sand around the dead pixie. Several other pixies flew over and flew around and around above the circle of sand. The head pixie flew away and came back with a crossbow holding a golden arrow. The sand flew around and around in the whirlwind created by the pixies. When they stopped flying the sand was still spinning like a tornado. After a few minutes, the sand settled, but the air was still whirling. Kami watched as time seemed to reverse inside the circle. A very large wasp flew backwards into the circle and the stinger came out of the pixie and into the wasp. At that very moment, the head pixie shot the golden arrow straight and swift. The wasp instantly fell, landing next to the frightened little pixie on the stump. Fluttering her wings wildly she tried to fly out of the circle. Air was still swirling around her, and she could not break through the time warp. The other pixies flew around the circle in the opposite direction. The sand swirled again around and around until it finally settled, and the little pixie flew up and to the head pixie, who hugged her tightly.

Aimee and Becka watched in amazement.

Erik came running up behind them. "What's going on here?" He asked. "We heard Kami scream. Are you girls okay?"

Becka pointed to the circle of sand and the pixies. "They reversed time in the circle," she said.

"It was astonishing," said Aimee.

The head pixie flew to the stump and motioned for Kami to bring the hourglass. The pixies put the sand back into the hourglass. Kami helped and closed the lid tight.

The pixies motioned for Kami to follow them. Brian and Adam had caught up so the entire group followed.

"These pixies sure are fast," said Adam, after Aimee told them about the sand and the wasp.

The pixies kept getting far ahead and would send the little pixie back to show them the way. She got very impatient with their slowness and started pushing Adam from behind.

"I'll get there, I'll get there," he said.

The pixie flew close to Kami's ear. She sat on Kami's shoulder, tapped her fingers together, and whistled.

"Impatient little thing isn't she," said Brian.

The pixie flew around Brian's head buzzing like a fly.

Brian swatted at her, and Becka grabbed his hand. "She's not an insect, you know," she said.

"She's as annoying as a gnat," he said.

The little pixie started buzzing around Kami's head again. Suddenly she flew away. "What if we get lost, and she doesn't come back for us?" said Kami. "We'd better try to follow her."

Kami started running. The others followed. Only a few strides ahead Kami suddenly came out into an open area. The brush had been getting thicker and thicker under the trees but now they were in a clearing. In the clearing was a magnificent oak tree. The tree was lit up by tiny lanterns shining in hundreds of tiny windows. A thousand toadstools grew around the tree.

The little pixie flew to Kami's shoulder once again. Hundreds of pixies came flying out of the tree. They chattered at each other, speaking almost as quickly as they flew.

The head pixie motioned for the visitors to sit on tree stumps that surrounded a stage, which was in fact a rather large toadstool, across the clearing from the pixie home. The little pixie stood on the stage and acted out her own death with the help of a large pixie boy.

"He's doing a marvelous job acting the part of a wasp," said Aimee.

"That giant wasp was like a dragon to them," said Erik.

The little pixie clutched her chest and fell to the ground, holding a sword under her arm.

The crowd of pixies booed at the wasp, cringed in horror as the stinger went into the little pixie's side and cried out in agony for the little pixie when she 'died'.

"Dramatic, don't you think?" Brian asked.

"I think it's a very nice show," said Kami.

The head pixie flew over and tugged at the hourglass around Kami's neck. A hundred pixies swarmed around her head. "Oh, oh," said Kami as they carried her in the air to the stage. "At least it wasn't as far or as high this time," she said, as they put her down much more gently than before.

When the show was over the actors and actresses took their bows. The little fairy motioned to Kami to curtsey. The audience exploded in applause.

Adam covered his ears. "For little people they sure can make a loud noise," he said.

The head pixie motioned for Kami and the little pixie to follow her. When they got away from the noise of the crowd, the pixie queen hugged the little pixie and cried. The little pixie cried too. Kami decided this must be her mother or big sister or something.

The pixie queen took the little pixie by the hand. Together they flew to Kami. The pixie queen took Kami's hand and placed the tiny hand of the little pixie into it. Then she pointed to the little pixie and bowed to Kami. The little pixie flew to Kami's shoulder.

"You want her to come with me?" Kami asked, pointing to herself.

The pixie queen nodded yes.

"I would love that," said Kami. But when she glanced over to her shoulder, the little pixie was still crying.

"You can stay here with your family," she said, softly.

The little pixie shook her head.

The queen pixie flew next to the little pixie. She wiped the tears out of her eyes. She pointed at Kami and started acting something out. The other children came in time to see the queen pixie pantomiming that Kami was a witch and would protect the little pixie. Then she pointed at the little pixie and held out her chest and flexed the muscles in her arms.

"I think she's telling her to be strong," said Aimee.

"She's sending her with us," said Kami. "But she is very sad to leave her family. You boys will have to be very nice to her and protect her."

The pixie queen hugged the little pixie once more and flew away. The little pixie buried her head in Kami's hair and cried.

"We'd better get back to the path," said Erik. "We're losing daylight here."

"Looks like a storm is kicking up," said Brian, holding his hand up to the wind.

Kami tried to soothe the little pixie as the group walked back to the path. "I wish you could tell me your name," she said, reaching up and trying to get the pixie to climb into her hand. "I won't hurt you," she said.

"I think we're lost," said Becka, pulling the map out of her cloak.

"We don't need the map. The path is right this way," said Erik, pointing.

Suddenly the little pixie flew out and took Erik's finger. The force of her little winged body amazed him as she spun him around and firmly pointed his finger in the right direction.

Job done, she flew quickly back to Kami and hid once again in her hair. "Thank-you," said Kami, softly.

"She's a pixie with an attitude," said Aimee.

"I think I'm going to enjoy having her along," said Becka, tucking the map away.

"What are we going to call her?" Kami asked.

"Let's call her Flighty," said Erik.

The little pixie came out of her hiding place and flew in front of Erik's face. She shook her head frantically, as if to say, "No, no, no."

Flying back to Kami she motioned for her to follow. Kami followed the little pixie a short distance when she landed on what looked like a weed. Kami smiled as the little pixie mustered all her strength and pulled the weed out of the ground. "Do you want to show them that this is your name," she said.

The little pixie nodded.

Kami showed the plant to her siblings. "I think this is her name."

"It's a weed," said Brian.

"Her name is 'Weed'?" Adam asked.

"It's not a weed," said Aimee. "It's a hollyhock. It looks like a weed because the season of its blooming is over."

When Aimee said the name of the flower, the little pixie fluttered her wings frantically and pointed to herself nodding.

"That's a beautiful name," said Becka, smiling.

"I like 'Weed' better," said Erik, still rubbing his finger where the little pixie pulled on him.

The little pixie, Hollyhock, laughed. She covered her mouth and pointed at Erik.

"What do you find so funny?" He asked.

Hollyhock flew near Erik and pointed to a bunch of weeds that he was standing in. Then she pointed to Erik and laughed again.

"She's calling you, 'stinkweed'," said Aimee. Everyone laughed but Erik.

"Hilarious," he said.

As soon as the group found the path, it started raining.

"We'll have to find shelter," said Brian, calling to everyone over the patter of the rain.

The travelers ran along the path through the mud. Adam slipped. Brian put the little boy on his back. "I'm getting cold," said Adam, shivering.

Erik, who had run ahead to scout out some shelter, came running back. "There are some caves about a quarter of a mile up the road," he said. "We'll take shelter there while this storm passes."

16

Of Angels, Banshees, and Anamorphists

The group trudged along as quickly as possible in the mud. By the time they reached the shelter of the caves they were soaked to the bone.

"Yesterday, we took a bath in the lake and today we get a shower," said Brian.

"Yeah, we're never going to get good and dirty," said Adam.

The little pixie emerged from Kami's pocket, completely dry. She flew to Kami's hair and began wringing out water a few strands at a time.

"That's okay," said Kami. "I'm just glad you are dry and safe."

Erik and Brian were busy starting a fire at the cave entrance.

"I want to explore," said Adam, holding up a torch and peering down a dark tunnel.

"I don't think so," said Aimee, pulling him back into the main cave. "You never know what might grab you and eat you."

"Exactly why we should explore," said Brian. "I want to know what's going to eat me. Come on, Adam."

The boys ventured into the dark tunnel. "If we don't come out in an hour, send in a search party," said Brian.

"I'm not coming in after you," said Becka.

"Go ahead," said Erik. "I'll find you if you get lost."

"Any of Caoimhin's bread left?" Erik asked.

Becka pulled a loaf out of her pack. "It's almost as good as Mama's, right?" She said, handing a piece to Erik.

"I think it's enchanted," said Aimee. "See that's one case where a magical object gives a magical benefit without a magical person using it."

"Athena and Mama know that," said Becka, patting the bag of goodies she was collecting. "They had plenty of contraptions and gadgets saved from when she and Mama were young."

"Yeah, I think they just like to argue with her brothers about the origin of mag --" Erik was interrupted by Adam, who came running out of the tunnel and yelled, "It's a lady in glass!"

"Whoa Little Warrior," said Erik. "Show me."

"Is Brian okay?" asked Becka, following.

"She didn't want him to leave her," said Adam. "She said she's been all alone for a long time."

"That's horrible," said Kami, bringing up the rear.

"Be quiet," said Brian. "It's already difficult to make out what she's saying."

The others each pressed an ear to the glass. "She's trying to tell us how to get her out of there," said Aimee.

"I'll go get the book," said Becka. "Maybe there's a spell."

Becka returned quickly with the book. Erik held the torch while she flipped through the pages. The woman in white went completely berserk when she saw the book. She came very close to the glass and made a motion that Becka should keep turning. A page that showed a picture of someone frozen in a block of ice came up and the woman help up her hand. Becka held the book up so the woman could see the page better. Soon she waved her hand. She had a look on her face that told Becka that this spell probably wouldn't work.

Becka's arms were getting tired from holding up the heavy book. Just as she handed the book off to Aimee, the woman began pointing wildly. Becka looked in the book. From what she could tell the spell would have to be repeated at exactly the same time by the person inside the glass and someone outside the glass.

The lady pointed at herself and then at Becka. She held up one finger, then two, then three, and started saying the words. Becka started an instant too late.

"Let me try," said Aimee.

"Well, it's hard to tell whether she was going to start on three or after."

The woman looked at Aimee. They nodded their heads at precisely the same time. And said these words; *"aborisci vitrium"*. The glass cube disappeared, and the woman stood before them. "Thank-you, thank-you," she said, taking Aimee's right hand in both of hers and shaking it wildly. "I am Angelica. Who do I have to thank for saving me from this horrible prison?"

"I am Aimee, and these are my brothers and sisters."

Each of the children bowed and introduced themselves. When Angelica got to Adam, she picked him up and hugged him tight.

"It was this sweet little cherub that found me," she said, kissing his face.

"How did you get stuck in there?" Adam wiped the slobber off his cheeks.

"A hateful Banshee encased me in there many years ago."

"Banshee?" asked Brian. "They only have Banshee's in Ireland."

"The man that she was to warn of impending death was from Ireland," said the white lady. "The Angel of Death was sent for him by mistake, but once the Banshee heard the chariot on its way to take Marcus of Dublin, she set out to find him and deliver her hideous cry, warning him of the coming of death. She was not supposed to leave Ireland, but she has a horrible vendetta against this family and will not rest until they are all dead."

"Marcus of Dublin is our grandfather," said Kami.

"Your grandfather!" said Angelica, incredulously. "Do you know if he is still alive then?"

"An evil dragon captured him,16 years ago," said Aimee.

"We are on our way to rescue him," said Adam.

"I must go to him," said Angelica. "I don't know how he has escaped the Banshee and the chariot this long, but he is in grave danger."

"I'll say, grave danger," said Brian, smiling.

Aimee smacked her brother in the stomach, "Maybe the magic of Gwandoya's mountain protected him all of those years."

"Yes, that's it," said Angelica. "But as soon as he comes out of that protection it will be only a matter of a few days before the Banshee will sense his presence, find him, and sing her song."

"Then it's only a matter of a few days after that the chariot would come for him," said Erik.

"The second he comes forth, away from the protecting magic, the Banshee will be at his side. Knowing that he is still alive on this earth she will not spare another second. And the chariot has been searching in vain all these years and will be there with her. I am sure he will have only a matter of hours upon his emergence from the mountain."

"We have to warn him," said Kami. "Tell him to stay in the mountain."

"But you are going to have to slay the dragon, right?" asked Angelica.

The group nodded.

"A colossal task for a group of children," said Angelica.

"We are wizards," said Adam.

"The term 'wizard' connotes more than just a title," said Angelica. "The greatest wizards are those that have seen many days and nights and, because they have paid close attention, have gained much wisdom."

"Some of the youngest have wisdom beyond their years," said Aimee, putting her hands on Kami and Adam's shoulders.

"This will remain to be seen," said Angelica. "Now I must go send the chariot back, then the Banshee will have to return to Ireland until Marcus' actual time of death draws nigh. But first I wish to give you a gift. You all look very weary, except for this one who I see has a pair of magic boots."

"How did you know?" asked Erik.

"Magical things have an aura about them," said Angelica. "You'll be able to see it better when you are older and wiser. That's how I knew these boys could help me when I first saw them through the glass."

"We glow?" asked Adam, looking down at his arms.

"Everything with a spirit glows," said Angelica. "Those with magic have tapped into the forces of that spirit and they glow brighter and brighter unless they use the magic for evil. I wish I had time to talk to you more of these things, but I must be on my way if I am to save your grandfather. Now everyone, do you have all your packs with you?"

Angelica followed the children back to the main cave. They gathered all their things. "My gift will be waiting outside when you are ready to begin your journey again," she said.

Giving them all a hug she bade them farewell and was on her way.

"I wonder what our present is?" asked Adam. "I want to go and see."

"Better wait for everyone," said Aimee.

"I'm all packed," said Kami. "I'll go out with him."

Kami and Adam came running back into the cave. "Horses!" yelled Adam. "And they've got wings."

"Just in time," said Erik. "I was beginning to think I'd end up carrying you, Aimee of the land of Frailty!"

Aimee ignored him, helped Kami mount her magnificent, winged creature, and climbed up on her own.

"Finally, a bit of rest for my aching feet," said Becka.

"Hold on tight," yelled Aimee as the horses rose into the air.

"They will get us there in no time at all," said Brian.

Adam sat up straight and tall, holding onto the horse's mane.

"I'm scared," said Kami, laying her head down on the horse's back and hugging him around the neck. The little pixie came out and flew in front of Kami. As if to say, "See, flying is fun," she darted back and forth, glided gracefully through the air, and then dove past Erik's face.

"It's not fun for me," said Kami, closing her eyes.

Erik felt the exhilaration of flying high over the landscape. He marveled at the green fields below him. Then sighed heavily as everything appeared brown, dim, gray. This is how our hearts have been affected this last week. Everything in our lives felt so promising and happy, and now we have to conquer this terrible beast or have no life to live.

In a matter of minutes, the horses landed in a wide-open field. As soon as the children dismounted, the horses turned to go.

"Wait," said Kami. She took an apple out of her pack. "I wish I had one for each of you," she said. Instantly Kami felt her pack get very heavy. Reaching inside she found six juicy apples. "Here you go," she said as she fed one to each of the horses. The horses were happy for the treat but flew away as soon as the last apple was gone.

Erik and Brian had gone to investigate a stone wall. It was only about ten feet high and fifteen feet wide and didn't seem to be of any use stuck right in the middle of a grassy field.

"Doesn't seem to have much of a purpose," said Erik, running his hands along the stones.

"Suppose it's a portal?" asked Brian.

Becka had pulled out the map. "There's supposed to be a gate or a door," she said. "But it looks like part of the wall is missing."

They all ran their hands around on the stones. Adam was climbing up one edge of the wall. "Looks like something came along and knocked this part down," he said.

"There isn't a gate or door among these fallen stones anyway," said Brian. "It doesn't look to me like there ever was a door."

Hollyhock flew to the wall. She flew into a tiny hole between two stones. Kami ran around to the other side, but the pixie was nowhere to be seen.

"Where'd she go?" Adam asked.

Kami ran back around and looked in the hole where the pixie had gone. "Wow," she said. "Look at this."

Adam jumped up to get a look, Kami lifted him higher. "Look at all those people," he said.

"It's like Market in Caraigdun," said Kami.

The others came over and had a look. "Definitely a portal of some kind," said Brian. "Does it say anything on the map about how to make the door or gate appear?"

"Maybe it's a Think charm," said Adam.

"You go ahead and think," said Brian, patting his brother on the head.

"He could be right, you know," said Aimee.

While Adam's face changed expression with each food he thought about, the others tried different things.

"I'll look in the book," said Aimee.

"Maybe one of those keys that Athena gave us will work," said Erik, feeling around in his pack.

"Maybe we have to get small like the pixie," said Becka, holding up three bottles that she had picked up when Athena was cleaning out her cloak.

"Wouldn't try drinking any of those," said Brian. "You never know what they might do to ya."

"You didn't think I'd drink them myself, did you?" she asked, holding a vile of red liquid out to her brother.

"Not a chance," he said. "Try it out on Erik."

"I'd rather give the keys a try," said Erik, "Brian, where's yours?"

Brian fumbled around in his pack. He pulled out the large, rusted key. "Do you think a keyhole is just going to appear out of nowhere?" He asked.

"You never know," said Erik, putting his key in between the cracks of the stones.

Brian gave his key to Erik, "You can make a fool of yourself, if you want to."

Suddenly the bricks seemed to melt away. A wall of warped looking air stood before them. Hollyhock came flying back through and took Kami by the hand.

"Told you the key would work," said Erik.

"It wasn't the key," said Adam. "It was my thinking."

"Maybe," said Erik. "What did you think?"

"Can't say it out loud," said Adam. "But I know it was it, watch."

Adam turned around and looked at the portal that still lay open behind them. He thought a thought, and the portal closed.

"How did you know what to think?" asked Kami.

Adam pointed at Hollyhock. "I looked through the hole and she was holding something up. As soon as I thought about it, the door opened."

"Thanks Hollyhock," said Kami.

Hollyhock smiled.

"This is the market where we are supposed to meet Athena," said Aimee.

"Don't see any sign of her. Do you think we got here more quickly than she expected?" Becka asked.

"Possibly," said Brian, petting a large white dog that had come over and was licking his hand. "Aren't you a beautiful thing," he said, as he scratched her behind the ears.

Suddenly she was no longer a dog but a girl standing in front of him. "Thank-you," she said, brushing herself off. "I needed a good scratch behind the ears."

"I've seen everything now," said Becka.

"How'd you do that?" asked Adam.

"Do what?" asked the girl.

"Change into a dog," said Kami.

"Oh that," said the girl. "I am Akire and actually I think I am a dog that changes into a human, but it's been so long, I'm not sure if I remember any more."

Suddenly, Hollyhock was buzzing around their heads. When she had everyone's attention she landed on Erik's head and changed into a hedgehog.

She crawled down into his cloak, making him squirm and laugh. "That tickles," he said, trying to shake her out.

She crawled back up to his head. After changing back into her pixie form, she took a bow. Adam and Kami clapped.

"Very impressive," said Akire.

Hollyhock smiled and flew back to her place on Kami's shoulder.

Adam looked at Akire. "Can you change into anything else?" He asked.

"The little ones always have the most curiosity," said Akire. "How about this?"

Before their eyes Akire changed into a large white tiger. Hollyhock hid in Kami's hair. Kami jumped behind Erik's leg as the tiger roared.

"I didn't mean to scare her," said Akire, as she changed back into her human form.

"I can change into anything that I've had contact with," she said. "I like the dog the best, because it's the easiest to change in and out of since I'm always around so many of them."

Akire whistled. Six dogs came running. The children were petting them when a beautiful collie showed up with three small puppies running behind. Adam and Kami went to pet the puppies. They were soon on the ground rolling around as the puppies licked their faces.

"Can I keep one?" Adam asked, through his giggles.

"I don't think a puppy would last too long in a battle with Gwandoya," said Brian.

"So, you are the six children of Jaynea and Denis. I have a message for you from Athena," said Akire, looking around as if to see if the pebbles on the road had ears. "Better go somewhere safe."

Akire had them all pull their hoods up as she led them into a pub. "They'll not think that I would take children in here," she said, glancing around at the tattered, weather worn faces. "Spies, everywhere, you know."

The group sat down at a table far to the back of the room. Adam reached up to remove his hood. Akire put a hand up to stop him. "Keep your face covered. They will think you are a Halfling," she whispered. "The word has been out that six children are coming to slay the dragon. While most are on your side, Gwandoya has spies scouring the countryside for you. Athena took me aside two days ago at another pub on the other side of town. She had been waiting for you and could afford to wait no longer. She has gone to the east side of the mountain where Solon waits. They are ready to advance the army as soon as we give them notice that you have arrived."

"Solon?" Erik asked. "That's wonderful!"

"He is one of the most formidable sorcerers of all time. His magic will certainly come in handy as he and Athena gather the army...."

"Army?" asked Kami. "I thought we were going to have to fight the dragon alone."

"Oh, you are," said Akire. "The army will be a distraction to the thousands of goblins guarding the mountain. Once Athena draws them away, you will enter the mountain through the dungeons."

"Then we can finally save Mama," said Brian.

Akire looked at the tall blue-eyed blonde-haired young man. She put her hand on his shoulder. He knew it was a gesture of comfort, yet somehow, he felt more than comfort. He felt that this strange woman who could take the form of creatures great and small would prove very influential in his life.

"No one is certain of the fate of your parents and the others. There may be someone to help them or they may find a means of escape on their own. This cannot matter to you. Your focus must be on the dragon," said Akire.

"Maybe Caoimhin and Grog will help them," said Aimee.

"Possibly, Prestwick," said Kami.

"Maybe Didean," said Adam.

"Too bad Mathius and Mikos are stuck in the enchanted realm," said Erik. "They'd be helpful."

"Mathius and Mikos?" asked Akire. "Those two ne'er-do-wells would only cause trouble."

"As long as it is trouble for the dragons and not for us," said Brian, smiling.

Akire put a finger up to Brian's mouth, "Someone is listening," she said.

Aimee peered out from under her hood. "Everyone is on the other side of the room. Who could possibly hear from way over there?"

Akire pointed to a man who had his hood over his head like them. "His dog is listening for him," she whispered into Aimee's ear.

"Let's give them some misinformation," Erik whispered. "Just follow along,"

"Gotcha," Aimee whispered back.

"We should attack in three days," he said, keeping his voice low but loud enough that the large black dog's ears twitched.

"Three days to prepare and then we attack," said Aimee, winking at the others.

"I thought we --" Adam started before Becka clamped her hand over his mouth.

"We are pretending," she whispered as quietly as possible.

"We should go in on the west side," said Brian.

"Right," said Akire. "According to Athena she will distract the goblins to the south with her army. Dragons guard the air, so you will have to enter at the base of the mountain."

The group continued to spin a plan that was nothing like the actual plan they were going to implement.

Once settled they talked about how hungry and tired they were. "Athena arranged for you to stay at the Good Fellow Inn," said Akire.

When the dog heard this, he walked out of the pub, his master followed.

"Guess that'll confuse him a bit," said Brian.

"Where will we really stay?" asked Becka, who was exhausted and liked the sound of a fresh clean bed.

"I think my barn will do nicely," said Akire, keeping her voice very low.

"Sleep on hay!" Becka exclaimed, forgetting to lower her voice. "I'm glad we won't have to do that for a while," she said, trying to correct herself.

"I don't think anyone is listening now," said Akire, stroking the fur of the wolf looking dog that lay next to her on the floor. "Follow me."

The children followed Akire to the front of the pub. "Put it on my tab, old friend," she said to the man behind the counter.

"Akire, in the company of Halflings," said the man, peering down at Adam.

"I'll have to introduce you some other time," said Akire. "We're in rather a hurry."

Hollyhock was getting hot under Kami's hood and peeked out her head for just a second.

"Fairy!" yelled a lady that had come up behind the group.

Hollyhock put her hands on her hips and screwed up her face. She flew over to the woman and started pulling on the long braid that hung down her back.

The woman screamed. "No good, nasty creature! You'll not be taking my baby and replacing her with one of your wretched changelings!"

Kami was trying to get Hollyhock off the woman's hair. "She's only mad because you called her a fairy," she said. "She's a pixie, not a fairy!"

"Pixie or Fairy, they all bring bad — ahhhh!"

Hollyhock had given up on the braid and was now pulling on the roots of the woman's hair.

"Only if you speak unkindly of them," said Aimee, trying to pull the woman away as Kami, who didn't want to hurt the pixie by grabbing her, tried to convince Hollyhock to let go.

A man who had been standing next to the woman was frantically trying to turn his coat inside out. As he put it back on, Hollyhock stopped pulling on the woman's hair. Pointing at the man, she laughed hysterically.

The woman ran out of the pub, the man swift on her heels. "I won't be comin' back to a place that welcomes such evil creatures," she said, as she left.

"Didn't want the likes of her around anyway," said the man behind the counter. He looked at Akire, "But don't you be forgettin' to come and visit your old friend Samuel."

"I won't forget," said Akire.

Samuel reached out from under the counter and handed something wrapped in burlap to Akire. "Just a little gift for all those animals of yours," he said.

Akire tucked the package into her cloak and walked outside. She bade the others not to speak until they came to a place on the road far away from the market.

"Let's go to my barn," said Akire looking around. "We can make a plan there. Free of any spies."

17

A Plan to Conquer

In the barn of Akire, the animals were restless. "They're probably spooked by the storm brewing," said Brian. He took a pitchfork and began tossing fresh hay into the stalls. One horse whinnied, tossed his head in the air, and poked his nose into Brian.

"He is trying to tell you something." said Akire. Putting her hand on the horse's side she petted him softly. She took Brian's hand and placed it where her hand had been. "His heart is beating wildly," said Brian.

"This is not the effects of an impending storm," said Akire, laying her head on the horse. "There is a great danger."

The dogs howled in confirmation of her words.

"They probably just want the treat the innkeeper sent for them," said Aimee, picking up the package Akire had left on the ground.

Akire reached out to stop Aimee from opening it.

"It's just fresh meat for the dogs, isn't it?" Erik asked, noticing Akire's hesitation.

"Not exactly," she said. "Go ahead Aimee. It's time for you all to know."

Aimee unwrapped the package carefully. The others gathered around. Inside the wrapping were three smaller packages.

"I want to open one," said Adam, jumping up to see.

"Me too," said Kami.

Adam grabbed a package. The wrapping came loose, and two flat stones fell out.

"It's just some old broken rock," said Becka.

Adam picked up the two pieces. "These would make great skipping stones," he said. "Akire, can I take them back to the pond at our house?"

"Let me see," said Aimee. Adam reached out his open palm to his sister.

As the stones touched Aimee's hand, one of them glowed. "I don't think these are skipping stones," she said.

"That's for sure," said Erik.

"How come they didn't glow in my hand?" asked Adam, frowning. "Does Aimee have some special power?"

"The stone that is glowing is serving as an oracle for Aimee's power," said Akire. "Adam, if you are truly part of the chosen group, one of these stones will glow for you."

Akire took one of the remaining two packages from Brian. "Try these," she said, handing it to Adam.

Aimee held on to her glowing stone and passed the other one to Becka. It glowed brightly.

Adam opened the package. This time he was careful not to let the broken pieces fall. "I want to try," said Kami, picking up two of the pieces.

"Nothing," she said.

"Let me try," said Adam. He gave her the stone he had picked up and took the other. "Nothing," they said together.

"Better let your brothers try," said Akire.

Adam put the pieces in Brian's hand. One glowed.

"No fair," said Adam, stomping his foot.

"Are there any more pieces?" Kami asked.

Brian pointed to the large wrappings lying on the ground, "I think there is one more," he said.

Adam squatted down on the floor and opened the leather coverings. Kami bent over next to him. "There is one piece in here," she said.

"It'll glow for me," said Adam. He snatched the piece in his hand, closing his fist tightly around it. "Now you shall see the magic of my power," he said, holding his fist out in front of him. When he opened his hand, the stone was not glowing.

Adam frowned. "Maybe I just don't have any power," he said.

"It's okay, little brother," said Kami. "It looks like I don't either. I guess you'll just have to find a couple of other children to help capture the dragon," she said, looking at Akire.

"Better try this out," said Becka, taking the piece from Adam and placing it in Kami's hand.

"I'm sorry, Adam," said Kami, as the shard glowed brightly.

Adam shook the leather wrappings. "One has to be missing," he said.

Erik tried to pick up his little brother. He struggled and squirmed. "Let me go," he said.

Akire placed her hand on Adam's shoulder. "One piece has been missing for many years," she said.

"See, I told you," Adam said.

"That is one reason no one has attempted to capture the dragon. Legend has it that the correct placement of these pieces at three corners of the mountain will form a vortex of some kind which will cast the spirit of Gwandoya down to a place from which it can never return. Amazingly enough there are many who wanted to try with just these five stones. And until now, not even I knew they had to be used only by certain people with certain gifts."

"How will we find the other piece?" asked Aimee.

"Yeah, my piece," said Adam.

"If my guess is correct," said Akire, smiling at Adam. "Someone gave it to you on your journey here."

Adam ran to look in his backpack. He began pulling things out: "The puppet from Athena, bread from Caoimhin, The Primer Book of Wizardry from Mathius and Mikos."

"How about that little pouch from Caoimhin?" Kami asked. "He said it was a treat for us but we haven't opened it yet."

Adam reached deep into his knapsack. "Here it is," he said, holding up the little pouch triumphantly.

Adam opened the pouch and poured the contents into his hand. "Just candy," he said.

"Just candy?" said Aimee. "You would usually be thrilled with 'just candy'."

Becka took the pouch from her brother. She felt the bag carefully. "Maybe it's sewn into the bag."

"Maybe whoever had it didn't know they were supposed to give it to me," said Adam. "We should go back and ask everyone we met."

"That would take forever," said Brian.

"Are you sure that's everything?" asked Akire.

"I think so," said Adam, reaching around in his pack.

Akire helped him search.

"Could the stone piece have been given to one of us?" Erik asked.

"Possibly," said Akire. "That would protect it from glowing and giving off any power."

The others searched all the things that were given to them by their newly found friends.

"You don't suppose Caoimhin hid it in some of this crusty bread," said Brian, almost breaking a tooth as he bit into the hardened loaf.

"He didn't even know we were coming," said Becka.

Adam pulled his hand out of the pack, "It's just not here," he said.

"What's this around your neck?" asked Akire, reaching out and taking the amulet in her fingers.

"Just an old amulet, Mathius gave me," said Adam.

"Let's check it out," said Akire.

Adam took off the amulet. Akire examined it closely. She ran her fingers around the round edge at the top.

"It's just a fake sapphire," said Adam.

Suddenly the blue stone seemed to split in two. The top piece opened revealing a small shard of stone fit perfectly into the blue sapphire.

"My piece," said Adam, trying to pry the shard loose.

"It won't budge," he said.

"Possibly, it needs to remain in the ring, for protection," said Akire.

"There must be a spell to remove it," said Adam.

"Maybe in the primer," said Kami.

Adam and Kami opened the book and asked Biblion if he could help them find the spell.

"Mathius scribbled something in the back here, just before you left on this journey," said Biblion, flipping the pages until they came to rest on the last page.

"It's only two words," said Adam. "And they're not even very long."

"It's a strange language," said Kami. "I can't read it."

"Probably Latin," said Becka, looking over their shoulder.

Akire came over to have a look. She laughed at the joke. "Those two always were coming up with ingenious ways of doing things," she said. "This might be fun for you to figure out. I can tell you, it's not Latin."

Kami and Adam sat down in the soft hay. *"El-e -a sre Nos-te!"* said Kami, waving her hand over Adam's ring.

"Elazer Nasty," said Adam, trying to mimic his sister.

Akire smiled. "We'll leave the two of you to this task while we discuss a plan," she said. "As you can see you are each connected to a specific stone. By this connection you have been placed into three groups."

"There are two pieces in each group," said Brian.

"I don't like the idea of sending Adam and Kami to one corner of the mountain all alone," said Aimee.

"I don't like it either," said Becka. "Can't we all just stand together as soon as we get there, put our pieces together and call it good?"

"These are pieces of the mountain itself," said Akire. "These pieces collected the good that remained when Gwandoya drove the inhabitants out of the mountain. Three winged creatures gathered them:

Andor the great king of the eagles, Flaithir the hawk, and Branwen the raven. These three brave creatures were shot down as they flew away from the mountain. The stones broke into these pieces as you see them now. No one really knew if they were of use, but the wizard's council has speculated for many years that these six pieces carry the shattered soul of the mountain. As soon as they are restored, the mountain will live again, and all evil will be compelled to leave."

"So, are you saying that the mountain itself is evil?" asked Aimee.

"It's dead really," said Akire. "You will see as you get closer. Nothing lives near the mountain for miles around. No animals will go near it and the ones that have tried have come back with horrible tales if they've returned at all. Clouds do not rain on the mountain even though lightning strikes. All lakes, streams, and rivers dried up years ago. All the trees and plants died. Flowers that used to come back yearly, like tulips and daffodils, hide deep in the barren ground and may never see the light of day again. The hideous creatures that dwell there do not need vegetation or water. They feed on raw flesh and must venture into the nearby towns to find it."

"I would have thought that everyone would get as far away as possible," said Becka.

"That is ancient country, Becka," said Akire. "It is difficult for some to give up what their families have worked for ages to build. They hold fiercely to the legend that brave heroes will defeat Gwandoya and even more so to the idea that they will be a part of that battle. There are many who would have gathered armies and tried to attack the mountain years ago, but they all know that there would be something lacking in such an attack. Some power that none of them have."

"So, do they all believe in wizards?" asked Brian.

"And witches," said Aimee.

"They all believe in wisdom and inner strength and know that those who come to conquer the dragon will bring these things with them."

"Do they realize that their fate is in the hands of children?" asked Aimee.

"Speak for yourself," said Erik, sticking out his mail-laden chest.

"They believe that those who fight the dragon will be skilled warriors. There were a few wizards who told of the coming of the children at first, but the stories have changed over time."

"Like gossip in the market," said Becka.

"Mama said she never believed anything she heard in the market," said Kami. "She would hear the same bit of news at each stand."

"But with a unique twist every time," said Becka, smiling.

"Your mother is wise," said Akire.

"So, will the nearby farmers, herders and town's people fight in the battle?" asked Brian.

"They are waiting and ready," said Akire.

"Let's go then," said Brian. "Their day of redemption is here."

"Don't jump ahead too quickly," said Aimee. "We still need to figure out the entire plan. I won't leave Kami and Adam alone. It feels like there are pieces to this puzzle that are missing."

"Yes, it seems like there are a lot more pieces to this puzzle than just these stone shards," said Erik.

"I like puzzles," said Kami, "like these *eleasre noste* words. It was just 'release stone'."

"With the letters all scrambled up," said Adam beaming as he held up his glowing piece of the mountain.

"We all know how upset you get when you can't find a piece though, Kami," said Brian.

"That's true," said Kami. "If one piece is missing, it seems like a lot are missing. I never can believe it when it's only one piece at the end."

"All the pieces will fit together," said Akire. "There are many who have prepared for this day for many years. I think you will be amazed at all the helpers that come out of the woodwork at the last minute. Even those who were evil even before Gwandoya's arrival are looking forward to this day. They will give you their aid because the dragon has upset the balance of good and evil."

"Well, we will tip the scales a bit in our direction if I can help it," said Erik.

"Me too," said Adam.

"Now you all will need a good sleep tonight," said Akire. "Tomorrow, I will take you to the last village before the mountain. There you will meet Foster. He is a human."

"A mere human," said Erik. "What good will he be to us?"

"Do you forget that just three weeks ago you too were a mere human?" asked Aimee.

"Right," said Brian. "Sorry, it's just that we've met many magical people along the way. I guess it never occurred to us that men would be capable of aiding in the battle."

"Never underestimate the power of any creature you meet, magical or not," said Akire. "I expect you to treat Foster with the respect he deserves. He is from the oldest family in the area and has had a substantial loss because of the odious Gwandoya. He will be your best ally in the cause of conquering the dragon. Now all of you find a dry place and get some sleep."

Adam and Kami climbed into the loft. "Just like our barn at home," said Kami, snuggling down into the hay. "The hay is always drier up in the loft."

"Akire, aren't you going to get some sleep?" Adam yelled from his resting place.

"I will rest in my time," she said. "I'd just like to go out and see what final stirrings I can gather before the sun rises on the day of battle."

"Be careful," said Adam, yawning.

Brian and Erik were grooming the horses before lying down for the night. Brian walked over to the barn door to close the top half. "Look at this, Eric." Peering into the dark they saw three dogs running across the field. Above them flew a large black raven silhouetted in the moon.

{ **18** }

A Mixing of Minds

When Brian awoke early that morning, he took the invisibility cloak and stepped outside, hoping to get a glimpse of Akire changing from the form of a raven to herself.

What he saw startled him so much that he ran into the barn. "Everyone, wake up!" He yelled.

Erik was the first to stir. He turned over slowly and rubbed the sleep from his eyes. "What—are — you in such a quandary about?" Erik asked, stretching.

"The dragons are flying," he said, shaking Aimee. "You all must wake up."

"They've left the protection of the mountain," said Becka, as the children gazed into the sky where a hundred dragons took flight.

"We should attack now, before they go back into the mountain," said Brian.

Akire appeared in the form of a raven and landed on a post next to Brian, "That would be very foolish indeed," she said, changing into her human form.

"Wouldn't it be best if we just snuck up to the three corners of the mountain and quietly placed our stones there," said Kami.

"Then the dragons couldn't come back," said Adam.

"It's more complicated than that," said Akire.

"Always is," said Becka, sitting on a rock.

"I've been thinking about it," said Aimee. "The body of Gwandoya was created by good, for good and the means by which the spirit entered the body was good. However, his spirit is evil."

"So, the body and the spirit will have to be separated before we place the stones into the mountain," said Erik.

"All creatures who live close to the mountain know this. Many of them are becoming restless as the time draws near. The dragons and goblins also know this, and they know that someone is coming who will bring down the shield. Gwandoya has ordered them to leave the protection of the mountain and push the armies back so the plan to enter the mountain will be foiled."

Aimee looked into the sky at the sea of dragons. "So Gwandoya does not fly with them," she said.

"He will remain behind the shield with his bride-to-be and a few guards," said Akire.

"He is a coward," said Brian.

"This could be to our benefit," said Erik. "Once we get past the battles surrounding the mountain and bring down the shield, we should have no problem killing the body of the dragon and capturing his spirit."

"That brings me to this one last gift before I feed you and send you on your way," said Akire, pulling a small wooden box from her cloak.

"Once you destroy the body of the dragon, the spirit will exit. It will be Aimee and Becka who form a new shield around the mountain, keeping the spirit from escaping. When you place all six pieces into the mountain, the shield will come down and Gwandoya will be free to escape. One of your groups will have to open this box, hands on the box you will then recite these words: '*intro peior ferocitus*'."

"Oh rats, big words again," said Adam. "I hope it's not my group."

"Let me guess," said Brian. "The spirit of Gwandoya will enter this box, where it will stay, imprisoned for all of eternity."

"Actually, it will be rather easy for him to escape from the box," said Akire. "The bearers will have only a matter of minutes to reach the top of the mountain where they must drop the box into the depths of the molten sea within, before good takes over and seals the chasm."

"So, it should be our group that performs this task," said Erik, taking the box.

"The two of you will be engaged in the fighting. I doubt you'll be able to place the stones and deal with this," said Aimee, taking the box from Erik.

"The small ones will be responsible for this task," said Akire, taking the box and handing it to Kami. "They have neither pride nor distraction to hinder them along their way."

Kami looked at the box. "Don't worry, Erik and Brian," she said. "You are better suited to killing the body of the dragon. I could never do that."

"I would," said Adam, punching the air. "I wish I could be with them."

"I guess that's true," said Brian. "We will take the task of slaying the dragon."

"Will we have a special task?" asked Aimee.

"It will be enough for you girls to keep from being distracted by the handsome goblins along the way," said Brian.

Becka waved her hand at Brian. Everyone laughed as he sprouted long floppy ears. The next sound out of his mouth was the bray of a donkey.

"Nice job, Becka," said Aimee.

"Wish I could make it last longer," said Becka, as Brian's face returned to its rightful form.

"A disservice to a very intelligent animal," said Akire, smiling.

"Thanks, Akire, I am intelligent," said Brian.

"I meant the donkey," said Akire.

The others laughed.

"The girls will have plenty to keep them busy," said Akire. "But you boys are right, your task will be to slay the dragon so his spirit will leave, and the young ones will be free to capture its evil force in the box."

"Do we need to have brooms, so we can fly to the top of the mountain?" Adam asked.

"No dear one," said Akire. "There is someone who wishes to help you with this task."

"That's good," said Kami. "We aren't too good on brooms yet."

Akire stopped to look toward the mountain.

"I hope all animals that remain have found a place to hide," said Brian.

"There were only a few, but they all were my friends," said Akire. "The battle has begun. Those who can aid in the battle will and those who can't I'm sure, have left."

Aimee came close to Akire and put her hand on her shoulder. "You are worried about someone," she said.

"Is it someone who can't leave the mountain?" asked Becka.

"It is someone who went to the mountain to fight," said Akire. Staring at the mountain a minute longer, she shook her head and turned to Aimee. "I haven't seen him in years anyway," she said. "Don't know why it should worry me at all."

"You loved him once?" asked Aimee.

"It's a long story," said Akire.

"It always is," said Erik. "Come on Brian, we'd better check our weapons."

Akire clapped her hands. "Wait boys," she said, spreading a cloth on the ground. "First, we eat."

Fresh fruits of all kinds and steaming vegetables appeared before them.

"Guess I better not say anything about the absence of meat from our meal," whispered Brian.

"Unless you want to risk your life," said Erik.

As they ate, the children put their heads together and planned their approach.

"Foster will meet you somewhere along the path before you split into the three groups," said Akire. "You will know him by the medallion he wears around his neck. It is the crest of his family. In the center is the roaring head of a lion. He will direct each group toward the correct corner of the mountain."

"Will he stay with us?" said Kami. "The mountain looks kind of scary for just Adam and me."

"I will protect you with my crossbow," said Adam, jumping in front of his sister.

Akire laughed. "You are very brave, young Adam," she said. "However, your best strategy will be to stay in the shadows. Foster will take you as far as he can but will have to return to the battle."

"Draw as little attention as possible to yourselves," said Erik.

"That's right," said Aimee. "You are both very good at hide-and-seek and that is precisely what you are going to do."

"That's it," said Becka. "Stay in the shadows and make it a game. The goblins and dragons will never find the two of you."

"We need some sort of signal to let us all know when to place the stone shards," said Brian.

"Something that Gwandoya's spies will not detect," said Erik.

"How about a rainbow?" Kami suggested.

"A rainbow is a great idea," said Aimee, "but I'm afraid the allies of Gwandoya would think it rather strange indeed for a rainbow to appear above a place where it hasn't rained in all these years."

"You are right," said Kami.

"How about rain clouds?" Adam asked.

"That is another good idea," said Erik. "But there is no way to assure that real rain clouds will not form above the mountain. Dark clouds form frequently although rain never falls."

"I have an idea," said Akire. She closed her eyes and put her hands in the air. She called in the language of the birds and soon three winged creatures appeared.

A raven landed on Brian's shoulder, an eagle on Aimee's, and a falcon on Erik's.

"Allow me to introduce Flaithir, prince of the falcons."

Flaithir flew into the air and circled high above them. Gliding in on outstretched wings, he landed softly on Kami's shoulder.

"Branwen, princess of the ravens."

Branwen took flight and, swooping down, landed on Becka's shoulder.

"And Andor, the great eagle prince," said Akire, bowing low. Andor also took flight and, letting out the call of the great eagle, landed on a tree branch above Adam and pecked playfully at the little boy's head.

Adam giggled. "I'm glad you didn't land on my shoulder," he said, looking up at the humongous bird. "You could have killed me."

"They want a part in the battle." She spoke to them each in his own tongue and waited for their reply.

"They have agreed to accompany you along your way. As each group is in position to place the stones, your companion bird will fly above and circle the mountain."

"When we see all three birds circling, we will know to place the stones," said Erik.

"It is imperative that they are inserted at the same, exact time. When the third bird enters the sky, they will circle once again. When they hover over their group, this will be the exact moment that you will place the stones."

"So, we cannot allow our bird to fly until we are ready to place the stones," said Brian.

"That is correct," said Akire.

"This is going to be really tricky," said Adam.

"You can say that again," said Becka.

"This is going to be really tricky," said Adam, laughing.

"The sun rises swiftly in the sky," said Akire.

"It is amazing to think that by the end of this day the mountain will be free of the evil Gwandoya," said Aimee, looking at the black mountain.

"Not if we don't get moving," said Brian.

"I'm ready," said Adam, shoving extra fruit into his pack.

Brian reached over and took some of the fruit out. "Don't want to weigh yourself down now do you?" He asked.

"I'll be carrying it in my tummy before long," said Adam, shoving the fruit back into the pack.

"I could conjure you some along the way," said Kami.

"Not if we're supposed to be hiding," said Adam.

"That's true," said Erik, putting a large loaf of bread into his pack. "We will all have to hold out on the use of magic until it is absolutely necessary."

"I will walk with you down the road a few miles," said Akire. "Then I will have to take my place in the battle."

Kami hugged Akire, "We have made a lot of friends along the way," she said. "I think I like you the best of all."

Akire bent down and looked the little girl in the eye, "Remember, my friend," she said. "No matter what happens in these battles today, you must carry on. Even when Gwandoya is gone, evil will not cease to exist in this world."

"I will carry on," said Kami.

"We all will," said Aimee.

The group walked along. Brian took a chance to pull Akire aside. "You sound as if you don't expect to come out of this alive," he whispered.

Akire was quiet. "I can feel death," she said, "death of all different creatures. It is going on all around us and it is painful."

"I think I can feel it too," said Brian.

"I'm sure you can," said Akire. "It seems you have the same gift as I do."

"Doesn't feel like much of a gift, right now," said Brian.

"You are right," said Akire. "The others will not know the severity of the dying and pain. Your brothers and sisters will get a glimpse as we draw closer to the battle. They will hear the screams and see animals and people fall. Each will feel sad and mourn, but they will not understand the gravity of the loss as you do. Even as we speak, you feel the pain of all the animals that fall in the battle. You feel the pain of the men and the horses. The pain of the flying creatures and the pain of the small creatures of the forest who flee their homes."

"How can I make it stop?" asked Brian.

"I often wanted that myself," said Akire. "Those intense feelings were the beginnings of my communication with the animals. The first creature I saved was a unicorn."

"A unicorn," said Brian, incredulously.

"Yes, a beautiful creature. I was walking through the woods late one night and I felt a stabbing pain in my heart. The pain was so strong that I collapsed right on the spot. Then I heard a cry, the last cry of a dying animal. I ran to the spot and found a unicorn close to death. Instinctively I pulled out the arrow that pierced his side close to his heart. Already studying the healer's art, I carried some herbs with me. I shoved the herbs into the wound and said a few words that were taught to me by your friend Athena. I had no faith in my skills but went through the motions of the things she had taught me, hoping beyond hope they would somehow save this poor creature. To this day I don't believe that it was only the herbs or the pressure that I applied to the wound. I think it was having someone stop to help that gave this amazing creature the will to live."

"And so, he lived?"

"Yes, and he is healthy and strong and during his recovery I learned to speak to him in his own tongue. I see him once a year now and that is the only time I get to use that language."

"Have you ever taken the form of a unicorn, yourself?" asked Brian, fascinated.

"Once, I did, and Shorgan and I ran through the woods with the speed of lightning."

"When we have finished our quest, Akire, I want you to teach me the healer's art. I want to help the animals as you do."

Akire stopped and looked into Brian's blue eyes. "I believe you will begin this path today," she said. "When the time comes, remember your presence may be important in helping an animal or a man begin the healing process, but a good bit of pressure to a severe wound never hurt."

"I'll remember," said Brian.

{ **19** }

On the Side of Good

As the group moved closer to the mountain, the many forces of good took their positions. Eagles, hawks, and ravens covered the highest parts, settling in the few trees that were left at the base of the mountain. Wolves had come from many miles to answer the call of Akire's friend the half wolf Omen. The gathering had taken place over many days and nights. Goblins and dragons were only aware of a small portion of the foe. Gwandoya and his dragon army were confident that no dragons would come out of their hermit hiding places to fight a battle that was not their own. They never would have imagined that one little girl could cross over in her dreams and take the heart of Old Prestwick the iron hearted. Nor would they have imagined that this little girl and her little brother could melt his heart so much that he would gather an army of dragons. Prestwick had a grand time recruiting the very best dragons for the job. He was a sly one and used mind tricks on them making them each believe that theirs was the most significant part in the plan to conquer the evil Gwandoya. Some were easy to convince as they still had treasures hidden in the caves of Mount Ceo'ban. Others from far away had no genuine interest in the affair. When Prestwick finished with them, they thought it was their battle and a battle they would gladly fight alone if needed. The pride and arrogance of the species of dragon worked to Prestwick's benefit, and he was very proud of his own arrogant knowledge that he was the leader of this force of dragons.

As the children walked along the edge of the battlefields, they witnessed the terror of war. The battle of man and goblins had already begun. The other armies would not enter the battle until the children of Denis and Jaynea had arrived. Kami hid behind Erik.

"I don't think I like this as much as I thought I would," said Adam. "People are really getting hurt out there."

Brian and Erik ran ahead to help an injured man who was dragging an unconscious man across the fields and into a tent. Brian and Erik carried the unconscious man as Becka and Aimee helped the other to safety. Arrows went flying past their heads as they ducked into the tent.

"Get the children inside," yelled a tall young man with long brown hair hanging in a braid down his back. "You must be the children we have waited for," he said.

"That would be us," said Becka.

"You look rather normal," said the young man.

"Well, we're not abnormal," said Brian, who was trying to stop the bleeding of the man he had saved. "Akire said I might begin the healer's art today," he said. "I didn't think I'd get my chance like this."

A young woman came into the tent. She quickly assessed the status of the two injured men. "They've lost a lot of blood," she said. "We must stop this bleeding, or this one will be gone."

Brian reached into his pocket and pulled out the herbs that Akire had given him. He shoved half into the wound of the bleeding man and dumped the other half into the girl's hand.

"Where did you get these?" She asked.

"A friend," said Brian. "Sorry I don't have enough to aid every one that falls in battle today."

The girl looked in the pouch, "Well at least we haven't used them all up yet," she said. "May I use these for some other severely injured patients?"

"Sure," said Brian, trying not to let on his surprise that the pouch was full. Must be a trick of Akire's he thought. "Wait," he said to the girl. "I would like a handful for another patient."

Brian turned the injured man over to Aimee and ran out onto the battlefield. Lying where the two men had fallen was a beautiful black stallion. Brian pulled a black arrow out of the horse's side and shoved the herbs into the wound. "I'm here," he said, stroking the horse's blood-stained neck.

The horse let out a small noise. Brian was surprised that he understood the sound as "Thank-you."

The goblins had been busy elsewhere but noticed that Brian was a sitting target. Arrows flew in his direction. He quickly placed the invisibility cloak around his shoulders. The young man with the long braid came running out onto the field with Erik close behind. They both carried large shields. The amazed young man dove next to the horse. Erik held the shield up to protect them all.

"You were just here," said the young man with the long braid. He stood up to clear the shield and aimed his crossbow at the approaching goblins. "I don't know where you went, but it is my job to see that you make it to the mountain alive."

"He's here," said Erik. Planting the shield into the ground Erik sent off an arrow and yelled, "Centum scindo!"

"I am here," whispered Brian. "I have to save this horse if I can."

"His heart is beating, and he is breathing. I will send someone to bring him to safety once the goblins have turned their attention elsewhere."

"I will wait in my invisible form," said Brian. "Once you leave the goblins will too."

"I guess that's a good plan," said Erik, "but I wish we could make an invisible shield as well. You are still here even if they can't see you."

More arrows flew swiftly past their heads. "I will leave since you are invisible, and I am just drawing attention this way," said the young man. "But you must promise to come back to the tent as soon as there is a break in the crossfire."

"I will come as soon as this horse is ready to come with me," said Brian.

The young man and Erik crawled out of the line of fire and hurried back into the tent. "Your brother is crazy, or he's been hanging out with Akire too much," he said.

"A bit of both, I'd say," said Erik.

Adam peeked through an opening in the tent. "I never saw a horse move while lying down before," he said.

Erik peeked out the opening. Placing a single arrow in his bow he muttered the spell again and sent one hundred flaming arrows flying at the enemy. Running across the field, Erik grabbed the horse by the hind legs and pulled him behind the tent with Brian.

"Even invisible you're crazy to go out on that battlefield," said Erik.

Brian threw off the cloak, "No time to argue, this horse is trying to tell me something."

"Oh, now you've really gone off your rocker," said Erik.

Brian put his hand up to silence Erik and then laid his head by the horse's mouth.

"Thanks to you, I will live," said the horse. "There are few who would risk their life for an animal when men fall all around. There is a pack on my side. In it you will find a whistle. Blow the whistle and it will summon the strongest horses of my master. They will take you around the mountain to the place where you will place the stones."

"How do you know of these things?" asked Brian.

"Stable talk," said the horse.

"I will make sure someone gets you up for a walk soon," said Brian.

"Right," said the horse, "wouldn't want colic to settle in now that I've survived a mortal wound."

"What are the two of you saying?" asked Erik.

"You can't understand?" asked Brian, thinking for sure that he was still speaking English.

"Sounds like the neighing of a horse to me," said Erik.

"I'll tell you later," said Brian. "We'd better get the others and find this Foster guy."

"I thought he was supposed to meet us before the battle," said Erik.

"So, you think I've fallen back on me duties," said the tall young man with the long, braided hair.

"You are Foster?" asked Erik.

"At your service," he said, bowing. "Wasn't exactly time for formal introductions when you arrived then was there?"

"I guess there wasn't," said Erik, extending his hand. "I'm Erik and this is my brother Brian."

"I've met the girls and the little one you call Adam," said Foster. "Please go back into the tent for a minute, I must summon my lieutenant and let him know I will be leaving with you."

"Finally, an adult who is courageous enough to accompany us on our journey," said Brian.

"Adult?" said Erik, looking at Foster. "He can't be much older than Aimee."

Foster took the horn from his side and blew. Soon another young man came riding on horseback. "I am leaving with the chosen ones," said Foster.

"I will hold down the fort until your return," said the lieutenant.

"You can alert the other armies that they can enter the battle."

"We will draw the armies of Gwandoya away from the mountain," said the lieutenant.

When the lieutenant rode away Foster, Erik, and Brian went back into the tent. Foster pulled out a map of the area.

"We will go around the battlefield to the east side of the mountain," he said, pointing to the map. "Erik and Brian must place the stones on this side but they will have to ride completely around the mountain to position themselves for the battle of Gwandoya."

"The horse I saved gave me this whistle to summon two fast steeds," said Brian.

"Good," said Foster. "We have none to spare."

Foster pointed to an area on the map just to the east. "This is the last place you will find people," he said. "This is where the women and children are hiding."

"This close to the battlefield?" asked Becka.

"I should think you would have removed them all to a much safer area by now," said Aimee.

"It is as safe as it gets around here," said Captain Foster. "It's so dried up the evil creatures don't come around much."

"Well, I'm glad we have one more stop to meet people before we fight the dragon," said Kami.

"I wouldn't count on meeting anyone," said Foster, touching Kami on the cheek. "These people have lost family member after family member to the odious creatures that infest the mountain. They are not trusting of anyone."

Kami took the primer spell book and sat in a corner of the tent while the others planned the journey. "Hollyhock," she whispered. "You haven't peeked out your head in hours. Are you alright in there?"

Kami looked down at the pocket of her apron where the little pixie was hiding. Hollyhock's little head came up slowly but only her hand reached out of the pocket as she pointed at Foster.

"You are afraid of him?" asked Kami.

Hollyhock nodded her head. Kami smiled as the pixie twisted her beautiful face into a menacing scary one.

"He won't hurt you," said Kami.

Hollyhock dropped deep into the pocket and curled into a ball.

"I need you to help me spread some cheer to the last people we will see," said Kami.

Hollyhock flew out and did a little pantomime. She acted like she was planting seeds, watering them and watching them grow.

"That's a great idea," said Kami. "Now I just have to figure out where to get the seeds and I'm sure this spell book will have a way to make them grow fast."

Adam had curled up in a ball and was asleep in the corner.

Erik glanced at his little brother. "So, our first stop is here where we will drop off Kami and Adam," he said, pointing at the map.

"Then on to here where we will leave the girls," said Brian.

"Yes, and here is also where you will fight Gwandoya. By this time the other chosen ones will have brought down the shield and will join you."

"So, we will twiddle our thumbs while the boys do all the work," said Aimee.

"Don't count on much thumb twiddling," said Foster. "We are luring the armies away but Gwandoya will certainly keep his best men to protect him and his queen and to guard his valuable prisoners."

"So, we never know when some hideous creature might sneak up on us," said Becka.

"Exactly," said Foster. "You might be able to use your magic after the shield comes down, but we are not sure about that. I was going to return to this battle, but I will stay and protect you if you like."

Aimee looked at Foster. Then she looked at Becka. She leaned over to Erik. "Is this what I look like when I'm all gaga over some boy?" She whispered.

"Worse," said Erik. "Your tongue gets all loose and you giggle too much."

Just as Erik said this, Becka let out a little giggle at something Foster said.

"Okay, she's as bad as you!" said Erik.

"I'm glad we get to lose the giddy girls along the way," said Brian.

Foster looked over at Kami and Adam, who were both asleep now. "I don't want to delay, but we'd better let them rest," he said. "They have a long hard journey ahead of them."

The sounds of the battle had stopped by the time the group reached the pass that would take them to the town of Briarwood. After his long nap, Adam had plenty of energy. Once again, he ran ahead along the path. Suddenly he came running back to the group red-faced and screaming. "A giant, horrible, ugly, crea—ture --" he said, between breaths. "We can't get past that way. He's humongous, and he's got a club."

Foster charged past them. "I will save you from the hideous monster!" He called.

When they came around the corner, Foster was stabbing at the monster that blocked the way and stood as tall as the tallest house they had seen.

"He's almost as tall as Grog," said Kami, hiding behind Becka's leg.

"Protect yourselves! Save the little ones!" yelled Foster.

"He's not moving," said Aimee.

Brian and Erik brandished swords and ran forward. Then started laughing. "Adam, he's a statue," they said.

Foster sheathed his sword, "Just another tactic to keep unwanted visitors away," he said, winking at Becka.

"Is he a giant like our friend Grog?" asked Kami.

"He was a half giant, half troll," said Foster.

"Fierce and dumb, that combination," said Brian.

"That's about right," said Foster. "Unlike most trolls Keorgg here didn't turn to stone in the sunlight."

"What got him then?" asked Becka.

"I enlisted the aid of a wizard friend of mine by the name of Bruin, who turned him to stone with a powerful spell."

"Sir Bruin?" asked Aimee.

"He's real?" asked Erik.

"He fights in the battle as we speak," said Foster. "How do you know him?"

"I conjured him to fight a battle for me once," said Aimee, swooning.

"Right," said Foster. "I remember him mentioning a fair maiden that he saved from one hundred dragons."

"More like one dragon," said Brian.

"There were only six to begin with," said Erik.

"And we each fought our own," said Adam, slashing a pretend sword in the air.

"Ah, I should have known he would exaggerate."

"We must hurry and do our part so this battle can end," said Aimee, running past Keorgg.

"Yes," said Erik, flailing his arms as he ran after her. "We must make haste and save your brave Sir Bruin."

"From his next battle with one hundred dragons," said Brian, mimicking them both.

Kami gasped as they came around the other side of the statue. "This is worse than I thought," she said.

Burned-out houses, many with windows that were boarded up lined the street. There was a frosty chill in the air but no smoke rose from any of the chimneys.

Becka had been walking along with Foster. "Maybe they've all left," she said as they approached what used to be the market.

Suddenly they heard a baby crying.

"They are still here," said Foster. "They stay inside all day to avoid detection by the flying spies of Gwandoya."

Kami decided there was no time to be shy. She went up to the door where the baby was crying and knocked.

The baby stopped crying.

"I know there's someone in there," said Kami. "I have something for you."

Adam tried the door. It opened. "Anybody in there," he said. "We are on our way to slay the dragon today."

The room was dark, but after a minute a small boy about Adam's size crawled out from under the table. "Are you really going to slay the dragon?" asked a timid voice.

"Sure are," said Adam. "Well I mean, my brothers here get to do that. Then me and my sister get to capture his evil spirit."

"Then things will get better for all of you," said Kami.

Four other children came crawling out of their hiding places. They were thin and dirty and dressed in rags.

Kami looked at a girl that seemed about her age. She reached into her pocket and pulled out some seeds. "These are for you," she said, placing the seeds in the girl's hand.

The girl's eyes grew big. She ran to a dark corner of the room. "They are apple seeds, Mama," she said.

"We can't plant them outside," said a woman's voice. "They will know we are here."

Kami looked around and found a large old pot on a shelf. She waved her hand over the pot and it filled with rich black dirt.

The girl came over and carefully planted the seeds in the pot.

"It doesn't matter," said a boy that was just taller than Kami. "It will take years for these seeds to become a tree and years more before the tree bears fruit."

Kami took a pitcher from the shelf. She handed the pitcher to the girl.

"There's no water," said another skeptical voice.

"Pour," said Kami.

The little girl tipped the pitcher. Water seeped into the rich black soil. As soon as the water hit the soil, a tree began to grow. Within a matter of seconds, it was as tall as Erik and full of juicy red fruit. All the little children ran to the tree and picked an apple for themselves. The little girl picked one for her mother, who came out of the corner carrying a baby. "Thank-you," she said, her young yet old looking eyes smiling, as tears formed.

"I have enough seeds for everyone in the village to have a tree like this," said Kami. "I wish I had time to help you go around and hand them out, but we really have to fight the dragon."

"I will take them to all the people," said the little girl.

"We will help," said the once skeptical boys.

"Just bring this water pitcher too," said Kami. "It will keep pouring water for the trees and you can fill everyone's water barrels."

"And here is a bucket of dirt," said Adam. "It should keep filling up too."

"I wish we had something to give to you," said the mother.

"You have given us a good reason to go through with this," said Aimee.

"That's right," said Erik. "We will think of you and your young children as we battle Gwandoya."

All the children hugged them before they left. "Thank-you."

The place where Kami and Adam were to place their stones was only a few miles from the town. "I don't like the idea of leaving them here, alone," said Aimee, looking around at the dark and dreary place.

"I don't like the idea of us being here all alone," said Kami.

"I should have thought to bring someone to look out for them," said Foster. "But this is the safest part of the mountain. The battle will not come any closer because of the dead forest."

"I could summon Bruin to stay with them," said Aimee.

"Can't use your magic," said Erik. "Gwandoya would surely detect it out in the open like this."

"Perhaps we could help," said a loud raspy voice.

All the boys immediately pulled their swords, but as they turned, two familiar faces met their gaze.

Adam couldn't believe it, "Caoimhin!" he said, running to hug his friend.

"At your service," said the wizard, bowing low.

"What do I be? Chopped liver?" said another voice.

"Grog!" yelled Kami.

"Okay, you guys can go now," said Adam, waving off his older siblings.

"How did you know where we would be?" asked Aimee, smiling at the wizard.

"We'll just say, a little raven told us," said Caoimhin.

"We were on our way to help with the battle and Akire came along and said we were needed for a special mission," said Grog, putting his thumbs in his suspenders and sticking out his chest.

"She also wanted us to remind you that before the six of you part for your respective tasks, you must say the spell together to bring the shield down."

Becka pulled the mirror out of her cloak.

"Gather around everyone," said Erik.

"I hope your reflection hasn't completely faded away," said Aimee.

"I read something in the book that said the mirror and reflection will recharge if it isn't used for a while. That's why I haven't tried to contact Mama again."

The children of Denis and Jaynea of Caraigdun gathered around the mirror. Becka looked into the reflective glass and saw through the eyes of her reflection that she was in the caves with their family.

"Mama!" Kami yelled.

"There is no time to talk with her," said Brian, placing a hand on his little sister's shoulder. "We must bring down the shield so our family can escape."

Erik began the chant as the others joined in.

"Contego Distraho. Contego Distraho. Contego Distraho."

The group repeated the words as Denis attempted to use magic inside the caves to unlock his cell.

"Contego Distraho. Contego Distraho. Contego Distraho!"

"It worked," yelled Denis. "Children! It worked, our magic works!"

"You must hurry," said Marcus. "There won't be much time before Gwandoya realizes that the shield is no longer in place."

"We will stay put so he won't realize..." started Guelder.

"I love you all!" Yelled Jaynea. "Be caref....."

And with that the reflection of Becka faded. She was no longer looking through the reflection's eyes but saw her own image in the mirror.

"Better be on your way, daughters of Jaynea," said Caoimhin.

"Better let me hug my little sister," said Becka, motioning for Grog to put her down.

After hugs all around, the older group started on their way.

Aimee breathed a sigh of relief. "Those two won't let anything happen to Adam and Kami," she said.

"Now that we've got that taken care of you boys best be on your way," said Foster.

"I'm not so sure about leaving him alone with Becka," said Erik, nudging Brian.

"I'll serve as chaperone," said Aimee.

"Right," said Erik. "Well Brian I guess we'll need those horses now."

Brian took the whistle that was hanging around his neck and blew. A long shrill sound came from the exquisitely carved piece of wood. Within a matter of seconds, two magnificent stallions came running along the path. Bolting, their braided manes flying behind them, they whinnied and stopped in front of Brian.

"It's okay," said Brian in the language of the horses. "I know I am not your master, but your friend, Flamethril, has given me this whistle."

"We know of your errand," said the black stallion with a star marking his forehead. "I am Windracer, and this is Branco."

"It is our honor to assist you in this task," said the albino.

{ **20** }

Of Loyal Friends

Kami and Adam were having a delightful time playing chess with Caoimhin. "You should have told me he doesn't have to follow the rules," said Caoimhin.

"No one's ever beaten him before," said Grog, laughing. "He cheats.""I cheat?" said Caoimhin. "He cheats. Jumping across the board like that and taking any man he pleases."

"That's the rule in our house," said Kami. "Mama says that we don't have to play by the rules until we understand them."

"Check mate," said Adam, knocking Caoimhin's king off the board. "I'm too little to understand the rules but she still thinks I should play."

"I think you could play an actual game with rules," said Caoimhin. "You just like people to think that you don't understand yet so you can win."

Adam smiled at the wizard, "don't tell anyone else," he whispered.

"Looks like we've got company," said Grog, peering into the sky.

"Let me see," said Adam.

Grog picked up the little boy and placed him on his shoulders. "Three dragons headed our way!" yelled Adam.

"I'll take care of the likes of them," said Grog.

Caoimhin took the form of a giant and, scooping Adam and Kami up, hid them behind a tree.

"I want to see," yelled Adam. "Put me in a tree and then I can watch."

"You'll be safer down there," said Grog.

"Dragons closing in fast!" yelled Caoimhin.

"Step aside," said Grog. He reached out his humongous hand and grabbed all three of the dragons by their tails. They breathed fire at him. "Wish I had some water to douse these dragons with," he said, patting out the flames in his beard with his other hand.

"Caoimhin, at your service," said the wizard. And with a wave of his hand a large pond appeared at Grog's feet.

"Thanks," said Grog, dipping the dragons into the water. "That oughta put these flamethrowers out of commission for a while."

The dragons came up sputtering and trying to breathe fire. All that came out of their mouths and noses were sorry wisps of steam and smoke.

Grog had a difficult time holding on to the dragons. "Seems these foul creatures are a bit agitated by their failure," he said, dipping them into the pond again.

"I believe they are more agitated by our success," said Caoimhin. "Hold them still for a minute."

Caoimhin returned to normal size and brought the children close to him. "How would you like to help me with a little restraining spell?" He asked.

"Does he have a good grip on them?" asked Kami, hiding behind Caoimhin's leg.

"Not to worry, my young friend."

"I want to help," yelled Adam, jumping up and down.

"Have you got any rope in your pack then, lad?"

Adam ran to his pack and pulled out his rope. "Never leave home without it," he said.

"This will be a fun spell indeed," said Caoimhin, taking the ball of rope. He directed the children to make a circle.

Grog placed the dragons in the middle of the circle.

"Should he really let go like that?" Kami asked.

"Don't you worry your pretty little head," said Grog. "They won't move as long as Grog is standin' over 'em."

Caoimhin threw the ball to Adam. Adam threw the ball to Kami. Kami threw the ball to Caoimhin. They continued throwing the ball like this until a spider web formed around the dragons and all the rope was gone.

"Now children, repeat after me," said Caoimhin.

Perfect web, weave it tight

Dragons have to stay the night.

If the spider comes this way

Sorry dragons they'll be today.

Kami and Adam repeated the rhyme transporting the rope holding the dragons between two trees, forming a perfect web. The more the dragons struggled the more they were stuck in place.

"Thanks," said Grog. "Now I can search the sky and the land for other foul creatures."

"I suppose that's what we have to do," said Kami. "Watch and wait."

"Yeah, we get to sit and twiddle our thumbs while the others have all the fun," said Adam. He walked over to a tree where Branwen, the raven, perched on a low branch. "You can fly now," he said. "It looks like we are the first ones ready."

Branwen took flight but came back and landed on Caoimhin's shoulder.

"She will wait until Flaithir flies," he said. "She doesn't want to draw attention to us yet."

Dragon Hunt

Erik and Brian rode swiftly up the side of the mountain. "I don't like this, Brian," said Erik. "The death of all these trees and under-brush have left this path too exposed."

"I know what you mean," Brian yelled back. "These horses run like the wind, but we could meet with the enemy around any of these bends."

"The scurvy goblin creatures could be slithering behind any of these rocks."

"We'd better be ready with our weapons," Brian agreed.

Just as each of the boys pulled out their cross bows a group of goblins came scurrying up out of the rocks and from behind the scraggly dead trees. There were fifty of them holding shields as they came. Brian's heart leapt in his chest. Out of the corner of his eye he could see Windracer rear up. Erik didn't get thrown and immediately sent one hundred arrows flying. The goblins' wooden shields protected many of them, only ten fell.

Erik turned to see that fifty more goblins came from Brian's right side. He yelled a warning to Brian and his brother was able to get a shot off just in time. Brian's hundred arrows took down another ten of the goblins.

"We need to get to high ground," Erik yelled. As arrows flew too close.

The brothers urged their horses on. Erik pulled up alongside Brian and yelled. "I have an idea. When I jump aboard your horse, wrap your rope around me."

Brian reached into his pack but had to let go of the reins so he could continue to hold his crossbow. He almost slipped off his horse as he tried to stay steady. Next thing he knew Erik was standing on Windracer. Still holding his crossbow Erik jumped onto Brian's horse and landed with his back to Brian. Brian quickly wrapped the rope around himself and his brother as they rode like the wind. Erik shot arrow after arrow and yelled the spell that split them into a hundred. "Hold her steady!" he yelled.

The goblins fell quickly and then began to retreat.

Brian blew the whistle to call Windracer. Erik jumped back on his horse and urged Brian to keep moving. Suddenly Erik heard Branco's loud whinny. She had stopped running and was calling to Windracer who turned around. Erik saw that Brian was hanging over the side of Branco's back. He was held only by the rope that had caught on the pummel and one leg in a stirrup. Windracer raced to Branco and Erik jumped down and eased Brian off the horse.

"Brian," he said, as he laid his brother down softly. Then he saw the arrow in Brian's thigh. "Brian, you must wake up." he urged, and patted his brother's face.

Windracer and Branco neighed frantically.

"I don't speak horse," said Erik. "Brian is the one who speaks horse and knows the healer's art."

Erik started rummaging in the packs on Branco's back. "He had this pouch of herbs that Akire gave him." Erik found the herbs. He looked at the arrow and was worried about how deep it seemed to have entered his brother's side. "Goddess of healing, please bless my brother," he said as he pulled the arrow out. Brian moaned loudly but didn't wake up. Erik was shocked when he saw green ooze pour out of the wound and then blood. "What do I do?" he asked no one. Erik tried to think back to all the healers he had witnessed. His mother,

Solon, Akire, and Brian. He couldn't fail his little brother now. "That green ooze must mean that the wretched Goblin arrow was poisoned," he said. The two horses nodded 'yes'. "When I got bit by that blasted snake last year Solon sucked on the wound." Erik put his mouth to the wound and began to suck as hard as he could. He spat the foul-tasting ooze out each time and sucked on the opening some more. After several times Erik finally tasted blood. Brian started to lash around, and his body convulsed. Erik held him close and when he calmed down placed more of the herbs into the wound.

He held his brother and rocked him in his arms. "Look little brother, I know I played all those tricks on you when we were growing up, but I didn't mean anything by it. I'd die too if you were taken from this earth. Not to mention that our mother would kill me, so I'd join you really quickly. Remember all those times we played on the edge of the woods hoping to see magical creatures. You were the best at climbing the trees and acting as our lookout. Remember when you told me there was a giant in the distance and I didn't believe you? I climbed up there with you and I never saw the giant and I gave you a hard time about it, but we sat up in the tree as it swayed, and we pretended we were on a pirate ship in a storm. Remember?"

But Brian didn't stir. Erik thought his brother's body was convulsing again, then realized it was his own body as he sobbed and swayed with his brother in his arms. Erik dug another handful of herbs out of the pouch and placed them on the wound. Then he took off the cloth that served as his belt and wrapped it just above the wound. The bleeding stopped. Erik heard a rustling sound and looked up. They were surrounded by goblins who had each raised a bow in their direction. Erik knew he had to act fast, but his bow was out of reach. He closed his eyes and thought of arrows flying from his bow into the air and aimed at each of the goblins. He didn't have to say a spell, or even physically aim and fire. He heard the yelps of the stricken goblins and heard the clunk of their arrows that landed on the shield above him. He looked up to see that many of the goblins had fallen and the others were running down the mountain. Erik looked down at his brother's face. He sat and held him for what seemed like forever and told him the tales he remembered from their many antics as children. Erik closed his eyes and sang the song their mother used to sing to them at night.

Good night precious one,
May angels guide you through your dreams.
Sleep tight little son.
This nighttime rest from all your schemes.
When angels hide and brightness shines,
Your rest will be complete.
Good night little son,
Til on the morrow again we meet.

"What are you crooning on about, Erik?"

"You're okay!" Erik said.

"I won't be alive much longer if you go on ruining our mother's song like that," said Brian.

"Yep, you're just fine," said Erik.

"My leg feels like a fire is trying to escape," Brian said, groaning.

"We need to wrap it," said Erik. "But I didn't…"

"Seems like you did pretty well," said Brian looking at his thigh and then at the arrow and noticing the green ooze that still stuck more than half-way up the shaft. "It was poisoned."

"I sucked out as much as I could," said Erik.

"And took out all these goblins while I was unconscious?"

"Yep." said Erik. "Now, do you think you're able to ride? We should try to get to the caves and out of the open."

"It looks like you put a lot of herbs in my wound. Look in that pack on the other side of Branco. You'll find a vial of red liquid."

Erik found the vial and handed it to Brian.

Brian opened the vial and drank it down.

"Medicine?" Erik asked.

"A tonic to take away the pain from the inside, and fight any infection," said Brian.

Erik helped Brian onto Branco. They rode more slowly as she would not allow them to urge her on too much. As they rode the horses would occasionally let out a warning neigh, and their ears would twitch. Erik learned to take this as a signal that danger was nearby. He was able to shoot at anything in the brush and kept the odd goblin at bay until they arrived at the cave entrance. The boys dismounted, thanked the horses, and Brian asked them to listen for the whistle in case they needed a ride again soon.

Following the map, they located the winding staircase. "Think you can make it?" Erik asked.

"My leg feels numb right now, so I'll make it alright," said Brian.

They climbed slowly to the great hall, slaying a few goblins as they went.

Brian hid behind a column.

"How are you feeling?" Erik asked. "Ready to slay the dragon?"

"I'm ready," said Brian, and they stepped into the great hall.

But what they saw as they emerged into the wide-open space was not what they expected. Jaynea sat on the floor, cradling Marcus in her arms.

"Mama!" yelled Brian as he hurried to her side.

Erik searched the room for Gwandoya's minions.

"The evil dragon made me sculpt a body for his decrepit bride Catara, and a new human form for him. But when I unveiled the statues your father, Marcus, and Guelder were hiding there, ready to fight."

"We thought we could kill them...." Marcus' voice was weak.

"Grandfather," said Erik. "You know the prophecy; it has to be us."

"Gwandoya took his hideous bride and tried to escape down that passage," said Jaynea. "Your father, and Guelder followed him. Athena is with them too. She appeared as soon as you took the shield down."

"I see you are wounded, son," said Jaynea. "Marcus, can you help him?"

Marcus raised his head. "Whoever dressed the wound did a good job, but this will help even more." Marcus raised his hand and said *"sana, medior."*

Brian winced as the pain came back. "It feels like my leg is on fire again," he cried out in agony.

"Marcus, what are you doing?" Jaynea was frantic.

"Wait, Mama. It feels better. It's no longer numb, but I don't feel the pain either."

"Now, you must go." said Marcus. "You mustn't let the beast escape."

Jaynea agreed, "you must go quickly, the only way to revive his wretched Catara now is to find children for her to feed upon."

Erik and Brian raced down the stairway. A horrible stench grew stronger as they ascended into the depths of Gwandoya's lair. There were tunnels going off in all directions. Erik pulled the Detectoral out of his pack. Following its eerie glow, they moved further into the depths of the mountain. Suddenly they heard footsteps approaching in front of them.

They stepped into a side passageway and waited for the goblins to pass. Three figures hurried by and then turned and stood in front of the passageway. Denis jumped forth and raised his hand to place a spell on the foe.

"Is that you, Father?" asked Erik.

"I was about to knock you out cold," said Denis.

"How did you find us?" asked Guelder. "We must have taken ten turns since we left the tower."

"We climbed to the tower, expecting to fight Gwandoya there and found Mother and Grandfather," said Brian.

"They told us you were in pursuit of the dragon," said Erik, "So we followed."

"I can't believe this old contraption still works," said Athena, taking the Detectrol from Erik's hands.

"I'm just glad that Becka thought to give it to us as we parted today," said Erik.

"Saved me from having to try out the Olfactorial," said Brian, scrunching up his nose.

Suddenly a hundred darts came flying in their direction.

Erik raised his hands and sent the arrows flying back the way they came. They heard yelps and whimpers as the goblins retreated.

"We keep running into goblins and have lost all sense of direction in this place," said Denis.

"We may never find Gwandoya now," said Guelder.

"We can use the Olfactorial," said Erik.

"Right," said Brian. "I suppose it's our only hope."

Brian placed the Olfactorial on his nose. "Ugh," he said. "There are so many foul smells in these caves, how will I ever be able to tell if I've found Gwandoya or not."

When he took the Olfactorial off and looked at the indicator, it was spinning wildly. Dragon, goblin, rat, troll.

"Let me see that thing," said Athena. "Where did you get this?"

"Mathius and Mikos."

"Those two clowns? They were playing a joke on you," said Guelder.

"Maybe not," said Athena. She turned the dial to 'dragon.' "This little latch should hold this detector in place and at least narrow the smells down to only dragons," she said.

"Maybe one of you would like to try it," said Brian.

"No, no," said Athena, handing the device back to Brian. "We wouldn't want to take this honor away from you."

Brian placed the Olfactorial on his nose once again. Erik walked along beside him, holding a torch, and reading the detector. "It's definitely registering dragon," he said, as they came to a fork in the path, "looks like the strongest scent is in this direction."

They all followed Erik and Brian to the right. "The smell is becoming unbearable," said Brian.

"I think we are really close," said Erik, "a little further."

Suddenly the Olfactorial ceased to glow. The detector barely registered anything at all. "What happened?" asked Erik.

"It malfunctioned just in time," said Brian. "I was about to vomit from the putrid stench."

Denis was close to the boys. He walked in front of them and held up his torch. "This is what happened," he said.

The group had reached a great stone door. "The lair of Prestwick," said Guelder.

"Gwandoya found a way in."

"We need that map that Prestwick gave to you children," said Athena.

"I thought about that before I put the Olfactory on, but I'm sure Kami has it," said Brian. He looked at Erik. "We'd better check our packs just in case."

"A map won't tell us how to enter," said Erik.

"It may have a clue," said Athena.

"I don't know how it got in here," said Brian, holding up the map.

Erik held his torch above the map while Athena inspected it closer. "I believe this place on the map marks the treasure room. There are no words in the area."

Denis was trying to get a look at the map. "What about these words along the side here?" He asked.

"Just scribblings," said Guelder.

"Dragon scribblings," said Athena.

"Scribblings that even silly Prestwick himself can't read," said Brian.

"Prestwick is anything but silly," said Athena.

"He's a crafty one alright," said Denis.

"So he probably has been pretending that he couldn't remember how to get in the lair all these years," said Guelder.

"To keep everyone else out," said Erik.

"That would be my guess," said Athena. "Years ago when the dragons learned to put their language down on paper, they extended their sharp claws and dipped them into indigo ink."

"Or the blood of their most recent prey," said Guelder.

"Right," said Athena. "They never wrote with one clawed finger."

"That's right," said Denis. "The dragons that write have always written with two or even three pointed nails."

"That's why their writing always looks like scribbles," she said. "And if the writing is in the dragon's language, there is only one who can read it."

"Glad I can be of service," said a voice in the dark.

"Solon, is that you?" Athena asked.

"As soon as the shield was down, I made my way into these caves from the south side of the mountain."

"I don't know how you found us," she said. "But I'm very glad to see you."

Solon didn't tell the group, but he later let on to Erik, and Brian that he was actually quite lost and was delighted when he heard the voices of his friends and family.

"I am glad to be reunited with all of you," he said.

Erik held up a torch for his old friend. "It's a kind of riddle," said Solon, rubbing his long, gray-streaked beard.

"What else," said Erik and Brian, exchanging looks.

Six sailors stood at the door.

Six sailors no less no more

Six tongues that day they shared.

For the sixth tongue, they stood not prepared.

"Well, there are six people here," said Erik.

"We aren't sailors though," said Brian.

"Riddles are symbolic," said Erik. "We have to think about what sailors do, or what they stand for."

"You don't suppose we have to have our tongues cut out and cooked or something, do you?" asked Brian.

"Once again, it means something else," said Athena, who was thinking hard. "Denis, you are the only thing we have that is close to a sailor."

"Right, what do you think?" asked Guelder.

Denis leaned against the cold hard wall. "I'm thinking," he said. "But just because I'm a merchant sailor doesn't mean I know anything...."

"Wait," said Erik. "Maybe 'tongues' means languages."

"Right," said Athena. "Sailors travel the world and ships pick up sailors from all around the world."

"So, we have to speak in six different languages," said Erik.

"But what do we say?" Brian asked.

"Here are the last two lines of the riddle," said Solon.

A simple word, it's clear and plain,

Begin the games and you'll get in.

"That doesn't even rhyme," said Brian. "'Plain.' 'In.'"

"Complaining about Prestwick's lack of poetic genius won't get us anywhere," said Erik.

"He should have written, 'plin' and 'in,'" said Brian. "What kind of sense would that make? Or 'plain' and 'ain'."

"His choice of words wasn't the greatest," said Athena. "But this is all we have to work with."

"Everyone, start thinking," said Guelder. "We have no idea what Gwandoya is up to in there."

"If he found a way out, his hideous bride Catara will have the whole town of Briarwood eaten by the time we figure out this puzzle," said Brian.

"You mean, conundrum," said Solon.

"It is quite the problem," said Denis.

"A veritable mystery," said Guelder.

Athena's eyes opened wide as the men wasted time with their little game, "a regular enigma!" She shouted.

They all looked at her. "'The word to speak is plain and clear'. We have to think of a word that means plain or clear."

"Well, they both sort of mean the same thing, don't they?" asked Erik. "If it's plain it's clear to see and if it's clear it's plain to see."

"I always knew my apprentice was a genius," said Solon.

"That doesn't tell us anything," said Brian. "They define each other. That's a big, 'so what'."

"What one word is synonymous with plain and clear?" Athena was thinking aloud.

"Shhh." said the rest of the group.

They all sat and rubbed their heads. The men pulled on their beards. Athena paced.

"Plain, is how I would describe the daughter of that blacksmith that lives in Caraigdun," said Brian.

"Ordinary," said Erik.

"Unadorned," said Denis. "Like your mother's daily dresses compared to the ones I bring from my travels."

"But these things don't mean 'clear'," said Solon. "Let's try 'unpretentious.'"

"Don't think we could come up with that word in six languages," said Guelder.

"The riddle says that the word is simple."

"Maybe we forget all of this and just say 'simple' in six different languages," said Brian.

"Do we even know six different languages?" asked Erik.

"I know four," said Denis.

"I know three," said Athena.

"I know enough," said Solon. "Let's proceed."

"A simple word for clear and plain," said Guelder. He looked at the door. "It's certainly plain that the way isn't clear, right now," he said.

"The way is obstructed," said Denis.

"Blocked," said Brian and he grimaced as a sharp pain shot through his thigh.

"Here we go again," said Athena, who had gone back to her pacing.

"Closed." said Solon.

"It's not open. That's evident," said Brian.

"If the way is clear, the way is open," said Erik.

Athena stopped pacing. "If someone is being plain with you, they are being open."

"This all makes sense," said Guelder. "Denis, remember the wizarding trials?"

"The head wizard always said, 'begin the games' at the opening ceremony," he answered.

"You'll have to teach each of us how to say 'open' in a different language," said Erik.

"I'll take English," said Brian.

"We'd better get moving," said Guelder.

"I hope Prestwick didn't have six specific languages in mind," said Denis. "I'll say it in French," said Denis, "and tell Erik the word in German."

"I'll speak the word in the language of our mothers," said Athena.

"I'll speak it in the language of our fathers," said Solon.

"What do you recommend I use?" asked Guelder.

Solon glanced at the map. "'For the sixth tongue they stood unprepared.'"

"What do you think it means?" asked Athena.

"What is the one language that none of us would be prepared to speak?" asked Erik.

Brian was picturing the large yet somehow beady eyes of Prestwick, hater of boys and men. "Dragon language," he said, almost to himself.

Athena caught his mumbles. She looked at him. "Dragon Speak," she said.

"It is impossible for a human being to speak that language," said Guelder.

"Impossible," Denis agreed.

"Unlikely," said Solon, "but not impossible."

"There is one here who can duplicate the language," said Athena. Her eyes scanned the dimly lit faces of her companions. Her gaze stopped on Brian.

He was holding his injured leg and leaning against the stone wall. "Who? Me?" He asked, pointing to himself.

"You are injured," Athena whispered.

"He was hit by a poisoned goblin arrow," said Erik.

"Why didn't you say something right away?" Denis asked, rushing to Brian's side.

"I'm fine," said Brian. "We need to take care of the task at hand."

Denis and Solon examined the wound. "It looks like it's been well tended to," said Solon.

"It does seem that someone with healing powers dressed this," said Denis.

"Did you do this to yourself?" Athena asked.

"It was Erik," said Brian.

"It was nothing," said Erik, holding back the emotion that he had felt at almost losing his brother.

"Back to this door," said Brian. "How can I possibly speak something I have never heard?"

"You have heard it in your dreams," said Athena.

"In my dreams?" asked Brian. "What are you...wait." A faint memory entered Brian's mind. It was not a memory of a dream but an actual encounter with a dragon. "When we all left Prestwick back at his cave," he could see the dragon in his mind. Prestwick was walking over to the outside entrance of his cave. He said a word and a great stone moved so the dragon could enter. Brian could feel the word forming in his throat, but when he said the word, it came out too much in his mouth. "*Kri-ahc-th-ahc-th*. No. No. That's not it," he said.

"The sounds of dragon speak come only from the throat," said Solon. "You almost had it but you, like all other humans, are using your tongue to make the 'th' sound."

Erik put his hand on Brian's shoulder. "I have faith in you, brother," he said.

"You didn't even say little," Brian said. Closing his eyes he could see Prestwick standing by the stone; he could hear the guttural sounds coming from deep within the dragon's throat. "*Kri-ahcth-ahcth.*"

Solon stared at Brian. "Amazing," he said. "I never thought I'd see the day. Denis, you have a truly amazing son here."

"Guess you'll have to take over the English one for me," said Brian to Erik.

"I'll be glad to utter the word in my own tongue," said Guelder. "*Open,*" and he waved his arms dramatically in front of the door.

"*Offen,*" said Erik, waving his arms with equal drama.

Denis moved his hands slowly in front of the door, "*Ouvert,*" he said.

Solon dragged his Swahili word out long and lean, "*Ku-fun-gua,*" he said.

"*Vula,*" said Athena, rolling her eyes at the dramatics.

"*Kri-ahcth-ahcth,*" said Brian, with not as much flare as his father but a bit more than Athena.

The group scrambled to get out of the way as two enormous stones swung slowly out toward them.

"I suppose we weren't considering that this door was going to be the size of a full-grown dragon," said Guelder.

The stench that arose from the lair was almost more than anyone could bear. "Quick, find anything you can and cover your mouth and nose. Breathing this stuff in directly could very well kill you," said Denis.

The entrance to the cave was dark but as the group rounded the third corner, a bright light shone at the end of the tunnel. Erik ran ahead to face the dragon, but when he came around the corner it was not the fire of the dragon's breath but the warm rays of the setting sun that shone in his face.

"The back door of the lair stands open," said Denis, who was close on his son's heels.

"We are too late!" yelled Brian. "Gwandoya has escaped!"

{ **22** }

Two Youngsters, a Dragon, and a Witch

When Gwandoya came flying out of the lair of Prestwick, Grog and Caoimhin were caught completely off guard. Gwandoya was thirsty for the blood of children and headed for the town of Briarwood, being aware that the town wasn't completely deserted. Seeing two children below gave his evil heart great joy. "It will not be long now, my love," he said to Catara.

"Put me down in the apple orchard," she said, weakly. "How I loved apples long ago when I was mortal. Now I must have children."

"I will bring a tasty child back for you."

Gwandoya flew high into the sky and cloaked himself in invisibility. Flying past Grog unnoticed, he snatched Adam and Kami up into his filthy claws. Grog and Caoimhin were helpless as the children became invisible as soon as they were in Gwandoya's grasp.

Grog tried to follow the voices of the screaming children. He was reaching out for them waving his hands in the air in front of him.

"You may knock them to their death!" yelled Caoimhin. "Just follow him. We will --"

"Caoimhin!" Kami yelled.

"Grog, help us!" yelled Adam.

Grog tried to reach out a long arm and pull back the children, but Gwandoya was swift as he flew up into the clouds.

Caoimhin sent great streams of fire into the sky.

"You're telling me I may knock them out of the sky!" yelled Grog. "You're going to burn them to a crisp."

"Oh, sorry," said Caoimhin, "I panicked."

"Be still, Adam," said Kami. "You're going to make us fall to our death."

"I'd rather die of falling than to have my bones broken by this evil creature," he said, trying to kick the beast.

Gwandoya laughed a wicked laugh. "Normally I would enjoy dealing with such a feisty catch," he said. "But Catara is dying. I must get you to her as quickly as possible."

"I have an idea," whispered Kami to Adam. "Stab the dragon with your knife. I have a hunch that if Catara drinks his blood, she will turn to stone."

So, Adam did. The dragon's blood dripped down onto Adam's arm and Gwandoya dropped Adam next to the evil witch. In no time at all, they were landing. The dragon uncloaked himself and, holding Kami tightly in one hand, cut Adam on the arm with a sharp claw and bade Catara to drink.

"No!" Kami screamed.

Adam didn't struggle.

"Such a brave little boy," said Catara, leaning over and putting her mouth to the wound.

Adam closed his eyes, and after a few seconds fainted on the ground.

"You'll kill him! You wretched creature!" yelled Kami, kicking as hard as she could.

"It won't be long now until my beloved is back to full strength," said Gwandoya. "Here is another tasty morsel for you Catara."

"Now, I'll -- drain --. h-e-r-r --" Catara didn't finish her sentence. Her grip was still around Kami's arm. Her hand and all the rest of her had turned to solid stone.

"Evil child!" yelled Gwandoya, "What magic is this? What have you done?!"

Kami tried to break free of the stonelike grip of Catara. "I will drink your blood before you move another step," said the evil dragon.

"Not if I can help it!" yelled Adam.

"Adam! You're alive!" yelled Kami.

"Strategy!" yelled Adam.

"What is this you say to your sister? Strategy? Strategy, is it? We shall see if the strategy of two small children can outwit the great Gwandoya. None have escaped the child eater."

Gwandoya swooped down and snatched Adam in his claws and immediately popped him into his mouth. His great jaws came crunching down.

"Argh," said Gwandoya, spitting profusely all around the orchard. "What was that? Bits of wood in my teeth; splinters in my gums. What trick have you played now, young master?" He yelled.

The real Adam started throwing apples down from a tree. His aim was perfect as he hit Gwandoya smack on the head with every throw.

"You expect to injure the great Gwandoya with apples?" he said.

While Gwandoya looked away, Kami raised her right hand and mumbled one word over and over. "Golden," she said, concentrating hard on each apple that Adam plucked off the tree.

The next apple that hit Gwandoya was solid gold.

"That actually hurt," said the dragon. "I am getting annoyed at your little games." He flew up to where Adam was sitting.

Adam closed his eyes and reappeared in another tree closer to Kami.

"Over here!" he yelled.

Gwandoya was amazed that such a young child could have the ability to teleport himself like this.

Kami was amazed too.

She kept to the plan and continued to turn the apples into solid gold as Adam threw them at the approaching dragon.

Kami was even more amazed when one apple grew to four times its size and flew much faster than Adam could throw it. It hit Gwandoya squarely on the nose. The dragon spun out of control and landed in a heap.

It wasn't long before he got up, this time Adam was not fast enough and Gwandoya grabbed him as he flew past.

"You will not take him as long as I stand alive," said a powerful voice.

It was Guelder, with Athena swift on his heels.

Gwandoya turned and with red eyes glowing cast his gaze upon them. Kami and Adam watched in horror as Guelder and Athena were imprisoned in a Circle of Flame. Guelder's sword lay on the ground just outside the flame.Denis was right behind them. "Let him go!" He yelled as he drew his bow and aimed at the neck of the dragon.

The arrow bounced off the mail of Gwandoya, who turned his gaze upon Denis. Denis rolled as the flame came searing down and although he escaped the prison, his clothing was on fire. Rolling until the flame extinguished, he tried to stand and face the dragon again. His body was badly burned, and he collapsed at Kami's feet.

"Father!" she yelled, struggling with no avail to break free of Catara's grip.

The next to try his luck with the dragon was Erik. He appeared seemingly out of nowhere and, drawing his sword, dared the dragon to do the same to him. "Your gaze is not hazardous to me," he said. "You are a coward to use it. Stand and fight."

Gwandoya did not hesitate, Erik felt his fiery breath hit his shield but did not back down.

Suddenly another Erik appeared behind the great dragon.

"I'm over here!" he yelled.

When the dragon turned, an arrow hit his arm loosening his grip on Adam.

Adam ran to the circle of fire that imprisoned Guelder and Athena and tried to remember the spell to free them from the circle of flame.

Both Eriks were fighting fiercely. Gwandoya faced the first Erik throwing flame in his direction while he swung at the second Erik with his gargantuan tail. Both Eriks used their shields well. Gwandoya swung around to breathe fire at the Erik behind him and sent the first Erik flying through the air with a swift flick of his tail. This Erik, which of course was just the 'Doublasphere' version, disappeared before he hit the ground.

"A mere reflection," said Gwandoya, turning to face the real Erik.

"Ahhh, but I'm no reflection!" yelled Brian.

Brian could see that Erik was very hot and exhausted. While he drew the dragon's attention away from Erik, Erik studied the dragon.

There must be a flaw. Mama never finishes her sculptures. Erik remembered that his father's arrow had bounced off the neck of the dragon. Perhaps he located a bare spot. Dodging the enormous tail, Erik ran around to the front of the creature. The dragon spewed forth fiery flames but when the smoke dissipated Erik found it, a tiny opening in the dragon's mail, just below his jaw on the left side of his neck.

"To the left!" he yelled to Brian.

Brian tried to get the dragon to turn to the left, but Gwandoya turned to his right. Just as Erik had planned. Not pausing for a second, Erik lifted the crossbow and reached into his quiver. Empty. Thinking quickly, Erik pulled the sword of Guelder out of its sheath. Placing the long sword onto the crossbow he aimed for the neck of the dragon. Gwandoya reached up a claw and pulled the sword from his neck. Greenish-brown blood oozed out, turning to stone as it ran down the dragon's side.

But Gwandoya was not to die of this wound. He turned and swung his tail into Erik and Brian, sending them both flying. Just as the boys hit the ground, Gwandoya heard a loud shattering sound from behind.

"No!" he yelled.

It was too late. Using a chain mace, Adam had shattered the body of Catara with one swift blow. Kami ran to her father's side, burying her head in his chest as she cried.

The pixie had kept hidden the entire time but could no longer stand to see her friend in pain.

Flying out of Kami's pocket, she hovered in front of Denis.

Denis awoke to a breath of fresh air. He looked up at Kami and the small pixie that was flapping her wings as fast as a hummingbird. It looked like she had no wings at all.

As Hollyhock passed over Denis' body, the burns felt the cool breeze made by her wings and soon most of the pain subsided.

"Hollyhock, you stay with him," said Kami. "Adam, we have to save Athena and Guelder!" Kami searched the trees. Suddenly Adam appeared floating through the air. Then Grog appeared holding the little boy in his hand. Grog put Adam down next to the circle of fire.

"Ohhhh, I hope I remember this," said Adam.

"I'll help," said Grog.

Together two small children and one enormous giant recited the incantation.

"*Exstinctum Ignus Orbis!*"

Athena and Guelder collapsed from heat exhaustion as the fire disappeared.

Gwandoya turned and walked toward Erik and Brian. He was ready to breathe a wall of fire when Adam yelled, "Grog!" The giant picked up the little boy and put him down close to his brothers.

"Now the dragon will deal with the wrath of Adam of Caraigdun!" he yelled. "You will pay for what you have done to my family!"

Adam picked up the crossbow and raised it in the air. He could barely hold it up. Suddenly powerful hands came from behind. "Let us help you with that, Little Warrior," said Erik.

Together the three sons of Jaynea raised the bow. Together they pulled back on the trigger. Together they fell backwards as the arrow flew swiftly into the neck of the wicked Gwandoya.

Gwandoya laughed a wicked laugh as he breathed fire. "Your mere mortal weapons will never conquer the dragon," he said.

But he did not see that the crossbow that was used was not a mere mortal crossbow but one that was made by the grand wizard Marcus. Those who held the bow were not mere mortal children but the wizard children of Denis and Jaynea of Caraigdun. The arrow that was sent into the neck of Gwandoya was not a mere mortal arrow, but an arrow made by the great and powerful Mathius and Mikos and dipped into a poison especially made to destroy the hardened clay body of the dragon.

The dragon did not die as swiftly as the arrow flew. Athena, Guelder and Denis looked up to see him stiffen as the poison made his blood turn to stone. He uttered but one word in the dragon's tongue before he breathed his last hot breath.

"Quickly," Erik yelled, "We must make our way to the other side of the mountain before the spirit of Gwandoya escapes."

"Right!" yelled Brian. "No time to bask in our victory, for this is only one battle. We have yet to win the war!"

Everyone heard clapping coming from above. A great roar of applause rang out and a crowd of spectators appeared sitting in the clouds.

Two cloaked forms descended slowly in strange flying machines.

"Bravo," said Mathius, clapping loudly.

"Quite the show," said Mikos, landing beside the sons of Denis, the whirligig whirling away. "It will be our great pleasure to fly you to your next task."

"I'll stay with the adults while you children fly in this contraption," said Mathius, climbing out of the hovering machine.

"Seems like we ought to be able to get there by magic now that Gwandoya is gone," said Erik.

"All the evil still present on this mountain will distort magic," said Mathius.

"But I thought the whirligigs flew by magic," said Brian.

"They fly on their own just fine," said Mikos, peddling away to keep his whirligig going. "Just need a bit of magic to keep them up every once in a while."

Erik boarded one whirligig, while Brian climbed into the other with Mikos.

"Thanks, little brother," yelled Erik, as he looked down upon Adam, who was growing smaller and smaller on the ground.

Adam waved and tried to follow the flying machine. "Don't mention it," he yelled. And then ran back to get in position to place his shard.

{ 23 }

Giggly Girls and Brave Warriors or Giggly Warriors and Brave Girls

It is important for the hearer or teller of this tale to know that Aimee and Becka were not merely sitting pretty, examining the condition of their fingernails, and brushing each other's hair while the others battled the dragon. As a matter of fact, they had far better distractions to keep them from being completely bored out of their minds. Sir Bruin, upon hearing that one of the children who had arrived to battle the great Gwandoya and clear the mountain of evil was none other than the fair maiden Aimee of Caraigdun, had left a lieutenant in charge on the battlefront and traveled by foot as not to attract any unwanted attention by using magical means of transport, to see this lady. So, for a long moment the girls had been occupied gratifyingly with listening to magnificent tales of the conquests of their brave men, as they sat and made brooms out of long branches and tall grass.

When Gwandoya left the castle, his band of goblins found the quickest paths out of the castle, off all sides of the mountain and down into the dead woods below. The goblins knew of the legend that, when Gwandoya was killed, all evil would be exorcised from the mountain. They didn't want to hang around to see what horrible death might befall them and so they fled. So, it was mere happenstance that a

{ 242 }

band of thirty goblins ran into Aimee as she gathered berries for her group. She heard them coming, recognized the growling language of the goblin, and passed the red scarf over her face. When they saw her, they pushed past and motioned for her to join them. She growled for them to stop and motioned for them to follow her. She hoped they'd think she had some way of protecting them, but she lured them smack dab in the middle of her camp. "Get them!" she yelled in English.

The goblins came running into the clearing and were immediately captured by Sir Bruin and Captain Foster, proof that the two did not jest when they spoke of their prowess in war.

Sir Bruin was holding onto Aimee, about to tie her up with the other goblins when she yelled, "You can let me go now!" and changed back into her human form. Sir Bruin did not let her go, but he loosened his grip before turning her face to his and planting a tender kiss on her lips.

"It is so nice of you both not to slay any of these poor creatures," said Becka, as she glanced at the lot of thirty goblins bound to each other and against trees in the area.

"Amazing that you didn't have to make use of any magic to capture them all," said Aimee.

"You were both so quick," said Becka. "I scarcely had time to be afraid."

"That was quick thinking on your part, Aimee," said Bruin. "Changing into a goblin, just in time."

"Ah, but my brave knight is wounded," said Aimee, noticing a rip in Bruin's shirt.

"'Tis, but a scratch," said Bruin, not too convincingly though. He didn't want to dissuade the fair one from extending her nurturing hand.

"Oh, you must lie down here in the shade," said Aimee, taking him gently by the arm.

"As you wish," said Bruin, gazing intently into her deep blue eyes.

"I'm sure you are famished after such a battle," said Becka, looking at her brave Foster.

Becka decided that since the goblins had already found them, it would be okay to use her magic to aid in preparing the feast. She had a blanket overflowing with pies and crusty buttery breads, vegetables, and roasted rabbit in no time.

It was during this picnic that one of the goblins awoke and moaned something in Goblin-speak.

Bruin spoke to him in his own tongue.

"He wishes to strike a bargain," he said.

"Poor wretch wants his freedom, I suppose," said Captain Foster, ripping off a piece of roasted rabbit with his teeth.

Becka smiled. She was very pleased that he noticeably enjoyed her cooking.

"Exactly," said Bruin. "He says he has some information that we may find valuable."

"What's valuable to a goblin may or may not be valuable to us," said Foster.

"He says he has seen Becka in the dungeons of Gwandoya's castle, just minutes ago," said Bruin.

"But she is standing here before us and has never ventured into the mountain," said Foster.

"My reflection," said Becka.

"I had almost forgotten," said Aimee. "She must not have completely faded."

"She is still trapped in the mountain," said Becka.

Bruin looked at Aimee. "Ahha, the original battle with the dragons," he said. "Your sister used a decoy."

"Yes," said Aimee.

"Do you have the mirror with you?" asked Bruin.

Becka pulled the mirror out of her cloak. "As you can see, I have no reflection," she said.

It was at this point that Flaithir, prince of the falcons took flight to the northwest of the mountain. Almost immediately thereafter Branwen in her majesty soared high in the south.

"They have destroyed the dragon," said Aimee, clapping her hands.

"I knew they could do it," said Becka.

The goblins began to squirm and cringe.

"They want to leave," said Bruin.

"The exorcism of evil from the mountain will very well kill them," said Foster.

"Let them go," said Becka.

"We have to at least give them the chance to run," said Aimee. "I don't believe they meant any harm to us."

Bruin waved his hand and loosened the ropes. He grabbed the goblin who had spoken of Becka's reflection.

The goblin spoke three words. Bruin let him go.

"Foster, you and I will have to bring back Becka's reflection," he said.

Foster looked at Becka.

Aimee looked at Bruin.

Each brave knight grasped his lady in his arms and kissed her for a long moment.

"Girls are magic," said Foster.

"Yup," said Bruin.

The girls seemed in a trance as the warriors left them standing and hurried off to the mountain.

"Better keep your wits about you," said Becka, snapping her fingers in front of Aimee's face.

"Oh, right," said Aimee, coming to her senses.

Becka smoothed her skirt and put a hand to her hair. "What were we supposed to do next?"

"Say the spell to raise the shield around the mountain so the spirits of Gwandoya and Catara cannot escape."

"Better do that right away," said Becka.

The girls mounted their brooms and flew close to the shield that surrounded the mountain.

"Magicis Clypeo!" both girls commanded. *"Magicis Clypeo!"*

"Next we must send Andor into the sky," said Aimee, when they were certain the spell had worked.

Becka called to Andor who perched comfortably in a nearby tree.

He flew into the sky and hovered over the girls for a minute.

Then all three birds, noticing the others, flew around the mountain at a steady pace. They arrived back to their spots at precisely the same time.

There was a stillness in the air and even those on the battle front felt it. All motion seemed to cease. The sands in the hourglass froze in their narrow hole for a second in time. The only stirring was the breeze made by the wings of Branwen, Flaithir, and the king of the Eagles, Andor.

All six of the children of Caraigdun watched.

All six held the magic shards in their hands.

All six children reached out at exactly the same time to place the stones.

Alas, before the children could place their pieces, the Banshee let out a cry, shrill and strong and echoing from every corner of the mountain.

Kami hesitated for a second and looked up. The white flowing dresses of the transparent Banshee waved high above the castle.

Kami's hesitation was just long enough to keep her from placing her piece at just the right moment.

"Kami!" yelled Adam.

Kami looked at Adam. She saw he had placed his shard. She noticed her piece still in her hand. "I'm sorry," she said, turning to her father who was standing close by. "Father, the Banshee has come for Grandpa."

Adam looked up at the Banshee. Just as his eyes fell upon her, she let out a terrible screech. Adam felt a chill run through his veins. "Hideous creature," he said.

"We have to go to him," said Kami.

"You must complete the task," said Mathius.

"We must send the birds up again," said Caoimhin.

"As soon as you have placed the shards," said Grog, looking down at Kami. "I will run you to your grandfather."

Kami took the shard in her hand. It seemed like an eternity as the birds circled the mountain. Finally, they stopped directly above the children at precisely the same time. Six hands reached out and placed the shards. A glowing white flame rose from the stones that were placed and slowly engulfed the entire mountain.

"The fire doesn't feel hot at all!" yelled Kami.

"No, but this wind could blow us away!" yelled Adam.

The children ran to hide behind Grog.

He bent down, scooped them up into his hands, and shielded them from the fiery wind. "I hope I've been good enough lately," he said.

"Don't worry," said Caoimhin, as he ran to hide behind his giant friend. "You are protecting two valiant children. That will surely make up for the chickens you stole from Ingrid the Ogre last week."

Denis, Athena, Guelder, and Solon followed Caoimhin and hid behind the great legs of the giant. Great gusts of fiery wind came rushing around the mountain.

"Weren't really prepared for this were we," said Guelder, holding on to Grog's shoelace as the wind lifted him up off the ground.

"Just glad that Jaynea is safe inside the castle," yelled Denis, who was trying to keep his grip on the hem of Grog's rather large britches.

"We can only hope she is safe," yelled Athena, who was hanging on to Guelder's belt for dear life.

"The cry of the Banshee has stopped!" yelled Solon.

"Well, she is evil," said Kami.

"Maybe she'll be ex-ee-sizzed," said Adam.

"I almost forgot," said Kami, pulling the wooden box from her cloak.

"Quick, get that thing opened," said Adam.

Kami opened the box. The wind almost sent it flying from her hands. She gripped it tightly.

"Just doing her job, that banshee," said Grog, trying to search through the flaming sky for the white figure. "I see another white figure with her," he said.

"It must be Angelica," said Kami.

"She will stop the Banshee," said Adam.

"Let's go," said Kami. "I want to be near my grandfather through all of this."

Grog held Kami and Adam in one hand, shielding them from the wind with his other. They held onto the box together.

Grog started to walk forward. "Better do something with us first!" yelled Denis, as the wind and the forward motion sent him and Solon flying off the right leg of Grog's britches.

Grog picked up all five adults and tucked them into his shirt pocket.

"That's much better!" called Denis. "Thanks."

Inside that huge pocket, a disconcerting thought was crossing the mind of Caoimhin. Mathius seemed to have the thought at the same time as they both spoke it at once.

"The evil," they both said, and looked at each other with trepidation.

"It is Aimee and Becka's task to form a shield around the mountain to keep the spirit of Gwandoya from escaping," said Denis.

"The children may be up to keeping Gwandoya confined," said Mathius, "but my nieces may not be able to hold the shield. There will be a lot of evil trying to escape the mountain."

Athena understood their line of thinking.

"We must form a circle of power around the mountain," said Caoimhin.

All the wizards looked at him.

"How did I not think of this," said Athena.

"No time to waste," said Solon. "We must transport ourselves immediately around the mountain."

"When you are in position, stretch out the energy of your hands until it reaches the wizard on either side of you," said Mathius.

"Then we must all focus on the chasms deep in the center of this mountain," said Caoimhin.

"We must keep the evil from escaping and consuming the land for many miles around," said Solon.

"Send it deep into the abyss," said Denis.

"Take care of the wee ones," yelled Caoimhin to Grog, as the wizards left his pocket and positioned themselves around the mountain.

"I think even this rusty wizard can help with that one," said Guelder.

Aimee and Becka stood together on the Northeast side of the mountain, as they recited the spell of exorcism. They could feel all power drain from every inch of their bodies and souls as they fought to confine Gwandoya to the mountain.

"Something besides the evil of Gwandoya and Catara is fighting against us," said Aimee, weakly.

"We—must—hold — on," said Becka, struggling to concentrate.

Suddenly they felt a great burden lifted.

It was then that seven of the strongest wizards known in all of time came together to aid in the exorcism of evil from the long-defiled Mount Ceo'ban. Solon and Athena of the land of Afrike; Caoimhin, friend of Jaynea; Guelder the Grand and Denis the Great of Caraigdun; Mathius, brother of Jaynea (who had grabbed Mikos on his way to the spot on the east side of the mountain, didn't want his little brother to miss all the fun.) And, into the circle of power there stepped Akire the tender heart with Omen the half-wolf at her side, Didean the centaur and Prestwick the dragon.

After several big steps, Grog had reached the highest point of the mountain. He found the room where Jaynea still kept watch over Marcus.

"I have to see him," said Kami. As she looked in through the window, she noticed the drooping head of her mother but could not see her grandfather whom she loved so dearly.

"Can you put us in through the window?" asked Adam.

The children climbed in.

Kami was devastated at the sight of the old man. She was still struggling to hold the box that was to capture the spirit of Gwandoya and could not even extend her arms to embrace the man whom she knew was dying.

Jaynea had been crying.

"Mama," said Kami. "He's not."

"No, my sweet Kami," said Jaynea. "He is not dead, but he is close. An angel came in a while ago and tried to intercede by healing his wound."

"Angelica," said Kami.

"Yes," said Jaynea. "Angelica tries to hold back the cry of the Banshee and convene with the chariot of death as we speak."

Suddenly the box in Kami's hand started shaking. Kami held tightly, but an unseen force was trying to pull the receptacle from her grasp.

"I need help," she said, as she struggled with all the might her little arms could muster.

"Oh, sorry," said Adam.

Adam came forward and grasped the box in his hands.

A force tugged and pulled but the children held their ground. Outside at the foot of the south side of the mountain the battle raged on. Pitting human against goblin, beast against beast, dragon against dragon, good against evil. In opposition to evil, the seven wizards held their circle of power strong. Angelica engaged in a battle overhead, contending with the Banshee and keeping her from screeching the last mournful cry.

The children stood their ground as the maddened spirit of Gwandoya swirled around the chamber, dodging the force that tried to pull him into the box as he focused all he had left on trying to cause them to lose their grip. Catara's spirit aided him as she too darted around the chamber in her rage. The presence of evil did not outweigh the presence of good in the room that day. With one last effort, the spirits of Gwandoya and Catara charged the children together. "The spell!" yelled Kami. "Now!" Two small voices joined together, "*Intro Peior Ferocitus*," they said. "*Intro Peior Ferocitus*," they repeated. "*Intro Peior Ferocitus!*" With the third recitation of the spell, the power of the children and the receptacle they held was released into the room. The evil that was Gwandoya and the evil that was Catara were sucked into the vortex of the box. Captured in eternal torment; together.

The box fell from the hands of the children. Adam pounced on it to keep it closed tight. "Where's that lock?" He yelled.

Kami pulled a lock from her cloak and ran over to fasten the box while Adam held it down.

A swirl of fire and wind entered the room and took the box into the evil that was being forced toward the fiery furnace in the center of the mountain. Around and around went the box; the box that held the worst evil ever to live upon the land. Those in the circle of power felt one last tug on the strength that had almost gone out of each of them. The birds flying high overhead struggled to keep from being pulled into the chasms of death. With one last breath, all evil was taken into the mountain. The box swirled down and down and disappeared out of sight. The spirits of Gwandoya and Catara sent once and for all to their doom. (And don't worry; they aren't coming back in another tale. They are toast.)

Suddenly the room filled with light; a bright piercing warmth of all that was good in the world. The light woke Marcus, and for a moment, he basked in the glow before Kami ran to him and kneeled by his side.

"Grandfather," she said, as tears swelled in her eyes.

"You're not dead," said Adam, sinking his head into the chest of the brave man.

Jaynea could feel the goodness in the room and knew that it was time to use magic. She needed her family together to say goodbye to this good man.

"*Familia proximare!*" she said.

Aimee, Becka, Erik, and Brian appeared in the room.

But Jaynea could feel that her husband could not come. Denis would not be there to say goodbye to his father.

The others came and hugged Marcus. And he spoke a few words to each of them.

"My Aimee," he said, as she held his hand. "You are my beautiful, feisty girl; soon to be on your way in the world. There will be many choices to make, my girl. Make none in haste. Give your heart away only when he has a whole heart to give back to you in return."

A tear came forth and fell on the hand of Marcus, "I will remember you with love," Aimee said.

"Becka, our sweet, beautiful hazel-eyed girl," he said, as he reached forth his hand to the second daughter of Jaynea. "Your amazing talents will propel you forth into all that life offers. Focus your mind and a world of wonders will be yours."

Becka leaned down and hugged this man, whom she had only known for a short time but already loved so much. "I will Grandfather."

Marcus put his hand out to Jaynea. She leaned close to the old man. "You must get Becka's reflection back soon," he said.

"I will," said Jaynea, "I can see that she is fading."

Jaynea motioned for Erik to come to his grandfather's side. "Grandfather, you are tough as nails. You'll be up and around before sundown tonight," he said, trying to lighten the hearts in the room.

He looked into the eyes of his mother who tried not to weep. She did not have to say a word, for just then he could see into her soul. Marcus would breathe his last breath, soon.

"Grandfather, I wish I had known you many years ago. That you had passed on to me all the secrets of wizardry that go with you now upon your death."

"Erik, oldest son of my oldest son, it is enough for me that I am here to see you at your best, in the destruction of the evil dragon and restoration of good to this mountain. My wisdom to you is to keep your humor. Marry a girl who has as much wit and humor as you do. Many of your words will hurt if not, but if she does, she will counter them and never take you too seriously."

Erik smiled. A thought of a very feisty dark-eyed girl he had met in Pharris, the town south of his apprenticeship, flashed through his mind. "I know just such a girl," he said.

"Marry her and pass on the name and tell my great-grandchildren many stories of their old grandfather."

"I will," said Erik. "I will."

"Bring my Brian to me now," said Marcus. "My sight is dimming."

"I am with you," said Brian, squeezing the old man's hand.

"Remember the power within you, young Brian," said Marcus, struggling to see the lines of Brian's face. "Hold on to everything that is you throughout your life."

Marcus took Erik's hand and placed it together with Brian's. "Never take your brother too seriously and make sure he treats the dark-eyed girl from the land of Pharris well."

Erik's eyes opened wide. His grandfather had read his thoughts!

Brian smiled. "Grandfather, as my brother said, there are so many secrets that you take with you in your death."

Marcus smiled one devious smile as he thought over his life and remembered the dreams he had at Brian's age of thirteen. "We would have had fun together wouldn't we," he said, closing his eyes for a moment.

Kami was eager to have her turn to talk to him. She glanced at her mother for evidence that he wasn't gone yet.

Jaynea smiled at the little girl. "He will not go until we hear the last cry of the Banshee, and the chariot comes," she whispered.

Marcus opened his eyes. "But all is not lost," he said, with one last burst of energy coming from deep within the soul of a feisty man. "I have written many of my schemes on parchment brought to me in this very mountain. The papers are hidden in a crevice under a large rock at the far corner of the cave where Guelder and I were held captive those sixteen years."

"We will find them," said Brian.

"We will share them with the family of Caraigdun for generations to come," said Erik.

Adam jumped in for his turn. "You aren't going to die are you grandfather?" He asked.

Marcus mustered up all his strength to wrap his arms around the little boy. "You are too young to understand my Adam; my energetic little man."

Marcus thought for a moment how to tell this young boy about death. "Think of the flowers that come forth each spring. They have slept in the earth all winter and grow again and bloom when the sun warms the air and earth, and the melting of snows and falling of rains moistens them. My body will sleep like a bulb in the earth. One day my spirit will bring life to it again like the sun and rain to the flowers in spring."

Adam stared at his grandfather. "Just as long as I get to see you again," he said.

Marcus smiled at this simple response compared to his lengthy explanation. "We will see each other again; as I know that today I will visit with my beautiful Bethina in her garden."

"Say 'hello' to my grandmother for me," said Adam. "Tell her I hope I get to see her soon."

"Yeah, and tell her to keep you out of trouble," said Erik.

"Right," said Brian. "Maybe she can keep you from haunting us."

Marcus was sad to leave this group of funny, intelligent children. "All that we could have shared and all the fun we could have had," he said, and then with a big smile and a glance at Brian. "There will be hauntings," he said.

All was suddenly quiet except for the sobs of one little girl that had not stopped since the capture of the dragon.

Marcus could hear the sobs and could feel the lifeforce leaving his body. His spirit that was strong soon could no longer inhabit the body that was so weak.

"Come to me," he said, reaching his hand out to the child. "My Kami. My curly topped blue-eyed child. Come now and stop crying. The one who has visited me the most in my dreams. Allow me to look for once and for real into those glistening eyes that are so much like the woman you have never met. I will see her today and tell her of you and how much you are like her."

"Grandfather, I will miss you so much. What if my heart breaks without you?"

"Hearts cannot be broken when held gently but firmly in the hearts of others," he said. Taking her hand, he opened it and placed his fist over her palm. "Hold my heart until you come to me again," he said.

"But Grandfather, in one of my dreams, it is you who teaches me to fly."

"The old and wise bird does not teach the fledgling to fly, Kami. The fledgling must test her own wings and when they are strong, they will carry her into the sky and beyond."

Kami buried her head in her grandfather's chest. "I just wish you could be here to see me fly," she said.

"You, my Kami, have made it to the end of the quest and made friends with a cantankerous old dragon, a rather large grumpy giant, and his friend the hermit sorcerer. You have helped others along your way and now defeated once and for all the great Gwandoya."

Kami looked up at him. She hadn't really thought about all they had accomplished along this journey.

"You are tired now my Kami, but after a refreshing sleep you will be able to more clearly see that you have been flying on your own for some time now."

Kami hugged her grandfather again then kissed him gently on the cheek. She could feel the grip of his hand going weak and squeezed it tight. "I will miss you," she said, tenderly.

"I will miss you all," said Marcus.

And it was then, after saying goodbye to the children of his son, that Marcus of Caraigdun took his last breath. The Banshee wailed one long mournful cry, but even her cry could not overshadow the sobs of the heavy hearts in the chambers of Gwandoya that day.

Kami could feel the spirit of her beloved grandfather leave his body.

"Look," said Adam, tapping her on the shoulder.

Kami looked up to see a chariot drawn by a dozen white horses coming out of the clouds.

Grog who had been peering through the window thought maybe he could block the chariot. But Angelica appeared and bade him move aside.

"It is time," she said. "Do not think of this as his ending, but as an everlasting beginning."

The spirit of Marcus appeared.

All in the room watched as this great man stepped aboard the chariot. Adam ran to the window. "See you later Grandfather," he said, waving his hand wildly.

Marcus leaned his head out of the window of the carriage and waved at the little boy. He blew kisses to all the girls in the room. Each felt the warmth of the kiss as if he were standing there next to them placing it on their cheek.

He saluted the boys who all bowed in his honor.

One last smile to Kami and the chariot flew over the clouds into the sky. The Banshee followed with her tale of gloom and woe.

"What did he put in your hand?" asked Adam, the only one who wasn't crying.

Kami didn't think her grandfather had actually placed anything there. Looking down, she noticed a gold chain hanging over the side of her still clenched fist. She slowly opened her fingers.

"A heart-shaped locket of gold," said Aimee.

Kami opened the locket. A smile and tears came simultaneously. "It's them," she said.

Two tiny engravings of a young couple met the eyes of all that looked.

"I'd bet he was difficult to handle," said Becka.

"If she really was as clever as Kami, I'm sure she could handle him," said Brian.

Jaynea stood back and looked at her six children. She was severely saddened that she would have to tell Denis of the death of his father. But her heart was light with the knowledge that all the children had survived. The evil that had so long tormented her heart and mind was gone from the world. The room was filled with light and so was her soul.

She walked over to the window and looked up at her giant friend that stood outside in the sunlight.

"Hallo, Grog," she said.

"Hallo, Jaynea," he said.

"I see you've met my children."

"Quite the cantankerous lot you've got there," said Grog, winking at his old friend.

"Thanks for helping them," she said. "When I heard you were with Kami and Adam, I knew no harm would befall them."

"Ah. They could've taken care of themselves," he said. "Chips off the old mum they are."

Jaynea turned to look at the children, then back to Grog. "Will you give us a ride to meet the others?" She asked.

Grog held his palm up to the window. "Glad to be of service," he said.

{ 24 }

Of Wins and Losses

When Jaynea summoned her family to be with Marcus upon his death, Denis was busy taking care of a very pressing matter.

Two young men had come running out of the mountain just as the evil had been consumed. It was Foster and Bruin carrying the reflection of Becka. When he saw how she was fading, Denis knew he couldn't answer the summons of his wife Jaynea.

"We got to her as soon as we could," said Foster, leaning on his knees and breathing deeply, still recovering from the strain of being so close to the evil as it was consumed. "What can we do to keep her from fading completely?"

"We will have to get Becka," said Bruin, who was not in the least out of breath.

"Right, I will stay here with Becka's fading reflection," said Denis. "The two of you go to Becka and bring her back immediately."

"Should I use a summoning spell?" asked Bruin.

"In the weakened state of this part of Becka, we need to make sure we focus all magic toward Becka and the restoration of her reflection. They have been separated for a long time. Becka's personality is going to go flat if we don't hurry and put them back together."

Just as Jaynea and all the children were heading down the mountain with Grog, Foster and Bruin appeared in front of them.

"Don't know if I'll ever get used to that," said Foster, his head swirling from Bruin's favorite method of travel, transportation. "I've never felt so dizzy."

Bruin looked at Foster and then at Becka. "You've been dizzier," he said.

Becka came over to see her friends. "Nice of you to come," she said.

"Well, either her personality is going flat, or she's decided that she's not into you anymore," said Bruin.

Aimee came over and gave her brave wizard knight a hug. "Our grandfather has just died," she said, a tear rising.

Bruin took her in his arms and held her tight.

Foster tried to comfort Becka. She stood with a blank stare on her face.

Jaynea came forward and waved her hand in front of Becka's face.

Becka pulled the mirror out of her cloak and gazed blankly into it. "I am nothing," she said. "I am gone."

"We must find her reflection," said Jaynea. "How could I have let her go without it for so long?"

Aimee put a hand on her mother's shoulder. "We have been a bit preoccupied, haven't we then," she said.

"Her reflection is on the other side of the mountain," said Foster.

"You didn't leave it there all alone, did you?" asked Jaynea.

"Denis is with it, umm, her," said Bruin.

Jaynea turned quickly to Grog, "take care of them," she said, putting her arm around Becka.

Kami ran to their side, "I want to come!" But before she reached them Jaynea and Becka had disappeared.

"Oops," said Foster. "Hope the spell works, since their mother just used magic on Becka."

"No time to lose!" exclaimed Bruin with a dramatic wave of his sword, (as he strategically kept one arm around his lady fair.) Instantly he whisked the entire company to the other side of the mountain.

Becka and her reflection were laying side by side, both with eyes wide open, staring straight into the sky, yet seeing nothing.

"I'll need everyone to help," said Denis, as if he knew they would be coming. "Repeat after me, *Restituo Imago de Speculum.*"

Adam stumbled over the words. Becka's reflection shook. Everyone looked at Adam, "So-r-ry," he said. "I had to practice with Kami for like an hour to get that *Intro Peior Ferocitus* thing right!"

Jaynea thought quickly, "Everyone, say 'restore the mirror image' instead."

"Much better," said Adam.

"*Restore the mirror image,*" they all said together.

After they repeated the spell seven times, Becka's reflection rose. It hovered over her body for a few seconds and then slowly descended.

"Wow!" said Adam.

Jaynea held the mirror in front of Becka's face. The dazed expression left her. "I'm back," she said. Taking the mirror from her mother's hand, she slowly stood up and looked around. She blushed when her eyes fell upon Foster. "Thank-you," she said.

"Yep, she's back," said Brian, "in all her giddy glory."

{ 25 }

Of Endings and Beginnings

Although the entire group could have returned quickly to Caraig-dun now that they were free to use magic, the children were none too eager to leave their newfound friends and very eager to have new adventures. While Jaynea and Denis, and Athena and Guelder used a transport spell to quickly take the body of Marcus back to Caraigdun to prepare for a funeral, the children all traveled by foot, taking their time, enjoying the countryside along the way. Brian and Erik retrieved the writings of Marcus from the caves of Mount Ceo'ban. Grog and Adam had a grand time digging up a buried treasure. Kami and Caoimhin flew on the back of Prestwick as he took them far and wide across the land. He showed them many unique flowers and edible plants that they collected to take back for the funeral feast. Aimee and Becka were of course busy with two fine young gentlemen. They walked along talking and laughing together and almost didn't remember to return in time for the funeral. Jaynea was actually very worried indeed about the group of young people when Foster, (polite young man that he is) thought to send a note held in the talons of an eagle friend, which calmed Jaynea's worries immensely and let her know that all was well and they would be home soon.

Men and wizards, princes and kings, peasants and nobility, all creatures great and small were represented at the funeral of Marcus the Great. Many had known him as teacher and friend and many came out of respect for his grandchildren, the hero wizard children of Caraigdun.

Vandea came with a heavy heart and sat for a long time listening as her nieces and nephews told her of her father's last days and the words of wisdom that he left to each of them. Brian and Erik gave her the pages of writings that came from the caves of Ceo'ban. Vandea opened the pages and laughed as she read. "Father always had a way of exaggerating," she said. Then with a wave of her hand she formed the pages into a leather-bound book and presented it back to the boys. "There are many adventures written in this journal, and many more to be embarked upon from the writings of my father. I'm sure he would want his grandsons to know of secret hiding places for treasures, evil beasts that remain to be conquered, and damsels in distress."

A grand procession passed by the body of Marcus that lay on a pyre. Each visitor embraced Denis, Vandea, and Jaynea and then placed a branch or twig on the pile of dry wood.

If anyone was crying or frowning, Adam was the first to run to them and tell them to "Put a smile on your face. My grandfather wants you to be happy!" or "Why are you crying, we will see him again!"

The last to make their contribution to the woodpile were Athena and Guelder. Just before the fire was lit, Denis called for a moment of silence to say a few words about his father.

"Alas, we are here to say goodbye. Here's a bit of wisdom my father shared with me many years ago upon the death of my mother. An ending is just a door to a beginning. Step through the door with curiosity and a smile and before the next door comes; you will find joy in the journey."

Denis paused and looked at the sea of faces. "Marcus has stepped through a door. I'm sure he is smiling now as he strolls through a garden with my mother. He would have us find joy in this life until we meet him again. He will want to hear of the adventures of his grandsons and the lives of his beautiful granddaughters."

Adam ran to Denis's side at just that minute. "He would want you to stop talking and let the party begin," he said.

Denis laughed and put the little boy on his shoulders. Together they yelled, "Let the party begin!"

Denis touched a torch to the pyre. A warm glow pierced the night and radiated heat out to the crowd.

Adam jumped down and grabbed Kami. They danced around the pyre and sang a merry tune.

Becka and Aimee smiled at Jaynea and Vandea and they all went to Athena and pulled her away from Guelder. "Now we can begin plans for the wedding," said Aimee.

"But the period of mourning," said Athena. "I cannot ask all of you to partake of the joys of a wedding during this sad time."

Jaynea looked at the children dancing around the fire. Her eyes swept across the sea of faces. They were all smiling and happy as Adam had told them to be. "Marcus wouldn't want you to wait," she said.

"You both have waited so long," said Becka.

"I think we should have the wedding in a month on the eve of the next full moon," said Aimee.

"My garden at my home in the south is just the place," said Vandea. "The most beautiful blossoms will bloom in a month. And if we hold the wedding at nightfall there is a special flower that blooms only at night."

"I'll have to make sure Venus is --"

Guelder had come up next to them with Erik and Brian, he put a hand over the mouth of his beloved. Erik was holding the book of the writings of Marcus. He held it open to a specific page. He pointed and said simply, "Read this."

Athena took the book and read out loud. "Again, as it has occurred so many times over the last ten years, Guelder dreams of Athena. He calls her name all night in his sleep, keeping me awake. If we ever escape from this wretched confinement, I shall not waste one day or one minute. I will, myself, as an ordained priest, find Athena and marry them immediately. There shall be no wait this time for the rising of Venus."

Guelder interrupted, quoting from memory. "There shall be no full moon or flowers of June; just Guelder and Athena under sun, or clouds or stars. I will make them man and wife for perhaps these night fits will stop if Guelder can just have a bit of Athena's good cooking in his belly each day."

Guelder took Athena and kissed her by the fire's glow. Brian stepped forward. "Seems like this is my grandfather's dying wish," he said, "to see the two of you wed."

And he and Erik stepped upon the platform and blew the horn to bring the party to silence. "I bid you all to listen," Brian announced.

"We have had a funeral, and by the wish of my grandfather Marcus the Great we shall now have a wedding!" Erik exclaimed. "Solon, brother of Athena, my friend, will marry Guelder and Athena on this day!"

A great cheer rose from the crowd. A thousand pixies flew overhead dropping flowers upon the ground where Athena and Guelder stood. Instantly the magic of Mathius and Mikos was felt as the crowd was suddenly sitting in floating stands where all could have a good view of the beloved. The dragons circled above, lighting the torches that were sent into the dark night sky by Vandea and Jaynea. Grog held the little children aloft in his hand. "Best seat in the house," Adam said. Denis and Jaynea stood by their friends as Solon led Athena of the land of Afrike and Guelder of the land of Caraigdun in the exchanging of the long-awaited vows.

"My love is eternal," said Athena.

And Guelder took her in his arms and kissed her.

Two voices were heard above the crowd.

"My very best wishes to you," said Clare.

"Take good care of our Athena," said Matilda.

And the spirits of two loving friends were finally released from the prison that is in between and allowed admittance into an eternity of joy.

Caoimhin lit up the sky with fireworks.

Jaynea waved her hand, a sumptuous feast appeared, and she bade the party to eat.

They celebrated through the night. But before the wee hours of the morning came, Jaynea and Denis found the smallest of their children. Jaynea lifted Adam off the great belly of Grog, whose snoring shook the land. Denis picked Kami up carefully; he did not want to disturb the peaceful dreams he knew she was having from the look on her face. Jaynea stopped and smiled at Aimee and Becka who were still dancing with their brave young men. Then she gave Erik and Brian each a kiss.

"Good night, Mother," said Brian.

"Yes, sweet dreams," said Erik, watching them walk up the hill toward the cabin.

"So, what do you wanna do now?" Brian asked.

"Just as Aunt Vandea said, there are secret hiding places for treasures, evil beasts that remain to be conquered, and damsels in distress," Erik commented as he pulled the writings of Marcus from behind his back. When he opened the book, the pages turned frantically and stopped on a glowing page. "Grandfather?" he asked.

Brian met his brother's wide-eyed gaze. "Looks like he's sending us on our next adventure," he said.

About the Author:

Jane Cleere Johnson is the mother of six children. She is also blessed with two sons-in-law, one daughter-in-law, and nine amazingly incredible grandchildren. She has an English Lit degree from Brigham Young University where her favorite class dealt exclusively with the writings of C.S. Lewis and J.R.R. Tolkien. She has a master's degree in special education from the University of Kansas and is now a retired teacher.

If you would like to know the answers to the riddles in Chapter 13: "A Pair of Grumpy Wizards," visit our website at:

Mushroommanorbooks.com